Will Kostakis is an award-winning author for young adults. His first novel, *Loathing Lola*, was released when he was just nineteen, and his second, *The First Third*, won the 2014 Gold Inky Award. It was also shortlisted for the Children's Book Council of Australia Book of the Year and Australian Prime Minister's Literary Awards. *The Sidekicks* was his third novel for young adults, and his American debut. As a high school student, Will won *Sydney Morning Herald* Young Writer of the Year for a collection of short stories.

# WILL KOSTAKIS
# MONUMENTS

LOTHIAN

A Lothian Children's Book

Published in Australia and New Zealand in 2019
by Hachette Australia
(an imprint of Hachette Australia Pty Limited)
Level 17, 207 Kent Street, Sydney NSW 2000
www.hachettechildrens.com.au

A catalogue record for this
book is available from the
National Library of Australia

NATIONAL
LIBRARY
OF AUSTRALIA

ISBN: 978 0 7344 1922 4 (paperback)

Cover design and illustration by Guy Shield 2019
Author photograph courtesy of Dion Nucifora
Typeset in 12.1/16.5 pt Minion Pro by Bookhouse, Sydney
Printed and bound in Australia by McPherson's Printing Group

MIX
Paper from
responsible sources
FSC
www.fsc.org  FSC® C001695

The paper this book is printed on is certified against the
Forest Stewardship Council® Standards. McPherson's Printing
Group holds FSC® chain of custody certification SA-COC-005379.
FSC® promotes environmentally responsible, socially beneficial
and economically viable management of the world's forests.

*TO DANIEL MOCHAN,*
*FOR MAKING AN ADVENTURE OUT OF THE PAST TWENTY YEARS*

# ONE

This is my first friend divorce, so forgive me if I'm doing it wrong.

It's probably – definitely – against the rules to text. But it's Monday, 30 March. Olly's sixteenth birthday. I can't ignore that. I won't. We met when the glue we used at school was edible; we have history. Sure, part of that history's him being very clear about not wanting to hang out anymore, but ignoring that little blemish . . .

He thinks I'm boring. I only ever do what adults tell me to. He's wrong. I'm messaging him to meet me on the Founders Block rooftop in seven minutes. I'm not allowed to let anyone else up there. I'm breaking a school rule for him. That's not boring. He'll see that.

I check the text once over for typos before sending it. I set down my phone and exhale. The cafeteria is buzzing. It always buzzes when pancakes are the breakfast special. I look to my plate, my overflowing plate. I told Olly to meet me in seven minutes.

I should have given myself more time.

Whoops.

I dart out of the cafeteria with a folded ricotta pancake hanging from my mouth. I spy Mr Wilson under the jacaranda, chastising students who wear creative interpretations of our school uniform. He's a stickler for presentation and I frankly don't have the time. I can avoid him by taking the back entrance into Founders Block – an offence punishable by stern lecture. I hesitate, remind myself I'm not boring, then sneak inside.

The service corridors of Charlton Grammar are treated like poorly managed backstage areas, littered with props and forgotten artefacts of past productions. I run the gauntlet of rolled carpets, trophy cabinets and framed student artworks. At the end, a door. I pop it open a smidge, check the coast is clear and then leap out into the hallway. This is centre stage.

Founders Block is the oldest building on campus. Once the entirety of the school, it is now the place where the important people have offices and host functions. The ceilings are high and framed by decorative cornices, and the floors are marble.

Ms Rowsey must recognise my frantic footsteps because she's waiting in her office with the keys held out. Nobody knows her exact role at the school, but she has the temperament of someone perpetually interrupted.

I greet her in Pancaklish: regular English spoken through more pancake than any person should have in their mouth at any one time.

She sighs. 'Chew, Connor. Honestly.'

I grin at her and a piece of pancake falls to the floor.

Ms Rowsey arches one eyebrow severely. She doesn't need to say anything. I scoop up the food, drop it in the bin and I'm out of her office before she thinks I'm up to anything.

I scurry towards the disused stairwell. A teacher I don't recognise tells me to slow down. I do, only until I pass him. When I get to the door, I fumble with the keys. They're long and heavy and stained by time, made for locks that should've been changed by now. I separate the one with the more ornate head, twist it in the lock and push. The hinges creak. I slip inside and prop the door open with my shoe, ready for Olly.

There's no railing so I hug the wall on my way up. After six flights, one wall comes to an end. The rooftop stretches the full length of the building. I ignore it and instead climb the cast-iron spiral staircase in the corner. I keep my head ducked until the spiral stops.

Students aren't allowed in the belltower. It's expressly forbidden. Whatever. I'm in the belltower. Sydney stretches out for miles, a patchwork quilt of roads and roofs disrupted by defiant bursts of green. The city marks the horizon, all spiked and silver. I watch the shells of skyscrapers and the cranes that fawn over them. I wonder what the view is like from there, if people in skyscrapers even look this way.

The bell is twice the size of my chest. I reach in and feel around – I've taped a whole world of contraband to the inside. The bell hasn't rung since some bright spark proposed a less tiresome way to signal the end of class than sending some poor soul up a mountain to bash a bent piece of metal. Come to think of it, the poor soul was probably the bright spark. Last week, while brainstorming ways to demonstrate to Olly how not-boring I can be, I realised the bell was perfect for hiding snacks. Charlton Grammar has waged a war on taste, and certain foods can't be consumed on campus without prompting several petitions from the militant Parents and Friends' Association and a passive-aggressive mention in their newsletter. They want us to live fuller, healthier lives, and I get that, but counterpoint: junk food is incredible. I pocket the peanut brittle for myself, and a packet of chocolate-coated almonds for Olly.

I pull back and soak in the view again – roads, roofs, green, silver, got it – and descend the spiral staircase. I forget to duck and whack my head. My skull throbs.

'Nice one,' I mutter.

At the foot of the staircase, a garbage bag is tucked under a brick. I leave the brick and drag the bag out onto the rooftop. It whips violently in the wind. I stop at the first pole and fish out the correct flag. It's the school's emblem: a black wyvern with its forked tongue poking out, stitched on white polyester.

When students are old enough, the teachers assign us chores so we can share in the thrills of maintaining a centuries-old building. I got off lightly with flag duty. All I have to do is raise the flags of a morning and lower them in the afternoon. Some kids have to mop. And this at least has its perks. Two flags raised in the correct order . . . It's a ten-minute job I can stretch to twenty and miss the beginning of my first class. That's not to say I've ever missed the beginning of my first class, I haven't, but the potential's there.

I rest the brick on the empty bag and return to the rooftop. I lean against the barrier and empty my pockets. I watch my phone. I swipe one finger across its screen. There are no new notifications.

Olly's late.

Okay, maybe that's unfair. I didn't give him much notice. He has until the bell. That's plenty of time. He's had three weeks to come to terms with the fact that life without me isn't too crash-hot. He'll want to repair things and the door's open. Literally. I've propped it open with my shoe.

My phone vibrates. My heart punches my chest. I assume it's him, but ... It's Mum. I exhale and answer the call on speaker. 'Yo.'

'You didn't call this morning.'

I wince. It slipped my mind. 'We were running late.'

'Well, run later and call me.' She isn't mad, but she's dangling the fact she *should* be. 'How are you, darling?'

'I'm well thanks, darling.'

A pause. 'It's weird when you say it.'

'That's why I say it.'

'Did your father feed you?'

'He gave me money.'

'That's not the same,' she says. 'Did he wash your clothes or did he accidentally throw them in the bin again?'

Mum's bids to win Best Parent are never subtle. 'He washed them.'

'Not as well as me.' She clicks her tongue against her teeth. 'Am I on speaker?'

I stare at the phone that is definitely on speaker. 'No?'

'It sounds like I'm on speaker.'

'You're not.'

5

She drops it. 'How was your weekend?'

As far as weekends at Dad's go, it was pretty standard. There was a lot of lounging on the couch, unless Dad wanted to watch sport, then there was a lot of vacating the couch.

I tell Mum the weekend was fine. 'Yours?'

'It was . . . I visited your grandfather.'

I imagine Pappou, his receding grey hair slicked back. He sits upright on a stool in the sprawling backyard of his place in Carlingford. He has an apple in one hand and guides a knife through it with the other. He motions me closer with a tilt of his head. He holds out the slice between his thumb and the blade.

'How is he?' I ask.

She's silent. It's a silence that says too much.

'I think you should see him, Con,' she urges eventually.

That's worse than the silence. I know what she's hinting at.

I sink deeper into the barrier. The patchwork quilt of roads and roofs stretches over the hills to the north. The nursing home is out that way. He moved in after we sold the place in Carlingford. When I last saw him, Pappou was a frail man under wisps of white hair, hunched over on a plastic-covered couch. That was a while ago. Almost a year.

'It's Olly's birthday, isn't it?' It's her attempt to pivot the conversation away from her father, to safer territory. She doesn't know about the friend divorce.

'It is, yeah.'

'Knew it.' Mum's a freak with dates. She can't remember the names of streets or movies, but tell her somebody's birthday and she'll never forget it. It's usually helpful. But not today. 'Are you all going out tonight?'

Seeing the biggest, loudest action movie on Olly's birthday has become our annual tradition. He brings his friends, his twin brother brings his, and we almost take up an entire row. It's epic. This is the first time I haven't been invited.

'Yup.' I regret it as soon as I've said it.

'Were you going to tell me or were you going to keep me up till midnight worrying?'

'I was going to keep you up till midnight worrying.'

She stifles a laugh. 'Tell me you bought him something nice.'

I look at the packet by the phone. 'Chocolate-coated almonds.'

'*Con.*'

'They have special meaning.'

'They mean you bought them on special when you should've spent more than five dollars on your best friend,' she says.

'You can pay me an allowance.'

'You can pay your own school fees.'

'I'm going to hang up now.'

'Thought so. Don't be later than twelve.'

'I won't.'

'Be good.'

'Always am.'

The call ends and I breathe it out. I've just committed myself to being out until midnight, and I have nowhere to be. The door might be open, but Olly isn't walking through it.

'He'll be here,' I tell myself, unwrapping the peanut brittle. 'It's his birthday. He'll invite me to the movies. It'll be like these three weeks never happened.'

I finish the peanut brittle and the digital bell rings. The students in the courtyard below begin their slow dawdle to class.

Olly isn't coming. I'm tempted to take a photo of the almonds and send it to him, one final 'I smuggled these in last week to prove I'm not boring', before I accept that sending a photo of chocolate-coated almonds is possibly the most boring way to prove you're not boring.

I tape the packet of almonds back inside the bell. While I'm up here, I look over to the city again. In however many years, when I'm in one of those skyscrapers, Charlton Grammar will be a speck in the distance. I wonder if I'll even remember the taste of the glue we used in kindergarten. Probably.

I descend the disused stairwell. I slide my foot into my shoe, shut the door and . . . linger. In a Connor first, I don't want to go to class on time. I don't want to see Olly. I don't want to walk past the books he's stacked on my old seat so I can't sit there. I don't want to be reminded that my oldest friend doesn't want anything to do with me.

I separate the ornate key from the others, unlock the door, kick off my shoe, and wedge it between the door and the frame. I return the keys to Ms Rowsey. She scowls like I've just interrupted her. 'You've lost a shoe.'

I step over it when I return to the disused stairwell.

I fetch the chocolate-coated almonds I was saving for Olly, and head back down the stairs alone.

# TWO

I sit at the bottom of the stairwell, just by the door I've wedged ajar. I'm skipping class and . . . to be honest, it's nowhere near as thrilling as people have led me to believe. At Charlton Grammar, every second of your life is monitored and measured against learning outcomes. I should relish this free time. Instead, I'm spending it worrying about how I'll explain my absence. Mr Cheen will have taken the roll already. He's probably explaining some vital content that will appear in an exam. I'm a truant *and* I'm going to fail . . . I can rush over to G Block, say I'm late because I had a bathroom emergency. Nobody ever wants to ask follow-up questions about those. Mr Cheen will point me towards a spare seat up the back. When I pass his row, Olly will avoid my gaze. Everyone else will notice.

I can already feel the heat of their glares, their pity.

I push the thought down and summon a distraction: catching almonds in my mouth. I start relatively close. Like, I'm literally just dropping almonds into my mouth until I believe in myself enough to start throwing them. I believe in myself too much. I toss an almond high in the air and open my mouth. The almond rebounds off my cheek, rolls across the room and stalls in a groove.

I sigh. 'Brilliant.'

I suppose I have to retrieve it. I might as well limit the offences I'm charged with when I'm eventually found. I mean, truancy *and* smuggling in contraband? I'll have detention from now until the end of term.

I crawl over to retrieve the rogue almond.

The stairwell floor is tiled with irregular stones, roughly the size of my shoes. They're cold to the touch. I stretch ahead and a stone shifts beneath my palm. It's weird. I check the stone beside it. It rocks with the slightest pressure. I examine the neighbouring tiles. About a metre from the back wall, a cluster of stones hasn't been set in grout. The almond is nestled between two of these loose tiles. I pop it in my mouth and . . . remain. Interest piqued, I raise a stone and set it to one side, exposing a timber panel beneath. I run two fingers across the grain.

Charlton Grammar has its legends. They're scratched into the backs of locker doors, texted between friends, relayed by older students with a flair for storytelling . . . Somebody heard something from some Old Boy about a treasure trove, a secret tunnel or a wartime bunker, that kind of thing. Everyone's heard the myths, but nobody ever admits to believing them. Back in Year Seven, we had peer support every Tuesday. They'd trust a group of us with a Year Eleven student for a period. It was envisaged as a way to help us build relationships, but in reality, it just gave the Year Elevens some impressionable minds to corrupt. Mark was our peer-support leader. He was a nugget of a guy with a wicked sense of humour. He had us convinced there was something buried beneath the cricket pitch. All we had to do was dig. We had swiped the groundskeeper's shovel before Mark felt bad and fessed up.

But yeah, Charlton Grammar has its legends. They're *legends*. You're not supposed to hang out in a disused stairwell, shift loose tile after loose tile and encounter a wooden trapdoor. I loop four fingers through the latch and pull. The door is exactly as stubborn as I expect. I get it open eventually, revealing steps carved roughly into the school's sandstone foundations.

'Wild,' I mutter.

As foreboding as a stairway descending into darkness is, I'm itching to know where it leads. I'm thirteen again, striding across the oval with the groundskeeper's shovel. I hover my foot over the opening.

What if I get caught down there? I jerk my foot back.

I'm already a truant though. I can close the trapdoor, scramble to replace the tiles, ignore the secret tunnel and still get in trouble. And when guys ask what I did when I skipped first period, what am I going to say? That I binged on almonds to avoid the thought of my ex-best friend?

I wanted a distraction. *This* is a distraction.

After one last glance back at the door and the shoe propping it open, I begin my descent. The steps are uneven; they sink in the middle. It's like they're goading me to twist an ankle. I run my fingers against both walls to keep my balance. The tunnel narrows. The steps corkscrew deeper. The darkness swallows me.

I reach the bottom. The air is thick. I activate my phone's flashlight. Like a seasoned adventurer, I illuminate the passageway with one sweeping gesture, collide with a cobweb and shriek. I scratch the stubborn silk from my hand.

Right. Take two. I hold the phone close to my chest. The passageway extends past the beam's reaches. Dusty webs hang from . . . I want to say sandstone bricks, but science is my weakest subject so don't quote me.

I march. To what specifically, I have no idea. With every step, tiny anxieties grow more confident. They use their big-boy voices and I begin to wonder if this is wise. There's no mobile reception down here. If something happens, no one will hear my scream – or, more realistically, my dying quip.

I catch a glimpse of a chamber at the end of the tunnel. My pace quickens. I step over the threshold and tumble down two steps with a lack of grace that anyone who knows me will tell you is entirely on brand. I wasn't expecting the chamber to be lower than the tunnel because I'm accustomed to rooms not actively trying to hurt me.

I pull myself to my feet and look around. Ceiling to floor, the room is tiled with tessellated coloured shards that glimmer when I wave my phone in their direction. A naked bulb hangs from the ceiling. Exposed wiring connects it to a wall-mounted car battery and then to a switch. The set-up looks slightly less shoddy than my attempt at an electrical circuit in science. I flick the switch. The bulb buzzes to life. I deactivate my flashlight and soak everything in.

Tiny rhombuses of varying shades of green swirl across the ceiling. They spread down the walls to a point where they meet the tiny blue rhombuses that rise from the floor. I'm standing in a circle of golden tiles. I step back. It's the sun, and the blue is the sky, and the green . . . I'm standing in a room that's upside down.

Its furnishings aren't though. In the centre, there's a dust-coated, wooden chest. To my completely untrained eye, it's roughly ninety centimetres tall and deep, and two metres wide. There are two iron ring pulls on either end that seem way too small to help anyone carry the thing, and not to denigrate artists from the olden days, but the chest looks like it was decorated by a toddler with a knife. Each face features a different crudely carved figure. The longer sides spotlight women; one has a tiny tree sprouting from the palm of her left hand, and the other has a golden chalice hovering above the palm of her right. On the shorter sides, there are young boys; one cups a fireball, the other a large snowflake. Carved into the top of the chest is a bearded, burly man. He lies with his eyes shut and a sword clasped over his body. There's a series of scratches near his head. I brush the dust aside with my sleeve to reveal a message engraved carefully into the reddish-brown timber.

BEVAN WAS HERE

I guess I'm not the first student to find this place. I wonder if Bevan was the one who installed the light.

Countless videogames have taught me that unattended chests in secret rooms contain rare treasures, but alas, I can't get this one open. I try for a solid ten minutes. I'm not strong enough. At one point, I push my whole weight against it out of sheer frustration and it doesn't even budge. The chest is bolted down, which is a bold choice in a room already filled with bold choices.

I approach the cupboard centred against one wall. It's the only other piece of furniture in the room – also wooden and dust-coated. I'm relieved I can actually get the door open. That soothes my bruised ego. The cupboard's empty, save for a leather-bound journal on its sole shelf. I flick through the book's blank, brown-spotted pages until I arrive at the sheet at the end – both sides are covered in a script I don't recognise. I bring the book closer, as if distance was what was keeping me from understanding the language. It's just a collection of neatly arranged squiggles and strokes.

I carry the journal back to the chest and sit up on the edge. I plonk the packet of almonds beside me and pull up a playlist on my phone. It's one of the finest I've curated in my sixteen years. Its aesthetic is boppy Euro electro-pop that sounds fun until you actually listen to the lyrics and realise everyone on the dancefloor has a bad case of the sads. I pass the time mouthing along to one upbeat-yet-depressing track after the other, and then a particular track comes on. I know it from its first bar. It's *my* track. Some songs pass through you; others seep into your soul. They tether themselves to memories, and the moment you hear their pulsing synths, those memories are conjured one after the other like handkerchiefs stuffed in a magician's sleeve. This is one of those songs. I remember the first time I heard the chorus, the night I pored over its lyrics, and the day I played it for Olly. I told him it showed me who I was with words I'd never thought to use before. His forehead creased. He didn't understand its significance, but he listened the whole way through. He always—

'Nope!' I unlock my phone and skip the track. I'm not letting any of that down here.

Another song starts. It's one that passes through me.

And then the sound of a door slamming reverberates down the tunnel.

I pause the track. That sounded too much like the door I'd propped open with my shoe.

I don't hear anything else. Enough time passes that I believe it's possible I just imagined the sound.

But then I hear footsteps.

Someone noticed the shoe, the trapdoor. They descended the stairs and now they're striding down the tunnel. They're following the light. They've come for me.

I think exclusively in expletives.

I spring to my feet. I tuck the journal into the back of my pants and cover it with my shirt. My eyes dart around the room's dark edges. I need somewhere to hide. I clear the space between me and the cupboard, pull both doors open by their rusted handles, and reorganise my limbs and internal organs to fit under the shelf. I guide the doors shut, and through the crack between them, I see the bright orange packaging on the chest.

I left the almonds out.

My heartbeat thumps in my ears.

I feel my offenses rack up: skipping class, venturing out of bounds, consuming banned goods. Even if they don't find me now, they have my shoe. They can *Cinderella* it, travelling from classroom to classroom to see whose foot it fits.

This isn't a matter of if I'll get caught, but when.

I move a fraction to the left to better spy on the tunnel opening. I hold my breath. A prefect emerges. I recognise the block colours of the senior uniform. Prefects are incentivised with gift vouchers and co-curricular credits, so the school has an army of pubescent monsters willing to improve their standing by throwing younger kids under the bus. There's no appealing to a prefect's better nature – it's impossible to compete with the allure of a gift voucher.

The prefect sets my scuffed shoe down beside the almonds. 'Hello?'

It's not the voice I expect. It's melodic. Then the prefect cap comes off. A brown mane unravels. I peer closer and . . . The prefect is a girl?

She removes the blazer, folds it over the chest and looks directly at the cupboard.

Okay, so this wasn't a particularly great place to hide.

I guess I should say something. 'Hi.'

Her brow creases. She steps around the chest. 'Why . . . are you in a cupboard?'

'I'm hiding.'

'From me?'

I nod. Then I realise she can't see me. 'Yeah.'

'You uncomfortable?'

'Little bit.' My whole body is cramping and my elbow is crushing an organ that feels important. I nudge open the doors and begin the process of unknotting myself. As soon as I'm free, I look back at the cupboard and I'm proud I managed to squeeze in there in the first place.

'I would've just pulled out the shelf to make more room,' she says.

Okay, I'm less proud now.

She smiles. She has a face full of stars. It's a constellation of amber freckles.

I don't get nervous around girls. We tend to have the same taste in music and boys, so there's lots to talk about, but this still feels weird. Charlton Grammar is a single-sex school and I can count the number of female staff members I know on one hand. Sometimes an English teacher slips through the cracks, but honestly we'd be less surprised to see a gazelle on the oval than a Giselle.

A girl has never snuck into Charlton Grammar disguised as a prefect before. At least, not to my knowledge.

I should probably introduce myself. I extend a hand. 'I'm Connor.'

'I'm trespassing, so hard pass on identifying myself, but I'll . . .' She checks her hand, wipes it down the front of her pants and then shakes mine.

We pull apart and I have no idea what comes next.

She asks if I'm the only one down here. I nod.

She asks if I come down here often. I tell her I only found the trapdoor this morning.

She asks if I know where *here* is. The way she drills into the word for emphasis makes me wonder if *here* is more special than I think it is. I shake my head.

'Well,' she says, 'I didn't see you and you didn't see me, all right?'

It takes me a second to catch on. 'You want me to leave?'

'Bingo.'

I don't want to go, not yet. There's so much I still—

'It was nice meeting you,' she adds.

'You too,' I stammer.

'And next time, remember . . .' She mimes removing the shelf.

'Got it.' I slink over to the chest. I pocket the almonds and grab my shoe as questions tumble over themselves in my mind. Who is she? What is she doing down here? What exactly *is* down here? How can I get out if the shoe I'm holding was propping open the door? 'Problem.' I drop the shoe and slip my foot inside. 'I can't actually leave.'

'Why not?'

'The stairwell door locks when it closes. It can't be unlocked from the inside without a key. And you closed it.'

'Just chill out in the stairwell, give me an hour to do what I need to, then bang on the door until a teacher fetches you.'

She acts like that's the end of the discussion. It's not. I have an advantage. She clearly doesn't want anyone to know what she's up to. If I jeopardise that . . . I mean, I won't, but if I make her think I *might*, then maybe she'll be more inclined to keep me on a tighter leash.

'What if I bang on the door too soon – like, right-away too soon – and a teacher shows up, sees the trapdoor and comes down here?'

Her eyes narrow. 'You wouldn't.'

'But I might. Maybe the best thing for you is to keep me close.'

She makes a face. I know that face. She's thinking exclusively in expletives.

Eventually, she clicks her fingers. 'Right then, back in the cupboard.'

That's not what I was angling for. 'What?'

'You heard me.' She's biting back a smile. 'Hop back in and I'll let you know when I'm done.'

'If you need me out of the way, I can wait in the tunnel.'

'But you said it yourself. The best thing for me is to keep you close.'

I open my mouth to speak and she raises an eyebrow.

I will say, removing the shelf does make a big difference. Fitting inside the cupboard requires far less contortion. She props the shelf against the wall and closes the cupboard doors. I watch her through the gap as she tries to open the chest. She struggles with it for some time. I nudge the cupboard door and put her out of her misery. 'The chest doesn't open.'

'Thanks,' she snaps, before regretting how harsh she sounds. 'There's something in there and I'd like to get it out.'

'Can I help?'

She shakes her head. 'It doesn't open. It must be a decoy.' She sighs. 'Is there anything about this chamber that seems unusual to you?'

'Besides the chest that doesn't open?'

'Yes.'

'The room's upside down, for starters.'

She cocks her head to the side. 'What?'

'Look at the tiles.'

She does, and I watch it dawn on her that whoever was paid to lay the tiles held the concept sketch the wrong way up.

'It's upside down,' she breathes.

'Yup.'

'We've got to turn it the right side up.'

'Huh?'

Her eyes sweep the room. 'The chamber must rotate a hundred and eighty degrees.'

I picture the whole room turning on the narrow tunnel like a rotisserie chicken. It's absurd.

'I know how strange it sounds,' she adds, 'but this room is a puzzle designed to test us.'

'It is?'

She tries to move the chest. It's bolted down. It's *bolted down*.

Either the interior designer was incredibly paranoid about thieves, or they were furnishing a room that . . . Oh my god, the room turns on an axis.

She throws her weight into the chest. It doesn't budge. She squints over at the cupboard. I know what she wants to do. She asks if I mind. I don't. I'm pretty certain no matter how hard she pushes, she's not going to tip over the cupboard with me in it, because like the chest, it's fixed in place.

She makes three attempts to shift the cupboard and then steps back. 'It's fixed to the wall.'

'Thought so.'

She returns to the chest with urgency. She runs her fingers across the timber. 'There must be some sort of switch that initiates the rotation.' She works her way around the chest. She grabs at one of the iron ring pulls. It rattles.

'It's loose.' She yanks it.

'What happened?'

'Nothing. It's just popped out a bit.'

'Turn it?'

She does. The click, click, click reminds me of a wind-up toy. She releases the iron ring pull and steps back.

The room jolts like an elevator that enjoys reminding you of your mortality. Beyond the walls, a chorus of grinding gears sing their ancient song. Slowly, the entire room responds. The tunnel we walked down remains fixed while the chamber rotates. The pace is glacial.

Until it's not. I steady myself in the cupboard, my forearms against the sides. The loose wooden shelf slides away. The trespasser is rushing to keep from being swept off her feet, like a hamster in a poorly designed wheel. I'm getting higher, higher . . . And it occurs to me that the wall the cupboard is bolted to is about to become the ceiling. Not ideal.

Then there's the sound of smashing glass, and everything goes dark.

The hanging bulb has not survived, and to be honest, I don't like my chances either. I'm very close to being suspended from the ceiling. I can't see how far I might fall and that makes it a hundred times worse. I press my heels into the timber. My limbs are trembling.

I feel myself level off. The gears' song goes quiet. The room steadies.

That wasn't one hundred and eighty degrees. That was only ninety.

'Why did it stop?' My voice is laced with panic.

'Wait. Wait. We need a light. Where's the shelf?'

'Use your phone.'

'I don't have a phone.'

I'm struggling. 'Who doesn't have a phone?'

'Me. Ah!' There's the sound of timber being dragged against the floor. 'One sec.'

It isn't long before the room glows. She pulls herself to her feet. The end of the loose shelf is now on fire, and she's holding it from the base with both hands like some old-timey wooden torch. The chest is bolted to the wall between us, casting a long, dramatic shadow. The slightest shake of the flaming shelf makes the shadow dance.

Her eyes are wide; her jaw is slack. She's forgotten my little life-or-death predicament. 'I've never raided a sanctuary before. I didn't want to hype it up and get disappointed.' She swings the torch and the shadow stretches elsewhere. 'And then that happened.'

I estimate there are two metres between me and the chest, and another two or so between the chest and the wall-turned-floor. 'It half-happened.'

She laughs and then the seriousness sinks in. 'Right. *Right.*'

'We need to twist the ring pull some more, but I don't think I can climb up to it,' she says.

I have a bad feeling she's going to—

'You're going to need to fall down to it.'

Yeah, that's what I thought.

She adds, 'The chest will break your fall.'

'It'll break my face,' I spit.

She adopts a gentle if not mildly condescending coo. 'You're going to be fine. I'll talk you through this. I'll break it into steps.'

I think I already know them.

Step One. Let go.

Step Two. Ow.

My limbs are trembling more severely. She coaches me from below. With her guidance, I shift my forearms so they're lined up with the front frame of the cupboard. She tells me that so long as I'm strong in my upper body, there shouldn't be any dramas – problem is, I'm weak, and I live for drama. She explains I've got to bring my knees to my chest in a controlled movement, and then extend my legs down.

I lift one shaking foot, chicken out and plant it firmly back. 'I can't do it.'

'You can,' she stresses. 'Stop pressing through your feet and bring your knees to—'

I let my legs go limp and my lower body just sort of flops out. I'm dangling from the ceiling. My forearms are pressed against the inside of the cupboard, keeping me from falling the whole way through.

'And now . . .'

She doesn't need to tell me what happens now. I know what I need to do. When my body is steady, I let myself drop. I land on the chest, remembering to bend my knees on impact, because apparently I *have* learnt something in years of compulsory physical education classes.

I peer back up at the cupboard, its doors splayed open. I'm a little impressed with myself. 'I'm annoyed we didn't film that. I could've become one of those hot gymnasts everyone thirsts over online.'

'It didn't look how you imagine it did.'

'Ouch.'

And like that, my feat of athleticism is forgotten.

'If you just reach over the edge of the chest, you should be able to grip the ring pull.' She points with the flaming shelf.

I lower my centre of gravity slowly – I've been in my body long enough to know that if I ever plummeted from a great height, it'd be immediately after celebrating not plummeting from a greater height. I lie face-down and slowly extend one arm over the edge.

'It's the ring pull on your left.'

I move my hand.

'The other left.'

I move my hand the other way and clasp the iron ring protruding from the chest. It's cold.

'Turn it,' she instructs.

I look over the edge of the chest, down at her firelit face. I have another advantage to exploit. She can't climb up here, so she needs me to cooperate. And maybe my cooperation requires something in return.

'Before I do anything, I'd really like to know your name.'

She cackles. 'Well played.'

'Thanks.'

'I'm Sally.'

I honestly expected more resistance. 'Really?'

'What? Do you want to see ID?'

'Okay.'

'Are you kidding?' this supposed Sally asks.

'You could've made up a name.'

'Who'd make up Sally?'

'I don't know.'

She sighs and produces a wallet from her pocket. She flicks it open and riffles through its contents, all with the same hand. She plucks out a card and pockets the wallet once more.

'It's a library card that expired last year,' she says, angling it up to me. 'Sally Rodgers. Not that you can read it from there.'

She's right, I can't. But I can make out enough of it to know there's no photo. I tell her so.

'It's me,' she insists. 'Why would I carry around somebody else's expired library card?'

She has a point. I'm about to turn the iron ring pull when I realise I can get so much more out of her than just her real name. I ask, 'What is this place?'

Sally's face twitches. She's reluctant to tell me. 'It's a sanctuary.'

'For who?'

'No idea,' she says.

I play hardball. 'Well, I have no idea if I can rotate the room for you.'

She groans. 'I have a hunch, but I can't say for certain. There are five of these sanctuaries hidden under the oldest schools in Sydney, designed to test people. Only the worthy discover their secrets.'

'Are we . . . worthy?'

'Turn the ring pull and we'll find out, I guess.'

I do as she says. I turn it in bursts, and each time, I'm rewarded with a click. When I've turned it as far as it will go, I release it. There's another jolt. The gears' song resumes and the room turns. Shards of bulb glass tinkle. The chest will soon be suspended from the ceiling. I instantly regret not better preparing for my descent. I panic and drop to a floor whose slope is steepening. I follow Sally's lead and rush down the tessellated tiles. The floor is rapidly becoming a wall. I jump.

The room stills and the tessellated green field is beneath our feet.

'What now?' I ask.

The room answers. The wall facing the tunnel collapses. Unsettled dust curls in the air. We're looking at an annex with no tessellated patterns or bolted furnishings. The sanctuary has revealed its secret. A seven-foot statue stands against a bare wall, its grey-stone body scarred by chips and white cracks.

It's the burly man from the top of the chest realised in three dimensions.

Sally holds up the flaming shelf. 'Darroch,' she whispers, taking careful steps into the annex.

The statue's build and beard say the dude was some kind of warrior. The sword hilt poking out behind one shoulder all but confirms it. I still ask, 'Who was he?'

'*Is*,' Sally corrects me, reaching out to touch the statue.

It seems like a silly grammatical point to get hung up on – until the statue swings an arm, grips Sally by the front of her shirt and lifts her to his eye level. Her makeshift torch tumbles to the ground and is immediately engulfed by flames. The statue's expression is wild, half-lit from below.

Sally was right. Darroch definitely *is*.

# THREE

Every so often, I encounter an online advertisement for Charlton Grammar. It's always the same one. Four clear-skinned uniformed boys stare wide-eyed into the distance. They're partially obscured by a message written in the school's signature cursive font. *Equipping young men for every challenge.* The ad's corny, but some part of me has always believed it. Now, staring down the statue that has come to life and lifted a girl clean off the floor by her shirt, I'm realising there's one challenge they missed.

My Charlton Grammar-acquired skills include creatively justifying why all of my visual arts assignments look half-melted, salvaging poorly argued essays with bomb conclusions and hiding academic progress reports from my parents.

I am totally ill-equipped for *this*.

I check over my shoulder. The tunnel. I can retrace my steps. Seal the trapdoor shut. Forget all this ever happened.

For a moment, all I hear is my kick-drum heart. And then I hear Sally struggling in the statue's grasp. I can't leave her down here. That's a bit dark. I turn back. The statue releases her like a kettle that's hot to the touch. Her knees buckle. She sinks to the floor beside the flaming plank. The statue trains his gaze on me like I'm next.

I should have run.

When Sally pulls herself up, the statue asks her name in a voice like gravel grinding.

'Sally Rodgers.' If he doesn't believe her, she can produce the library card again.

'Sally Rodgers and companion, you have disturbed my stasis,' he booms.

Is there a word for being simultaneously terrified and awestruck? Should it even be possible to feel both at once? You'd think the terror inspired by a talking stone warrior would overpower any inner voice saying, 'Ooh, that stone warrior can talk!' Apparently not. He might beat us to a pulp, but I can't stop *marvelling*.

Sally pulls her shoulders back and clears her throat. 'I don't disturb you lightly. I've come to warn you, Darroch,' she says. 'I—'

The flaming shelf extinguishes, and the room goes dark. I'm quick to withdraw my phone and shine its flashlight.

'Thanks,' Sally whispers before straightening once more. 'I'm a Guardian. You and your kind are in danger. The Hounds are circling and they mean to destroy you.'

Darroch smiles. 'I fear no Hounds. I doubt they shall find me, I am interred deep enough that they will not sense me, but if they do,' Darroch gestures to the very large and very real sword strapped to his back, 'I shall greet them with my weapon and they shall die in pieces.'

That obviously isn't the reaction Sally anticipated. She frowns. 'With all due respect, you were hidden precisely because you are vulnerable, to not only the Hounds, but to anyone. And you're not as well hidden as you think,' she tells him. 'Anyone could wander down here. Connor found your sanctuary by accident.'

I chime in. 'It's true.'

'You will be discovered if you stay,' she adds. 'You might be able to defend yourself, but what about the others? This continent is no longer safe for them. We need to relocate all of you. It's time for the next Movement.'

The word is magic. Darroch is instantly pliable. He blinks. 'As my Guardian, I defer to your better judgement.'

'Okay,' Sally says. 'We need a way out.'

I remind her that she'd have one if she hadn't removed my shoe. She calls me a smart-arse and I graciously accept the compliment.

'We need a discrete escape route,' she clarifies.

The statue turns to face the wall, and after a measured pause he slams his fist against it. The chamber quakes. The wall fissures. He digs his fingers into the fresh crack and pulls the wall apart in chunks. He drops them at his feet.

He's digging a discrete escape route. It's pretty cool.

'There are four others like him, aren't there?' I ask. 'Talking statues?'

She tries to act coy. 'What makes you say that?'

'The chest carvings. And earlier, you said there were five sanctuaries. If each belongs to one . . .'

'You're correct.'

'And a Movement is when you . . . move them?'

Sally nods.

Darroch drops one final chunk of wall to his feet. 'Follow me,' he says, before disappearing through the opening he's created.

Sally and I lunge forwards. I shine the flashlight into the void. The rotating chamber is housed within a much larger cavern, cradled by an intricate system of gears and pulleys that allow it to turn on its axis. I can barely make out Darroch in the almost-darkness. Sally calls his name and he doesn't answer. He's marching towards the jagged rock face.

'I'm having a hard time believing this is actually happening.' I step back from the opening. 'I hit my head earlier. I'm knocked out and dreaming you, the rotating room, the talking statue.'

'Sorry, Alice. This is real,' Sally says. 'But obviously, if anyone asks . . .'

'It never happened.'

'No, it did not.' Sally looks at me and smiles slightly. 'I'd better follow the big guy.'

We rush our goodbyes, and then she doesn't leave. She leans out of the opening, probably nervous about the drop into the cavern below.

'Thanks, by the way,' she says eventually. 'I don't think I would've been able to manage that without you.'

'It was nothing.'

'It was a lot.' She surveys me closely. 'Do you . . . want to come? I have a feeling I might need some help finding the others.'

Her offer knocks the wind out of me. In the friend divorce, Olly won custody of our mutuals. They don't speak to me anymore. I'm not a total pariah, other guys still greet me in the corridors, make small talk in the cafeteria line, but no one's saving me a seat at lunch, or dragging me shopping after school. It's just politeness. This is more than that. This is an invitation. I'm wanted.

'You've probably got to go to class or something,' Sally adds.

'I don't.' I conjure a lie about it being an independent learning day. I figure, I'm already a truant and Mum isn't expecting me home until midnight. 'I'm game.'

'Sweet,' Sally says. 'Come on.'

She jumps first. The drop is a few metres, enough to allow for the chamber to rotate without disturbing the earth below. The soil is soft, and the air is stale. When I land beside her, Sally helps me up. We weave through the maze of archaic chamber-rotating technology, my phone lighting the way.

The jagged wall of the cavern that Darroch marched towards is now interrupted by a narrow tunnel. Sally and I draw nearer. The tunnel stretches the entire way to the surface – there are five flights' worth of steps, give or take a few. Darroch stands by the exit, a shadowy figure against the sky. He's waiting for us.

The tunnel is part discrete escape route, part miraculous feat of artistry. Darroch has carved relief sculptures into its left side. Near the foot of the stairs, three giant creased faces protrude from the rock wall. They watch us as we ascend. I raise my phone. The flashlight illuminates them. The creases aren't wrinkles, they're the outlines of clashing armies, swords and severed limbs. Stories of a warring world play out within the margins of each face.

The detail is incredible. I can't believe Darroch managed it with his bare hands.

'Darroch did all this in the time it took us to come down?' I ask. 'What is he?'

Sally doesn't answer immediately, like she's fighting against her better judgement to keep me in the dark. 'He's a Monument,' she says finally. 'A powerful being from the past.'

I stop to trace over the contours of the third face with my fingertips. I know it's only carved rock, but when I match its gaze, my surroundings evaporate. I'm drawn closer and closer by the wide, blank, unblinking eyes.

'You coming?' Sally calls.

I shake my head. 'Yeah. *Yeah.*' I climb two steps at a time to catch up. 'Do you think it's ethical for a Monument to do my visual arts major work?'

'No,' she says.

'Would Darroch do it anyway?'

She clicks her tongue against the roof of her mouth.

There's a larger scene carved into the rock beside her. The three intimidating faces from before, they have bodies now. The near-identical women sit on separate thrones. They look like sisters. Another scene follows, and another, like three-dimensional panels of an ancient comic strip. The sisters command opposing armies – humans fight alongside animals. When one sister is slain, the two others split her throne. In the background, the world burns.

Sally squints at the wall. This time, she shares without me prompting her. She uses Darroch's art as a spine to hang her words from. 'Thousands of years ago, the world was consumed by war,' she says. 'The five Monuments contained the feuding sisters in another realm. The world was saved, but at a terrible cost to the Monuments themselves.'

She brushes her hand against the five rock figures she passes. When I get closer, I recognise one as Darroch, and the others from the chest. They adopt the same poses, only they've been rendered far more competently.

'The Monuments each have different specialities,' she says. 'Darroch is strong. The younger-looking ones, Aiden and Finn, they regulate temperature.' That explains the fireball and the snowflake. 'Jivanta is a giver of life.' Hence the tiny tree sprouting from her palm. 'Nuo's always been my favourite. She controls the forces that keep the world intact, from binding the nucleus of an atom all the way to fixing our feet on the ground.' Darroch has attached the chalice to Nuo's front, so it appears as though it's floating above her outstretched hand.

The carved story continues. The Monuments break off pieces of themselves to build a barrier between the feuding sisters and the world. And then the battlefields clear. Crops grow over discarded armour.

'After containing the sisters, the Monuments were left as shadows of their former selves, so they entrusted themselves to humans – to the Guardians.' Sally leads me past a depiction of Darroch and the others being packed into ornate chests and carried away.

A thin man stands separate from the other humans. The sun sits above his left shoulder and a crescent moon above his right. He clutches an hourglass.

'Who's he?' I ask.

Sally stares hard at the thin man for a moment. She has no idea, and when I suggest he might be another Monument, she shakes her head. 'No, there are only five,' she says, moving on. 'They were hidden in the hearts of mountains, where they slept. The responsibility for keeping them safe was passed on: Guardians told their first-born, for generation after generation. If the times necessitated it, the Monuments were moved to caves by the sea, or to the treasure vaults of royalty. Over two centuries ago, they were brought to Australia. They were buried, protected and, for the most part, forgotten.'

She pauses. I assume her calves are burning as much as mine are, then she turns, and I realise the pause was for dramatic effect. 'The times necessitate they move again,' she concludes.

'The times?' I ask.

'The Hounds are circling.' She mentioned that earlier. 'There are the Guardians, who are responsible for keeping the Monuments safe, and the Hounds, who we are keeping them safe from.'

'Darroch's in danger, then?'

'He is.'

'And if he's in danger, am I in danger if I come with you?' I ask.

'I totally understand if you don't want to—'

'I want to,' I blurt out.

She exhales. 'You sure?'

I'm not in *love* with the idea of putting myself in danger, but I know one thing for certain. 'I don't want to be at school today,' I tell her.

That's good enough for her. 'Great.'

We reach Darroch. The daylight behind him makes my eyes throb. I glance back down the length of the tunnel, at the secret history of the world on its walls. It's an impressive achievement.

'I understand you're a Monument,' I say, 'but what *are* you?'

'A powerful being,' Sally reiterates.

'Yeah, but *what*?'

Darroch looks me square in the eyes and says, very plainly, 'I'm a god.'

I blink. 'A god?' I ask. 'Like, *god*-god?'

He nods. 'Yes.'

'I was thinking that for your safety, we probably shouldn't disclose that detail to everyone we meet,' Sally says.

The Monument – the *god*-god – shrugs. 'He knows now.'

Sally and Darroch ascend the final steps of the tunnel, leaving me standing, mouth agape, in their wake. Gods are real and I've met one. Gods are real and hidden and I'm going to help find them.

I rush and emerge in the middle of College Lane. The lane skirts the western side of the school campus. It's used for student drop-offs and pick-ups, and deserted in the hours between. That's lucky, considering the small mountain range of displaced earth and crumbled bitumen Darroch has just created.

Sally wants to get moving pronto, on account of Darroch being *made of stone*, but there's still the matter of the sanctuary to deal with. According to the god, it's standard practice during the Movements to destroy them.

'Then destroy it,' Sally says.

Darroch seems hesitant and I understand why. I point to the buildings over the fence – a lot of Charlton Grammar is built on top of the sanctuary. If we destroy it, we risk a decent chunk of the school sinking into the earth. We settle on a compromise: we'll fill the hole and then run away before anybody sees us.

The Monument leans his weight into the mounds of soil, toppling the displaced earth back into the tunnel. He's doing in seconds what would take a landscaping crew an entire day, and barely seems inconvenienced. But he *is* a god, I guess.

Watching him work, I'm reminded of Joshua Parks.

I took a semester of drama in Year Nine. When an improv scene partner would say something, no matter how inane, we were encouraged to accept and build off it. So, when my partner Joshua Parks exclaimed, 'Look! A dinosaur!' in what was supposed to be a Parisian café, I had to say, 'Yes, and . . .' That blanket acceptance only spurred Joshua on. The scene kept escalating, and by the end of our five minutes, we were duelling an alien warlord on the moon.

Basically, Joshua Parks is improvising my life. This is his latest escalation, after the trapdoor and the girl, and the cupboard, and the rotating room, and my feat of gymnastic excellence, and the talking statue.

My brain is just saying, 'Yes, and . . .'

*Yes*, Darroch is a god, *and* I'm skipping school with him.

Speaking of . . . I check my phone now that I have service. It's pushing half-past ten and there are no panicked messages from Mum or Dad, so the school hasn't notified them that I've been marked absent. Mr Cheen must have forgotten about the roll. He's distracted at the best of times, and my class . . . Well, we can be especially distracting. The guys in the back row have never been confronted with a lesson they can't derail.

'You're not texting anyone, are you?' Sally asks.

I wave my home screen at her. There are no apps open. 'Nope.'

'Good. Cone of silence.'

Darroch steps back. He's filled the tunnel and smoothed the surface over so the soil is even with the bitumen.

Sally takes the lead. She strides ahead, waving towards a distant intersection. 'My van's parked this way.'

Darroch's steps are uneven, like he's nursing an injury. He drags his right foot a little, but I only notice because I'm staring. And he notices my staring. 'Live as long as I have, and you will collect your fair share of ailments too,' he says.

I apologise. He shrugs it off.

Even with his ailments, I still have to alternate between walking and jogging to keep up with him. General politeness dictates I should probably make small talk, but is it rude to waste a god's time like that? My experience with gods is limited to the Greek Orthodox church services my grandparents dragged me to as a kid, the names Mum takes in vain, and the photos our school rowing champion Brent Ahmadi uploads online with the hashtag #god.

'Did you create the world?' I ask.

'With the other Monuments, yes. It was a collaboration. If the world were a mound of clay, Nuo bound it together, I gave it shape, Aiden and Finn tempered it with fire and ice, and Jivanta gave it life.'

Before they contained the feuding sisters in another realm and allowed humankind to flourish, the Monuments' big achievement was creating the world. No biggie. They started with their metaphorical mound of clay and . . .

'But who made the clay?' I ask.

Darroch laughs. 'And who made me?'

That's more uncertainty than I expect in a deity. 'Gods don't have gods, do they?'

'Gods have gods.'

'And they have gods?'

'Presumably, yes.'

I'm distracted by the mental image of a nested doll of gods within gods for a moment. 'Do you pray to them?'

He smiles wryly. 'Do you pray to me?'

That's a ridiculous question. I didn't even know he existed until this morning. I say so.

'Most gods worth their salt don't trouble themselves with being known or worshipped. Creating something, seeing that creation flourish . . . That is what satiates us, not the size of our followings.'

I don't know what makes me think of Pappou, but I do. It must be Darroch's vibe. He has the air about him of someone who's been around a long time. His words have weight. I could never understand the things Pappou would tell me, but judging by the way my distant cousins flocked to him for advice, his words had weight too. Once, anyway.

I exhale and try to think of something different.

'What are the other Monuments like?' I ask.

He sighs and his lips curl as he reminisces. 'Jivanta is wise, far wiser than me. She is the mother of all that live and breathe in this world, the creator of life. Nuo has a sharp wit and no patience for fools. She is loyal, reliable, but prone to cheating when one turns their back on her during a contest. Aiden is fiery and sometimes reckless. He is driven by his passions whereas Finn is calmer, more measured,' Darroch says. 'We are an unconventional family, and as dangerous as Movements are, it will be wonderful to see them again.'

'I'm still coming to terms with meeting one god, the idea of meeting more . . . I don't have words.'

'I must admit, a Guardian enlisting an accomplice is unorthodox,' he says.

'I specialise in falling from heights without spraining ankles, apparently.'

'Let's hope your luck lasts.'

We arrive at the intersection. Sally leads us to a van that has seen better decades – the body is dented and what paint hasn't been scratched off is fading. Darroch hops in the back. The vehicle buckles a little under his weight. Sally and I climb into the front. When I sit, I feel the journal I tucked into my pants press against my back. I'd forgotten about it completely.

Sally turns the key in the ignition and the van sputters to life. There's a persistent rattle. And no seatbelts. She says it's all part of the charm. If that's the case, I like my transport with a little less charm. She pulls out of the parking space in a hurry; I'm thrown to one side.

'You'll get used to it,' she says.

I look back at Darroch. He's marvelling at the machine, prodding his seat with the curiosity of a child. Past him, out the rear window, I see the Charlton Grammar belltower shrinking, shrinking. My chest swells.

I take back what I said earlier about skipping class. It's exactly as thrilling as people have led me to believe.

'I'd face forwards, if I were you,' Sally says.

'Right. No seatbelts.'

I face forwards.

# FOUR

Sally Rodgers does not have a driver's licence, and that becomes abundantly clear when she crosses three lanes without indicating because, and I quote, she could do with a burrito right about now.

'Are you hungry?' she asks. 'My shout.'

She's pulled into the drive-through of a chain that, despite lowering their prices since a highly publicised salmonella outbreak, is still the chain that had that highly publicised salmonella outbreak.

'Nah, I'm good.'

'Suit yourself. Darroch?' She peers into the rear-view mirror.

The god thanks her for the offer, but explains that gods don't have much use for food.

'Actually, I was going to ask if you can see a woollen blanket on the floor under my seat,' Sally says.

'Oh.' Darroch checks. 'Yes.'

'Could you . . . drape it over yourself so that—'

Darroch is looking daggers at her.

'Right, never mind,' she course-corrects. 'They won't look into the back anyway.'

The van rolls to the first window, where a man in a headset and a gaudy uniform waits hunched over the register. He greets us and his gaze instantly trails into the back.

'We're redoing the garden,' Sally snaps. She hurriedly orders herself a regular chicken burrito with extra guac, double-checks I'm not hungry, then asks for a side of wedges just in case.

She opens her wallet and a wad of notes bursts from the sleeve. It's a cartoonish amount of money, and I tell her so after she hands over a twenty, waves off the change and drives to the next window.

'I don't want anyone tracking my transactions,' she says.

'What, do you live off the grid or something?' I ask.

'As much as I can.'

I want to probe deeper, but there's a woman at the drive-through window holding out a brown paper bag and staring into the back of the van.

'A statue for the garden,' Sally says flatly, accepting the bag and plonking it down in my lap. 'Have a lovely day.'

The woman's stare follows Darroch as we drive off.

Sally swerves the van back into the flow of traffic and the driver behind us punches their horn. She tells me she's self-taught and I believe her. Not that I'm really in a position to judge. I'm not the most competent learner driver. Janice from Janice's Driving School is unflinchingly enthusiastic, but the best compliment she's given me is, 'I really thought you would hit that tree, and I'm glad you didn't.'

Sally reaches into the bag warming my lap and extracts her burrito. She presses it against the wheel and scratches at the aluminium foil wrapping as she drives.

'What do your friends think about you living off the grid?' I ask.

'Don't know.' She tries loosening the foil wrapping with her teeth. She's unsuccessful. 'This is a one-person operation. Fewer people to explain things to.'

'Now there's me.'

'And I'm spending a lot of time explaining,' she says.

'Still, it's a two-person operation.'

'Is it?' She doesn't take her eyes off the road, but she does scrunch up her face. 'I see you more as a temporary helper. It's not like we're going to get to know each other and become chummy.'

'We could.'

'No.'

'I have the time. I recently divorced a friend.'

Judging by her expression, she has no idea what I mean. 'You were married?'

'No, my best friend and I are no longer friends,' I clarify.

'Why not just say that?' She catches herself and shakes her head. 'Anyway, we're not doing this.'

I continue, undeterred, 'Basically, he got mad at me for not showing up to a party I never actually said I was going to. I don't drink. Never have. That's a lie. Dad's poured me a sip of beer before, but I don't *drink*-drink, so parties don't sound like fun for me. And Mum made me promise not to go anyway. I didn't show up – apparently that makes me boring – and we're not friends anymore.'

Sally glances down at the still very-much-intact burrito wrapping. 'This is too hard,' she mutters. She stops the van across the driveway of an auto repairs factory and puts on the hazard lights. With both hands free, she unwraps the burrito and relishes the first bite. She relaxes into the seat. 'So good.'

I try to sit with most of my face covered. I have this creeping fear that someone might spot me skipping school – Mum while visiting a client, Dad on his way to a long lunch. I look out for them, in case they pop out from behind a post box or something. I notice a guy in all black loading glass bottles into a recycling bin by the roadside. I recognise him by his dirty blond hair. I straighten. *Olly.* That's why he didn't come to the rooftop this morning. He's skipping school too.

I'm about to lower the window when I pause. What's he even doing?

He turns and it's . . . not Olly. It's a waiter. He walks an empty crate back into the café on the corner.

Darroch speaks up. 'We are waiting here in the open?'

'Mm?' Sally finishes her mouthful. 'Oh, right. The Hounds. They won't attack on a busy street, will they?'

The Monument sounds severe. 'They have before and they will again.'

'Right, I'll hurry with this.' She points to the half-demolished burrito. Then she turns to me and says, 'Keep an eye out, will you?'

I check the side mirror, but I don't exactly know what I'm keeping an eye out for. Regular dogs? 'What are they?'

Sally glances at the god in the back seat and asks if he minds.

'Before the world was torn apart by war, it was customary for gods to keep understudies,' Darroch says. 'We had two each at any one time. They would learn from us, but they were also confidants – we were better because of them.'

'Why would a god need an understudy?' I ask.

He looks at me like the answer's obvious. 'To take over if need be.'

I wait for him to elaborate, but he doesn't. Can gods . . . die?

'We didn't snatch people off the street and train them as our understudies,' Darroch says. 'These weren't ordinary humans. Ten were initially created especially for this purpose, two for each of us. They could sense our advanced power, they smelt it, and this was an ability they could pass on to their first-born. If we required them to take over, our understudies were willing and ready.'

Sally gasps dramatically. What's left of her burrito is collapsing in her hands and she's in a race against time to keep it from leaking everywhere. 'Sorry, sorry. I'm listening though.'

'We never required them to take over,' Darroch continues. 'Their senses waned when their first-born came of age and could sense us themselves. Each generation replaced the last . . . until five of our understudies were corrupted. They grew weary. They argued that their apprenticeships were long and pointless, because they would never assume our place. They were bitter, twisted by their ambition. We tried to reason with them, to restore them. We failed. When we were weakened, they struck. The faithful understudies, the Guardians, aided our escape, but their disloyal peers could sense us. They pursued us like—'

'Hounds,' I say.

'Exactly.' The Monument nods. 'They were ruthless hunters. We had to be moved quickly, stealthily. We were interred to mask our scents and relocated only when necessary. Every minute we are aboveground, we are in danger.'

Sally scrunches the foil wrapping into a ball. The burrito is gone. 'Got it,' she says, restarting the engine.

'And the Hounds are still around after all this time?' I ask.

'In some form,' Darroch says. 'Do not underestimate the power of a grudge to survive generations.'

Sally merges into traffic – again, with the confidence of a much better driver. It occurs to me that if she's a Guardian, then she can sense Darroch.

'Wait, can you smell him?' I ask.

'What sort of a question is—? Rude. Of course, I can. And I can smell you too,' she says with a shake of her head. 'Boys thinking sprays are the same as deodorants, I swear.'

She's kidding. I think she is. I hope she is. I make a mental note to check my underarms when we're out of the van.

'For what it's worth,' she adds, 'your ex-friend sounds like he's not worth your time.'

She was listening. My heart soars a little. 'I thought we weren't getting to know each other,' I say.

'Oh, we aren't. I just . . . It needed to be said. Pass me a wedge, would you?'

# FIVE

Sally lives two blocks back from one of the busiest roads in Sydney's inner-west. The distant thrum of traffic is like a threat – at any moment, cars can spill onto the street and we'll be caught. It helps that Darroch has warmed to the idea of the woollen blanket. Sally drapes it over him – well, the top half of him anyway. He looks like the world's tallest child in the world's weakest Halloween costume. She takes him by the hand and leads him through the gate and across the lawn of 71 McKenzie Street. I saunter a few steps behind. She avoids the front porch, heading down the right-hand side of the house. The land slopes gently to the crimson door of 71A McKenzie Street.

While Sally fishes around in her pockets for the key, I take it upon myself to be the entertainment. 'Is this the strangest way you've been transported in broad daylight?' I ask Darroch.

The world's tallest child keeps still. 'Surprisingly, no.'

'Sounds like a funny story.'

'Many men died.'

'Oh, that's less . . .' Trailing off is clearly the best card to play.

Sally pops open the door and peels the blanket off Darroch so he knows to bend a little to clear the frame. I follow them inside. The apartment is open plan, divided roughly into quarters. One corner is devoted to cooking, and the others dining, living and sleeping.

'This is the mansion,' she says, exhausting the world's entire supply of sarcasm in one hit. She tosses the blanket onto her unmade bed and starts tidying the place in the smallest ways: she picks a jumper off the floor, pushes in a dining chair, moves a dirty bowl to the sink.

I didn't think she was old enough to live alone. There's a lot I want to ask, but I know her policy on personal questions is pretty rigid, so I keep quiet.

She sits on her bed and exhales deeply as she loosens her school tie. She produces a sphere of lip balm from underneath her pillow and applies it with one finger. She offers me some. Tastes like blueberry.

A map of the city dominates the left side of the room. The wall and its two doors are tiled in pages torn out of two street directories. When I ask why one wasn't enough, she explains that the pages were double-sided, so to get the whole map flat, she had to buy two. The shoreline cuts a striking silhouette against the sea – like a face in profile, screaming at the blue.

I wander closer. Darroch does the same. He's a mountain beside me. Standing slightly hunched, his head still grazes the ceiling's exposed beams.

'This is Sydney?' he asks.

'Yup.'

'The history of a city is written by its streets,' he says. He lets the words hang a bit before he points to the shoreline. 'It was new and young and reckless once. You see that in the chaos of the roads that twist and mingle by the harbour. The city matured as it sprawled west.' He points closer to where we are and further out. 'Its lines become neater.'

I inspect the map closer. I spot Charlton Grammar. Sally's traced over the campus boundary in silver ink. I scan the map. There are dozens of similar silver boundaries, some with red crosses through them.

'I've been researching potential sanctuary locations for six months. Basically, every school I've marked up there was opened before the 1900s,' Sally explains. 'I didn't have much luck with the first couple.'

'You did not know where I was interred?' Darroch asks. 'You weren't told?'

'Mum only left me this.' Sally fishes out a leather-bound journal from under the swirl of bedsheets. It looks exactly like the one I have tucked into the back of my pants.

Wait . . . Her mum only left her that? So, she's . . .

'I'm sorry for your loss,' the Monument says, bowing slightly.

'Me too,' I add.

She accepts our commiserations with a nod. 'I moved to the basement after she died,' she says. 'I rent out the upstairs and it pays for everything I need. My neighbours don't know I'm their landlord. I told them I'm a backpacker from Europe, but they keep inviting me over for dinner and my accent keeps changing.' She laughs.

I don't know how we got from her nodding solemnly to laughing so quickly, but here we are. It's like she wants to get the mum conversation over as painlessly as possible.

'Your neighbours don't recognise you?' I ask.

'I avoid them.' Sally thumbs the journal open. 'Now, I've isolated the other potential sanctuary locations.'

'And they're all under schools?' I ask.

'Yes.'

I scrunch my face. 'Why?'

Sally shrugs. 'That's what the journal says. The sanctuaries were built beneath sites that were reserved for schools.'

'The five Guardians who participate in a Movement decide where we will rest. They know the world at the time better than we do,' Darroch says. 'The other four Guardians . . . Are they each aware of their Monument's location?'

Sally hesitates. 'I . . . haven't spoken to them. Or found them.'

Darroch glances back at the map, at the dozens of silver boundaries that indicate potential sanctuaries. 'This is highly unorthodox. Usually all Guardians consent to a Movement before a Monument is disturbed.'

'I only have this to go by,' Sally says, waving the journal.

'And you are my Guardian?' Darroch asks.

'Yes.'

'Then I trust you with this Movement,' the god says. 'We must find the others as a matter of urgency. My scent will attract our hunters soon enough.'

Sally springs off the bed and approaches the map. She asks Darroch if he knows where the other sanctuaries are.

'I was never told,' the Monument says, hunching a little more, so he can withdraw his sword from its sheath without knocking out a light fitting. He pulls back to his almost-full height. 'But I can find one.'

Darroch points the blade downwards and holds the hilt to the wall. He shuts his eyes and listens – not to anything we can hear. It's as if the sword leads him. He raises it to the north of the city centre and taps a small silver square with the green grip. 'There.'

He steps back so Sally and I can better make out the name: Eden Ladies' College.

To anyone south of the Harbour Bridge, ELC girls are renowned for their dizzyingly rich parents, hyphenated surnames and allergies to travelling south of the Harbour Bridge. The campus must be pretty close to paradise with a name like Eden. Somewhere beneath it, there's a god waiting to be discovered.

'Are we off, then?' I ask, eagerness radiating from my pores.

'Not quite.'

'Why not?' I think it's simple enough. We hop back into Sally's deathtrap of a van, sneak into ELC and have Darroch do his sword-magnet trick to find the next Monument. We'll be in and out in twenty minutes tops, give or take a chamber to rotate.

Sally lists her why-nots. First, if we're strolling through the gates during the day, she's going to need a uniform, and that means visiting the school's second-hand shop or paying a girl to borrow hers. Second, Darroch's made of stone. Third, I'm a guy.

'Schools like ELC are teeming with security guards. This requires *some* planning,' Sally says, returning to her bed. She reopens the journal and after a moment, she asks if she can borrow my phone to research ELC.

'Can't you use your computer?' The answer occurs to me as soon as I finish asking, and we both say, 'Off the grid,' in unison. I toss her my device.

Without my phone, I'm left to while away the time watching Darroch complete slow laps of the basement. Occasionally, he comes across an object that he can't quite figure out. He looks to me for help and I oblige him. I never thought I'd have so much to say about a tissue box – or ever need to have so much to say about a tissue box – but there you go.

This is a far cry from the dangerous adventure I expected when I followed Sally out of the sanctuary, but I'm not going to complain about getting to chill at Sally's, acting as a literal god's guide to the modern world.

As the hours pass, I'm surprised that I haven't once considered heading back to Charlton Grammar. Occasionally, I ask Sally if anyone has texted. She answers in the negative. No messages from my parents means that not only have I proven myself capable of mild rebellion, I've got away with it too. Maybe the school's sophisticated anti-truancy measures aren't as incredible as they're talked up to be.

I regret not testing them sooner.

I also regret turning down a burrito. Sally, guilty that she polished off the in-case-Connor-changes-his-mind wedges, invites me to raid the kitchen cabinets. I find a fire poker and the ingredients for a peanut butter sandwich, so I make a peanut butter sandwich and wonder why Sally has a fire poker when there's no fireplace down here.

Half an hour later, I make myself a second sandwich.

I'm rinsing the plate when Sally says, 'According to the ELC website, the historic Bryan Manor is hosting the debutante ball tonight.'

I turn to face her. 'The what?'

She's squinting at my phone. 'It's a manor. They say it's historic, I don't know why.'

I come closer. 'I meant, what's a debutante ball?'

Sally's smiling. 'I'm teasing. They're these fancy dinners where girls from posh families wear white gowns to be presented to formal society. Basically, it's an excuse to eat good food and dance. I've never been to one.'

'You've never been presented to formal society?'

'A shock to all, I know.' She's picking burrito out from between her teeth with the little finger of her free hand. 'But this is how we get in. You're going to present me to formal society. Well, not really. We'll pass security. They'll think we're going to the ball and instead, we'll look for the Monument.'

I perk up. This means I might actually get to meet another Monument before my midnight curfew.

'And Darroch?' I ask.

Sally starts, 'I'm not sure he—'

'They will not see me,' Darroch says, pretty sure of himself.

Sally doesn't argue with him, probably on account of him being a god and all. She hands back my phone. 'We'll need formal wear.' Her eyes widen and she excuses herself, leaving without explanation. It isn't until something – some*one* – lands heavily above us, that I realise she's broken in upstairs. Her footsteps cross to the other side of the house. When she returns, it's with two dry-cleaning bags slung over her shoulder. She unzips one to reveal a dark blue suit. 'What do you think?' she asks.

'You didn't swipe it from your tenants, did you?'

'I can tell you I bought it, if you'd like.'

That's a definite yes.

While she gets ready in the bathroom, I slip into the suit she *bought* for me. It fits pretty well – a little long in the sleeves, but nothing I can't work with. I feel bad for the grown man living upstairs with my string-bean proportions.

I fill the time.

This is the part they edit out of spy movies. In the fancy dinner scenes, the lady spies always look done up beyond belief. Nobody ever asks where they source their perfectly tailored designer gowns on such short notice, or where they've been hiding the professional hair-and-makeup teams. I guess that'd ruin the magic. Through the door, I hear what sounds suspiciously like someone knocking their makeup into the sink by accident.

I work my way around the basement apartment, and I'm struck by how few photos there are. Well, there are none. There's no sign of her parents, her friends. She just lives down here, disconnected from the world, with the map overwhelming one wall. I have a strong feeling her life revolves around the Monuments.

I'm drawn to the leather-bound journal Sally's left on her bed. I remove mine from the uniform I've piled on her dining table and compare the two. I bend back the covers. Someone's torn out the first page of Sally's – there's a jagged strip of paper down the inside of the spine. While the brown-spotted pages in the front of my journal are blank, the equally stained pages of hers are covered in handwritten notes. She's broken down each of the schools highlighted on the wall, detailing their histories and the notable features of their campuses. I flick to the end. Indecipherable words stretch from margin to margin, as they do in mine, only in Sally's, select words have been circled and translated. There isn't much in the notes that Sally or Darroch hasn't already told me.

I do learn that the Monuments arrived in 1788, a good piece of trivia. Not that I can ever raise it.

My eyes scan over the names of each of the Monuments – Jivanta's mention is underlined twice – and I wonder which one is waiting for us at ELC. I look up to ask Darroch if he has any idea. He's testing the structural integrity of the couch with one hand. He decides against it and sits on the floor.

Sally probably expects me to babysit him. I snap both journals shut, tuck mine behind the waistband of my suit pants and . . . How am I meant to babysit Darroch exactly? What am I supposed to do, engage him in a rigorous and stimulating debate? He's the very definition of not-on-my-level. He's a god. Plus, he's been buried for hundreds of years, and in and out of hiding for thousands. Everything ought to sound like gibberish to him.

Wait . . . How does he understand me and Sally?

'Question,' I announce on approach.

Darroch twists slightly. 'For me?'

There's literally no one else in here, but I humour him with a nod. 'Why do you speak like we do now? Shouldn't you be speaking Latin?'

'I can speak Latin, if you'd prefer.'

'Please don't.'

That makes him smile. He taps the couch with his structural-integrity hand. It's an invitation to sit. I take it. It's weird to look down on him.

He explains, 'Language came up from the earth as grunts and groans, and grew. Whenever people from different patches of earth met, their words would mix. One would leave with the other's turns of phrase. People kept colliding, and languages kept changing, but the earth kept constant. And the earth kept listening.'

My brow furrows. 'So . . . you heard it from the ground?'

He smirks. 'You should not be afraid to listen to what cannot speak.'

I look at the floorboards and imagine the earth beneath them collecting every word I say. Does it judge me? Mum can't handle the slang we use nowadays, so I can only imagine what the eternal earth must think.

'Do you, like, cringe when you hear how we speak?' I ask Darroch.

He laughs. 'If I were a purist, then every word beyond a grunt would be an aberration. I would have to consciously choose a moment when language was perfect, ignore its evolution prior, and condemn its evolution since. That is foolish. I learn a new phrase and relish it. It means the language is alive.'

I'm still stuck imagining the earth cringing at how many times I drop *like* daily.

Darroch's gaze is unwavering. 'May I ask a question now?'

That's how conversations tend to work. 'Sure.'

'Sally is a Guardian, but you are new to the fold and I find that fascinating.' He leans in. 'Tell me, what is it like to live in this world?'

It's probably the broadest question he could've asked and I try my best to answer it. My initial response is about one sentence long. I tell the nice deity who had a hand in creating the world that I very much like living in it. But Darroch looks at me with these big, expectant eyes and I'm encouraged to elaborate.

Those eyes . . . They're like Pappou's. They droop and make him look sort of sad. I focus on them and when I talk, it isn't to a creator god. It's to my grandfather. I'm filling him in on everything he's missed. My heart aches a little.

Darroch spoils the illusion when he finally speaks again. 'Fascinating.' I'm not sure the earth told him what it really means.

'Am I living right?' I ask him. 'Should I be doing anything differently?'

'Who am I to say?'

'Who are you? You're a god. Commandments are supposed to be your thing.'

'The world is not ours to play with.'

'But surely you have some advice?'

Darroch's reluctant to offer any, and he's saved by the bathroom door opening. Sally emerges. I rise up off the couch and she does a little twirl. She looks stunning. The gown starts with a sweetheart neckline – for some reason, Mum was surprised when I came out of the closet – and the white fabric crosses over at the front and then falls from her waist to the floor.

'You look amazing.'

'Really?' She stares down and inspects herself. 'I feel a bit bride-ish. Like, this might be my tenant's wedding dress.'

'It's perfect.'

Sally accepts the praise with a glowing smile. 'How much time do we have?' she asks.

I check my phone. 'It's pushing five o'clock.'

She exhales. 'We'd better be—'

There are three hard knocks at the door.

I freeze and turn slowly to face the entrance. Do god-hunting Hounds usually knock?

Sally doesn't seem particularly fussed. 'Go away, I'm busy,' she calls in an accent that can best be described as non-specifically European.

There's a slight delay before the muffled reply. 'Pizza delivery.'

'We didn't order any pizza,' she calls, her fake accent beginning to fray.

'Pizza delivery,' the visitor repeats.

He can't hear through the door.

Sally sighs. She apologises to Darroch, drapes the woollen blanket over him and procures the fire poker from the kitchen.

She holds it like a makeshift spear and strides towards the door. She reaches for the knob and checks behind her. When she sees I'm still standing in the open, she gestures for me to hide. I sink behind the bed and hold my breath.

Sally opens the door. A delivery guy's standing there, gripping a pizza box. His wide sunken eyes make him look endearingly hopeful. 'Delivery?' His voice shakes like he's new at this and a bride's answered the door holding a fire poker.

My fear subsides. I sit up. The guy's my age, drowning in a floppy fluoro pink shirt that features a four-wheeled cupcake: the logo of this month's trendiest food-delivery app.

Sally tells him that he has the wrong house and promptly closes the door. She looks to me and says, 'We should get going.'

I notice the poor guy's still in his car when we lead a blanket-covered Darroch back to the van. He hasn't found the right address. Sally jokes that we should take the pizza off his hands.

I catch myself grinning in the side mirror. This morning, I committed myself to staying out until midnight because I didn't have the guts to tell Mum about Olly and me. I don't know how I would've filled the hours, but I know I would've felt terrible.

I don't feel terrible now. The creators of the world are in danger. Sally is seeking them out and moving them, and I'm along for a bit of the ride.

What's watching the biggest, loudest action movie with Olly, when I can star in my own?

# SIX

The sign warning trespassers is too fancy for its own good. Every word has a long tail that loops and curls. We don't feel so much threatened as we do invited to a high tea. We walk right past, the loose pebbles of Eden Ladies' College's main drive swimming beneath our feet. Sally's heels wobble; she dips and grips my arm for support. She laughs.

'Lucky I'm here, hey?'

Sally gives me a little pat. 'You're proving as useful as I expected.'

'Wow. Don't let yourself get too sentimental.'

She smirks. 'What would you rather I say? That this is the longest I've spent with someone since I started looking for the Monuments?'

'I mean, to start.'

She clicks her tongue. 'I'm glad you're here.' She glances at Darroch, who's shadowing us. 'Are we going the right way?'

The god unsheathes his sword, points the hilt ahead and confirms that yes, we are.

The air is thick with the scent of freshly cut grass, not surprising considering the main drive separates two playing fields. A giant white building with too many columns dominates our line of sight, bathed in the glow of spotlights shining from its base. No prize for the person who guesses that's the *historic* Bryan Manor. I imagine the Monument is interred in a sanctuary beneath it.

Sally's heels wobble, and this time her stumble is more severe. 'Careful there.'

The voice doesn't belong to Darroch. Or me. Sally and I turn.

A security guard is climbing the bank of a field. We're trespassers. If he realises we don't belong, he'll be escorting us back out the gates.

This is our first test as debutante and date.

The guard stops between us and Darroch, who is doing his best impression of a regular statue on the side of the road. He switches on his flashlight and shines it in our eyes. 'You here for the ball?'

We squint and the guard lowers the beam to the ground. My eyes drift to Darroch, who gently mimes taking a swipe at the guard. I shake my head. I think we've got this.

'I've already phoned Mrs Johnson,' Sally says. 'She knows we're running late.'

'On you go, then.' The guard waves us towards the manor with his flashlight. 'Have a good night.'

'You too,' we answer in unison. She nods and I do this odd curtsey thing. We leave Darroch where he is and continue down the drive, feeling the burn of the guard's stare.

'Mrs Johnson?' I mutter. 'Was that in your journal?'

'Nope. Pulled it out of my arse.'

I stifle a laugh and peer back. The guard is inspecting the statue of a warrior that has seemingly sprouted from nowhere. 'Are we all right to leave him?'

'He'll catch up,' Sally says.

'And what about the Hounds?'

'He'll be fine.'

'What are they like?'

'Who?'

'The Hounds.'

She checks Darroch's well and truly out of earshot and then says, 'Honestly couldn't tell you. I've never seen any.'

That strikes me as weird. 'But this morning, you told Darroch he's in danger.'

'I made that bit up.'

My mouth hangs open. 'You made that bit up? But everything Darroch said about them, he seems to think they're dangerous.'

'Like, thousands of years ago maybe. Nobody's running around looking for the Monuments. Except me.'

'Well, the Hounds were enough of a threat for them to build the sanctuary under Charlton Grammar. They didn't just chuck Darroch in a hole.'

'They went overboard.'

I'm having trouble wrapping my head around all this. 'Why exactly are you looking for the Monuments if they're not in danger? You're a Guardian, you're supposed to protect them.'

Sally grimaces.

'You are a Guardian, right?'

Sally grimaces harder.

'You're not a Hound, are you?'

Her forehead creases. 'What? No. Don't be silly.'

'What then? Some random digging up all-powerful gods because you want to?'

She sighs. 'Sort of. Mum would tell me about them as a kid. She wasn't a Guardian, but she knew about the sanctuaries and everything. She died six months ago, and when I was going through her things, I found her journal. The idea got stuck in my head that I could find the Monuments.' She's not looking at me when she adds, 'Mum was the last family I had. This god stuff is all I have left of her and I'm not ready to say goodbye.' Her voice cracks.

I'm sad. Anybody who hears that and isn't needs their heart checked. But my chest is tight and I'm struggling to breathe. She lied to a god and she roped me into this. I'm angry.

'What's Darroch going to do to us when he finds out?' I ask.

'*If.*' Sally, ever the optimist.

'I saw him lift you clean off the ground. He could kill us with ease.'

She cocks an eyebrow at me. I'm not being overdramatic. If anything, I'm underselling it.

'We're on our way to wake another Monument. What are you going to do? Collect them all and hope none of them notice you're a fraud?' I stop just shy of the entrance to the manor. 'I can't be here for this.'

'Connor.'

'*Sally.* You're doing this for nothing.'

I turn and walk back the way we came, loose pebbles clacking together under my shoes. I don't want to be anywhere near this bomb when it explodes.

'I'm not doing this for nothing,' Sally says.

I pause. I should leave, but I look at her again. She's slouched, like she's trying to occupy as little space as possible. She swallows hard.

'I'm trying to bring my mum back, okay? Jivanta created life. She can resurrect her. She can resurrect both my parents. I'm not interested in the other Monuments, I'm just working through the list until I find Jivanta,' she explains.

'I wish she was the one hidden under Charlton Grammar, but she wasn't. When we found Darroch, I couldn't ignore him. He was my only lead. I knew about the Movements from the journal and what Mum told me. I pretended to be his Guardian and said that he was being hunted so he would help.'

'You lied to him, and then you asked me to tag along! Have you ever read a religious text? Gods do not take kindly to betrayal.'

'I wasn't thinking about getting caught when I invited you, and I absolutely believe we won't get caught,' she says.

'What if Jivanta's the second Monument you find? Or the third? What happens when you give up the Movement and ask her to bring your parents back to life? They're going to realise what's up.'

Sally waves off my concern. 'Then I'll find them all, complete the Movement, and just before Jivanta's sealed away in her new sanctuary, I'll ask for the favour. If you're scared, you can go. But don't, *don't* tell me I'm doing this for nothing.'

I should leave, but my feet are firm. I can't imagine losing Mum, and I can't imagine that if I had the chance to bring her back, I wouldn't do everything in my power to make that happen.

I can't leave yet. For Sally's disguise to work, she needs a date. I will do this tonight, and then I'm out.

'My curfew's midnight,' I tell her, 'so I can help with this sanctuary.'

She exhales. 'Okay.'

I hesitate. 'And you promise Darroch's not going to find out?'

She crosses her heart with one finger. 'Promise.'

There are a couple of metres between us. 'What now?'

She squints at something behind me. 'I can't make out the guard, but I can see the beam of his flashlight slowly travelling up the main drive towards us. I assume he's still watching, so I guess you're presenting me to formal society for real, until we can get away and find the sanctuary.'

'All right.'

Sally and I ascend the manor steps together. I hope I won't regret this.

The entrance foyer is unmanned. The room inexplicably smells of vanilla and is wallpapered with alternating white and gold stripes. I hear a horde of chattering teenagers but can't see them. The poster taped to the balustrade points debutante-ball attendees upstairs.

At the foot of the grand staircase is a trestle table with a few name badges that nobody's claimed. Sally snatches one up. Tonight, she's Taylor. I opt for Brent. I don't look like a

Brent. Brents are confident and use the hashtag #god on social media. I've always wondered what it's like to be a Brent.

The grand staircase coils upwards to a marshalling area on the second floor. The debutantes and their dates are crammed together. Past them are four French doors. Through the carved glass panels, I see the ball unfolding, tinted purple by the mood lighting. The debutantes are in white, clearly-not-wedding dresses. Most wear gloves that stretch right to their elbows.

Two adults by the French doors manage to clear enough space to get a pair of them open. Conversations, clanging glasses and student cellists become louder. The adult gatekeepers are all that stand between us and the party. The man – dressed like the midpoint between a lumberjack and a hipster barista – announces the names of the debutantes from a clipboard, and as they file into the room with their dates, the woman – a human-sized corsage with a voice like sharpening knives – assesses their attire and makes last-minute adjustments.

We'll have to get past both of them.

'You're not Taylor,' the girl closest to us says.

Sally laughs awkwardly. She turns her back on the girl. 'Do you see the exit sign on the far side of the hall?' she asks me.

The sign glows way off in the distance.

'Fire escape,' she says. 'Here's the plan. We keep to ourselves. They announce my name – Taylor – and we saunter in, cross the room and pop out.'

I have every intention of sticking to the plan and keeping to myself as the roster is called, but then I notice the most gorgeous guy to ever roam the earth. He has an athletic frame and stands relaxed against the radiator, one hand around the opposite forearm. His skin is a deep brown. He talks through a crooked smile. I want to get close enough to hear what he's saying and, if he's keen, marry him.

I clutch Sally's arm and surrender to his gravitational pull. She gets partway through asking me where I'm dragging her when she too notices the most gorgeous guy to ever roam the earth.

I read the name badges: he's Locky and he's here with . . . Violet. I take comfort in the fact they're not standing particularly close. It's *friend* close. Or maybe one-more-misunderstanding-and-we're-breaking-up close. I can work with either.

Violet notices Sally's name badge and says they're in the same maths class.

Sally goes with it. 'Sure.'

Violet asks, 'Are you . . . wearing a wedding dress?'

'No.' Sally reaches for a glass of water resting on a nearby shelf. She checks the rim for lipstick, then sips from it.

Violet persists. 'It looks like a—'

'*It's not.*'

Locky isn't paying them any attention. He's squinting at me.

'What?' I'm worried he thinks I don't belong here.

He asks if he knows me.

'I don't think so.'

'Thought you looked familiar, sorry,' he says. 'How's your night been?'

My answer's vague. I ask about his.

'Oh, pretty good.' He has these stunning eyes and, I kid you not, the cutest dimples. Basically, he has a face and I'm its biggest fan. 'It's all very strange,' he says. 'They're being debuted.'

Violet rolls her eyes. 'This is why you don't bring the guy you run track with to school functions.'

'So, you're not dating?' I hear myself and cringe at the audible desperation. 'That's . . . a weird thing for me to say out loud, I'm sorry.'

Locky laughs. 'Are you two –?'

'No!' I smile. 'I am super gay.'

Let the record show that I have never been this confident in my life. Maybe it's the suit. Maybe it's because I'm a Brent. Maybe it's because I know that when Sally's fake name is called, we're going to waltz across that hall and I'll never see any of these people ever again.

'*Super*?' says Locky. 'Wow, I wasn't aware we could earn adjectives.'

'There's a really tough accreditation process. I had to . . . Wait, did you say *we*?'

Sally chokes on her water.

'You right?' I ask.

'The window,' she mutters between coughs.

I look out the window over Locky's shoulder. A seven-foot statue is striding through the school.

The lumberjack hipster barista with the clipboard calls Taylor Lemke-Berry to the front. Sally tugs on my arm as she tells Violet and Locky to have a nice night. I might be reading too deep, but Locky seems disappointed our chat's ended abruptly. He tosses a coy smile. 'Catch you in there,' he says.

Was that to me? To us as a pair?

Sally yanks me towards the French doors before I get any clarification. The corsage and the lumberjack hipster barista are exchanging terse words. Apparently the real Taylor Lemke-Berry's parents called to say she wouldn't be coming, and it had been on the lumberjack hipster barista's to-do list to amend the call sheet and notify the MC. Now the night is ruined, absolutely ruined.

The lumberjack hipster barista is first to notice Sally and me striding past. When the corsage does, she stutters, 'That's not . . .' But it's too late. We're in and they're not going to start a scene to stop us.

The event smacks all of my senses at once. The MC announces Taylor, and we're met with loud applause and a short fanfare. Colognes mix in the air. Vibrant silks are draped across the ceiling and down the walls, no doubt to dull the school-ish vibe. There's everything you'd expect from an assembly hall – the trophy cabinet, the school captain honour board, the portrait of somebody old and important enough to warrant an oil painting – but with added luxe.

'There is way too much going on in here,' Sally says.

I can see the exit sign she pointed out earlier. We're walking right for it when a volunteer grabs Sally's shoulder and gently steers her towards the local member of parliament – a bundle of burst capillaries in a bowtie. She extends one limp hand for him to . . . kiss? He grips it and gives it a vigorous shake.

'Well done,' he says, stepping back for us to pass.

The debutantes who have already been presented are scattered around tables in the centre of the hall. Adults, presumably their parents, are seated on the fringes. We're pointed towards a table to the left of the dancefloor that's really just a square patch of parquetry that doesn't have tables on it.

Sally waves back at a parent who scowls when she realises Sally's not the girl she thought she was. The same confused look is plastered across several other debutantes' faces. Under her breath, Sally says, 'Keep acting like we're totally supposed to be here.'

At the nearest table, a guy with dirty blond hair leans into his date's ear. He's cracking a joke and she's trying not to laugh. I do a double take.

'Olly?' I ask.

The guy sits back in his chair. He's very much not Olly. He frowns at me.

I cringe and Sally quickens her pace. 'Less of that,' she says. 'My bad.'

We arrive at our table and then continue past it as the MC announces Violet Olsen-Smythe. I risk a glance. Violet enters, her arm interlocked with Locky's. Sally leads me behind an ice sculpture and through the exit. The stairwell is all grey and functional, with none of the opulence of the grand staircase. As we descend, Sally discards her name badge. I do the same.

We emerge from the building. The night air pricks at my skin. The ELC courtyard is bordered by the back of the manor and a horseshoe-shaped block of classrooms. At its heart, there's a monstrous Moreton Bay fig tree. Now, Moreton Bay figs are objectively terrifying. They're basically stranglers. They can begin life as seeds that drop onto trees and grow roots that enlarge until they overwhelm the host. I learnt all that from a plaque. I had my first kiss under a Moreton Bay fig in a botanical garden – there was too much tongue and it went on too long; my eyes had to look *somewhere.*

Darroch waits for us a few metres from the tree's base. The sight of him sends a chill down my spine. He's going to be furious if he finds out Sally's taking advantage of his unrelenting trust in the Guardians. I try to keep my expression blank, but inside, I'm falling apart from nerves.

Sally walks right up to him, completely unfazed. She asks him if the tree is the sanctuary's entrance.

The Monument nods slowly. 'Jivanta likes to build her own burial sites.'

'Jivanta?' Sally asks coolly.

'Yes.' Darroch gestures towards the mammoth trunk. 'After you.'

Sally eagerly steps over the sprawling roots to get as close as she can to the tree. She lingers for a moment and then checks over her shoulder. 'What am I supposed to do?'

'It should open for you, if you are who you say you are.'

There's a hint of uneasiness in her laugh. I think it dawns on her that maybe her subterfuge hasn't been as successful as she's believed. 'Should it?'

'The sanctuary recognises gods and descendants of the five Guardian families,' Darroch says. 'You are a Guardian, are you not?'

'Yes.' She swallows hard and says it one more time with feeling. '*Yes.*'

My heart's thumping in my chest. The jig is up. I should've left when she told me the truth.

I wonder how long he's suspected Sally was lying to him, how long he's planned to bring us here and test her word.

My voice cracks. 'Could it be broken?' I ask.

The Monument scoffs at the thought. 'That would be very unlike Jivanta.' He's waiting for a confession that doesn't come.

Sally stammers.

'Try touching the bark,' he says.

He *knows* she's been lying to him. He's just toying with her at this point. I want to blurt out the truth, but I don't want to be the one to anger Darroch.

Sally reaches out to lay a trembling hand on the tree.

'Is anything happening?' Darroch asks.

'Not yet.' She sounds hopeful, like the tree might recognise her as a Guardian.

'Maybe this isn't the entrance,' I suggest. 'Maybe your sword is wrong.'

The Monument ignores me. 'Are you my Guardian?' he asks Sally. He takes one step towards her and the earth crunches beneath his feet.

I am frozen, dreading what comes next and powerless to stop it.

And then Sally yelps. It's as if a glowing blue liquid spreads from her palm to flow through the cracks in the Moreton Bay fig, illuminating them like paths in a maze. She pulls her hand back and retreats as the roots begin to kick at the ground, spitting up soil and the courtyard tiles that were laid too close to the tree in the first place. The roots part, clearing a path to a fresh opening in the trunk.

Darroch strides towards it. 'Come.'

Sally doesn't budge. On my way past, I ask her how she managed that.

'I have no idea,' she whispers.

And with that, we follow Darroch into the belly of the Moreton Bay fig.

# SEVEN

Sally stops to peel off her shoes. The dark passageway is bounded by entwining roots and impossible in heels. My heart hasn't quite recovered from Darroch's little test outside. The tree opened for Sally. We're in the sanctuary. We might just get away with this.

'Hurry,' the Monument says.

We rush to catch up to him. There's a kink in the path, then I catch sight of glowing dots ahead. It isn't until we arrive that I realise what they are: the chamber is peppered with luminescent flower buds sprouting from the roots.

It's like nothing I've ever seen before.

'Look.' Sally's staring down at her hands.

I look at my own. They're tinted blue.

'Where's Jivanta?' Sally asks.

'Entrants must prove themselves worthy,' the Monument replies.

This room better not rotate, that's all I can say.

Darroch takes slow, deliberate steps through the glowing

garden. A single line of flower buds has spread up the rear wall and across the ceiling, making a large circle above us.

This place is unreal. I whip out my phone and take a photo. I remember Sally's warning about discretion the moment the flash goes off. She arches an eyebrow at me, and I know I should feel bad, but ... the flowers nearby opened to drink up the light of the flash. The others remain closed.

'Um. Check this out.' I walk deeper into the garden and take another photo. The flash goes off. The flowers around me bloom as soon as the light hits them.

Both Sally and I look to Darroch for confirmation that we're on the right track. He tells us that Guardians must prove their worth.

That's not particularly helpful.

'But,' the Monument adds, gesturing towards the circle of buds sprouting from the ceiling, 'Jivanta believes that Guardians are a shining light in darkness.'

Okay, that's particularly helpful.

I switch on my phone's flashlight and point it at the buds above us. They flower. In response, the entwined roots unknot to reveal the face of a statue lying among them. Her eyes are shut.

Jivanta. The god who created all life.

'Hello?' I say.

The Monument in the ceiling moves. The roots restricting her upper body recoil. 'Good evening, children.' Her speech samples the music of the world – the cry of a caged bird, the thumping gallop of a horse – chopped, warped and rearranged into words. Her syllables are alive.

'It's really her,' Sally mutters. Something's caught in her throat.

Jivanta notices Darroch standing off to the side. 'Good evening, my love,' she says.

I can't tell whether it's an affectionate *my love* or a we're-an-item *my love*, at least until he says it back, dripping sentimentality. They're definitely an item.

'Is it time for a Movement already?' Jivanta asks. 'It's come so soon.'

'It is, and it has.'

'That's a shame, I quite like it here,' she says. 'Do you like what I did with the place?'

Darroch's response is quick and dry. 'It's a tree, Jivanta, you've made your fair share. It would be alarming if you weren't this good at it by now.'

She huffs. 'You know, one day there'll be a Movement, and I'll make sure we leave without you.' The roots shrink back, and the now-unrestrained Monument drops down . . . but not all the way. She hovers inches from the floor, toes pointed.

'Whoa,' I whisper, partly because of the hovering, partly because coming face to face with real gods never gets old.

While she and Darroch both resemble statues come to life, I'm struck by how differently they're composed. Jivanta's brown skin is interrupted by concentric circular cracks that reveal sparkling green and blue opal. The folds of her long dress billow like real fabric, not rock. Hovering beside Darroch, with his chips and cracks, she makes him seem unimpressive.

Jivanta glances around, as if expecting someone else to be here too. She frowns, then asks our names. We give them to her. She greets us warmly. 'And the human loitering aboveground, what is his name?' she adds.

'Who?' I ask.

'Oh. We are not alone,' she says.

Sally blinks. 'We're not?'

'No.'

The Monuments wait for us to explain, but we're at a loss. It could be a security guard doing the rounds, passing through the courtyard by chance, or it could be . . . something more sinister. Sally might not think they're a threat, but what if one of the Hounds – bitter, twisted, and intent on destroying the Monuments – has sensed Darroch and tracked us to ELC?

'Hello?' a voice calls from the surface. I *know* that voice. 'Brent?'

The most gorgeous guy to ever roam the earth is roaming the courtyard looking for me.

Sally tells me to go distract him. 'We'll meet you at the van,' she adds.

I barrel up the tunnel. I have no explanation for leaving the debutante ball so soon or for hanging out inside a tree, but I'm eager to be aboveground. Locky's come looking for me. It all feels so romantic. There *is* the slight chance the corsage and the lumberjack hipster barista sent him after us, but I banish the thought.

I climb out of the opening. I'm met by the crisp night air and music wafting down from the manor, but no Locky. I step around the trunk and . . . there he is. He's standing under the sprawling branches of the tree with his back to me, hands buried in his pockets.

I take a moment. I need one. I just met the god who created all life; it's unfair for the universe to also spring Locky on me so suddenly.

He turns and his brow creases. 'Have you been there all along?'

'Yup.'

'No way. I walked past like three times.'

I commit. 'Yeah, you walked past me like three times.'

He asks what I'm doing out here. I tell him I felt like some fresh air, then ask what *he's* doing out here.

'I also felt like some fresh air.'

'You didn't come looking for me?' I ask.

He shakes his head. 'No.'

I don't believe him.

My heart flutters, and then I realise I'm not giving Sally and the gods much room to escape in. I need to lead Locky away from the Moreton Bay fig. I rush forwards and grab his hand with a boldness the situation necessitates. I tell him I want to show him something. I keep it vague so that my options are open.

I walk him past a water fountain. I consider the possibility that we might find something better, and then decide that the odds are stacked against me in the dark. I extend my free arm dramatically.

'A bubbler?' Locky asks.

My response is quick and dry. 'Because you're thirsty.'

'The sass! Okay. Night.' He motions to leave but I squeeze his hand tighter. He laughs. 'So, do you do this often?'

'Do what?'

'Impersonate people to attend fancy school functions.'

He knows I'm not really Brent. 'What gave us away?'

'Vi and the real Taylor are close friends, and she knows Taylor has gastro.'

'Ah. Poor Taylor.'

Locky deploys the dimples and my heart flutters some more. 'Where's Fake Taylor anyway?'

'She left already and I'm about to.'

'What? You're not staying?' he asks. 'They actually serve food at these things if you wait long enough.'

In an instant, a night unfolds in my head. Locky leads me back to the manor. I weasel my way onto his table. We lean into each other as we eat. I watch him dance with Violet. They break apart. He approaches me, hand outstretched, and asks me to join him on the tiny dancefloor.

'We only wanted to duck in, duck out, prove we could do it,' I tell him. 'Besides, I'm pretty sure we didn't fool many people.'

'That's a shame,' Locky says. 'There's this bubbler I really wanted to show you.'

'Oh, really?'

'Yeah.' He flashes me a smile. 'Will you at least walk me back to the fire escape?'

I can't exactly demand he hang out with me longer than he wants to, so I have to hope I've given the others enough time to flee. As we cross the courtyard, I notice a line of bulging tiles that stretches away from the tree towards the campus entrance. Darroch has dug their escape route.

'I swear, this campus is too large,' he says. 'I feel like I need to pitch a tent and complete the journey tomorrow.'

When I laugh, he asks me if I camp, and I answer, 'I *very* camp,' which is hilarious.

But he doesn't laugh, at least not immediately. 'Oh, I just got it.'

'There we go.'

He shrugs. 'I didn't pick up on the dual meaning. That's why I'm not *super.*'

I cock my head. 'I think you're super.'

'No, I was . . . Remember before? When we were talking about adjectives?'

'Oh!'

He scrunches his face. 'There we go,' he mimics.

'I sound nothing like that.'

Locky doesn't defend his impersonation. Instead, he just sighs. 'I'm dreading going back to the party.'

'Why?'

'The whole concept of a debutante ball is so old-fashioned, so ELC. I always feel like I've had to step into a wardrobe to get here,' he says. 'Every posh school has this Narnia vibe – they're fantasy worlds that are trapped in the past, where the magic is money and I'm just a mortal. I never feel like I belong.'

I feel instantly awkward, I ought to mention—

'Schools like this shouldn't exist,' he continues, his voice filled with passion. 'They swallow suburbs and erect high fences and pride themselves on selling opportunity, but why does any girl deserve less opportunity than Vi? I love her, she's a riot, but she gets a leg-up because of what her parents can afford. That's not right. I say, tear the fences down. What do you think?'

'I go to Charlton Grammar,' I admit.

He winces. 'Oh, that's fancy.'

'No debutante balls though.'

'Yeah, because you don't let women in.' He smirks. 'It's okay, the kids will go to public school.'

'The kids?'

'*Our* kids.'

'Oh.' I feel myself beginning to blush. I want to steer the conversation somewhere, anywhere else, but words have apparently failed me in my time of need.

'Relax, I'm kidding,' Locky says, opening the fire-escape door and stepping in. 'I barely know anything about you.'

'Right. Of course.'

'But it was nice to meet you . . .' He trails off because he doesn't know my name. My real one.

I help him out. 'Connor.'

He angles his name badge towards me. 'Locky.'

I tell him I've never seen it spelt like that.

'I thought this was how to spell it when I was a kid, and it stuck.'

That's the most adorable thing I've ever heard.

'Bye,' he adds.

And the door's closing – literally and figuratively. He's about to become the single most gorgeous guy to ever roam out of my life.

I reach out to stop the door. 'Would you want to hang out properly some time and maybe get to know more about me?' I ask without breathing first, so I come off sounding exactly as needy and vulnerable as I feel.

Locky doesn't mind the needy vulnerability. 'That could work.' He relinquishes his phone. 'Text yourself so I have your number, and you have mine.'

Cue my nervous laughter. The first text to a guy is usually something I labour over. It needs to be a direct hit, brief but witty. If it's stale, they're going to wonder if you're really the one they want to be texting during class. Locky's thrown me the curveball of writing *his* first text to me. It's a perfect opportunity to showcase my brevity and wit, but . . . I can't do it on the spot. With him *watching*.

He senses me struggling. He pokes his tongue out a little. 'Type this,' he says, before dictating the perfect message. It's a direct hit.

I send it and his phone vibrates in my hand. I read the message preview; it's from Violet. 'They've served appetisers,' I tell him. The phone vibrates again. 'You have three minutes before she eats yours.'

Locky shrugs. 'I'll eat her dessert. It'll even out in the end.' I give him his phone back. 'You should go.'

'You too, before they find you.'

The door closes and I'm grinning for a good minute or two before I hear the roots of the Moreton Bay fig shifting once more. I turn, expecting to see the tree returning to its usual, objectively terrifying state, but something different is happening. The tree sheds its leaves in an instant. They rain to the ground and almost cover the entirety of the tiled courtyard. The bare branches stretch to the night sky in one final, dying lurch.

And everything is still.

I should probably get going before a guard finds me.

I hurry around the manor, down the main drive, past the sign that warns trespassers in fancy cursive.

The van's parked a couple of blocks away, but I don't mind the walk. More time to bask in the glory of exchanging numbers with Locky. At one point, I throw my arms out and do a couple of musical-theatre spins in quick succession.

Feels great until I slap someone.

I tell him it's my bad, when really, it's a shared bad. I mean, who stands in the middle of the footpath at night? It's dark, people might want to celebrate their successful interactions with cute boys through dance. You can't just . . .

First, I recognise the shirt, fluoro pink with a four-wheeled cupcake. Then I recognise the eyes, wide and sunken.

Without saying a word, he rushes back to his car, parked two spots behind Sally's van.

It's him. The delivery guy from before.

It's weird. It's more than weird. It's . . .

I hurry.

# EIGHT

I hop into the front of the van and Sally immediately starts the engine. I check the rear-view mirror. The gods are in the back, looking every bit like a recently reunited couple. Jivanta rests her head on Darroch's shoulder. He has a hand in her lap. It's adorable, but I'm looking past them, trying to make out the driver two cars back.

I must be wrong. There's no way he's the same delivery guy who showed up at Sally's place. We're on the other side of Sydney. I watch the rear-view mirror closely, even though I'm definitely, absolutely wrong.

'What did your boyfriend want?' Sally asks as we set off.

I'm a little distracted. 'My what?'

'Locky,' she prompts.

'Oh. He's not my boyfriend.'

'Sorry,' she says. 'Didn't think you'd take it so literally.'

The delivery guy's car shrinks in the rear-view mirror. He doesn't leave the kerb before Sally takes the next corner sharply enough to remind me that the van has no seatbelts. I collide with the door.

'Sorry.' She means it this time.

'All good.'

There's no traffic behind us. We're not being tailed. I relax. Talk about getting myself worked up. This morning, I didn't even know what Monuments, Guardians or Hounds were, and now I freak out when I can't tell two delivery guys apart.

I notice a pair of headlights in my side mirror – small bursts of white light that bounce with the dips in the road. They don't faze me. Sure, it was a bit weird that guy was loitering near the van when I accidentally slapped him. And sure, he looked a lot like that guy who tried to deliver food to the wrong house despite using an app that tracks customer locations with GPS. But I'm definitely not fazed by these headlights that could belong to any car driven by anyone.

Okay, I'm a little fazed.

I wait for the headlights to veer down a side street, but they don't. They stalk us, maintaining their distance.

I can't see the make of the car.

What if the delivery guy didn't misread his map? He could've knocked on Sally's door because he sensed a god inside. He was still in his car when we left for Eden Ladies' College. He could've followed us to the other side of Sydney. He could've been the delivery guy I accidentally slapped. He could be tailing us right now.

'Can you take the next left?' I ask Sally.

'Hmm?'

'The next left, take it. I want to check something.'

She glances at the headlights in the rear-view mirror and then at me.

I mouth, 'We're being followed.'

She frowns. 'No way,' she mouths back.

'Humour me,' I say, sitting up taller. 'And don't indicate.'

Sally humours me. Without indicating, she turns down a street of modestly sized houses. It accommodates two-way traffic about as well as a two-seater convertible might accommodate a rhinoceros; with cars parked on either kerb, there's just enough room to scrape the van through without clipping its mirrors.

The van comes to a stop. I turn in my seat and keep my eyes on the intersection behind us. The headlights pass. I exhale.

When I look to Sally, she cocks an eyebrow, steers into a driveway and starts the involved process of turning the van around. There are nine points to her three-point turn. She straightens the van and clips the passenger window. 'Didn't happen,' she says.

We're almost at the intersection when a car turns into the street from the northbound lane and blocks our way. There's an awkward moment as each driver waits for the other to make room. Neither retreats.

My stomach drops. I recognise the car. He stalked us, and when we turned off the main road, he made a U-turn and came back for us.

'What's their problem?' Sally asks.

I squint. Beyond the glare of the headlights, I see the driver's face. 'It's the delivery guy from earlier,' I say.

Sally laughs. 'What? No.' Then she squints too. And it dawns on her. She sinks back into her seat. We exchange a look. The delivery guy showed up at Sally's house. He sensed Darroch and now he's here.

A Hound, ruthless hunter of Monuments, is here.

No, he's not a ruthless hunter. He had pizza and his voice shook when Sally answered the door holding a fire poker. He can't be a Hound. Which means he's a Guardian. Darroch's real Guardian, here to expose Sally as a fraud and me as her sidekick.

Sally clears her throat. 'We appear to have been followed by a Hound. Possibly.'

Darroch is assertive. 'We must keep Jivanta safe.'

He is quickly corrected by the other Monument. 'We both must be kept safe.'

'I have a sword.'

'You have a Guardian.'

'Yes.' Sally must feel the pressure. 'I will guard you.'

She reaches for her door.

If she heads out there to confront Darroch's real Guardian and the truth comes out, there's no way Jivanta's resurrecting her parents. But if I confront him, Sally can gun it in reverse and get the Monuments out of here. She can complete the Movement and ask Jivanta her favour.

She can see her parents again.

'I'll go,' I say.

Sally doesn't understand why. I want to explain that I'm going to distract Darroch's real Guardian so that she can get away and hopefully resurrect her parents, but the gods are within earshot. I need to be cryptic. 'I can't drive.'

Sally's expression is blank. 'Okay.'

'I can't *drive*,' I repeat, eyes wide.

'All right,' she says.

I hope that means she understands. 'All right.'

I open my door and squeeze between the van and a parked car.

I'm still annoyed Sally dragged me into this, but at the same time, I'm thankful. After weeks of being apart from Olly, today I was a part of something. It sucks that at the end of it, we don't get to say goodbye. If I do, the Monuments will realise I don't intend on coming back.

I get one last proper look at Sally and close the door.

I'm sandwiched between the van and a parked car. There's some manoeuvring involved to get through, then I have to squeeze between the front of the delivery guy's car and a parked truck. There's more manoeuvring.

I arrive at his window. It's open. 'Hi?'

He's definitely the delivery guy from Sally's place. He avoids eye contact when he greets me back.

'You might remember me from earlier. I accidentally slapped you. Again, totally my bad.' It's like talking to a brick wall. 'Are you . . . still trying to offload that pizza?'

'This isn't about pizza.'

I give him a chance to elaborate. He doesn't take it. 'I know why you're here,' I say.

'You do?' he asks.

'You're a Guardian.'

He has no idea what I'm talking about. 'A *what*?'

I open my mouth and words fail me for the second time in one night. He's not a Guardian. He's a Hound. But he looks like he's about to throw up. He seems nervous, first-kiss-under-a-Moreton-Bay-fig nervous.

He extends his neck and points with his nose. 'Who's in the back of your van?'

I glance at the van and it dawns on me that Sally didn't understand the hint.

My heart thumps. 'Nobody.'

'Can't you smell them?'

'Smell them?' I ask.

'My grandad said we'd know when they were loose. They smell like rotten eggs to us.' He looks to me. 'Your van smells like rotten eggs.'

His phone is mounted to an air vent by the steering wheel. The screen flashes – there's a stream of delivery jobs he hasn't accepted.

'This is weird,' he says. 'It's weird. Right?'

'I . . . don't know?'

'Grandad would point to his scars and tell me stories about them before bed. Some were from bar fights, but one of them . . . He said our family was special. We could smell evil. It smacked our nostrils. One time he smelt it, he sought out a monster. Had his cheek slashed. I always thought he was just trying to scare me. But I smell it now. There's a monster in your van.'

He thinks the Monuments are monsters.

'What do I do?' he asks. 'Grandad said it is our family's duty to kill the monsters in the world, but he never told me how. I guess he didn't know. He confronted one and had his face cut up. I don't want my face cut up. I *like* my face.'

His story makes no sense. The *monsters* have been buried for over two hundred years.

'There are no monsters in the van,' I explain.

'The smell is so strong.'

'Mum uses the van sometimes to . . . transport eggs to her . . . shop. Maybe that's what you're smelling?'

'It's not.'

I need a different approach. I try sincerity. 'Look, you can drive away. Forget the smell, forget family duty. You can drive away. Trust me on this.'

'I'm not afraid,' he answers meekly.

'I'm not saying you are.' But he definitely is.

The delivery guy chews on his bottom lip and shakes his head. He releases the brake, determination now etched across his face. His foot hovers over the accelerator pedal.

'You have to put the car in reverse first,' I tell him.

He shakes his head. 'I'm not reversing.'

'Oh.' I don't understand and then I *do*.

I scramble, climbing onto the bonnet of the nearby parked truck the moment before he accelerates. He drives into the front of the van. The crunch is loud. Sally slams into the wheel without a seatbelt to restrain her. The delivery guy reverses his car. Its front has been misshapen by the impact. The van is dented. Its headlights are smashed.

Sally sits back, shaken but all right. I relax a little. Only a little.

'What was that?' I shout at the delivery guy.

He seems surprised at himself, like even he thought he got a bit carried away.

I hear the scrape of the van door sliding open. Nobody steps out; there isn't enough room. Then the closest parked car – a shiny, black, luxurious number – is heaved onto the nature strip. The side is damaged. The alarm sounds. The hazard lights flash.

Darroch emerges from the van and unfolds to his full height. He draws his sword and strides towards us. There is no sign of his limp, and his chips and cracks only make him seem more imposing. He looks . . . monstrous.

'Darroch, no!' I say.

The Monument stops, his brow furrowed. In his mind, a ruthless Hound has attacked him, but the reality is very different. The delivery guy doesn't know what he's doing.

Darroch waves his free hand and Sally retreats. The van speeds backwards, clipping mirrors the whole way down the street.

The Monument blocks the road. He glares, as if daring the delivery guy to pursue the van. He's protecting Jivanta. The delivery guy accelerates once more, this time driving straight into the god.

Darroch gasps. He releases his sword. It falls, clanging against the road. He glares at his attacker through the windshield, then slams his clenched fists on the front of the car. It crumples like paper. He raises his hands to strike a second blow. I call out for him to stop and he does.

The delivery guy loses his nerve. He reverses. His bumper bar dislodges and irritates the bitumen as he swings back onto the main road.

He drives off.

Darroch blinks down. The impact has left a mark – a crack splits his legs. There's a spatter of dust by his feet.

'You all right?' I ask him.

He nods, but when he attempts a step, his leg snaps at the knee. His strength evaporates and he collapses.

I rush to his fallen body.

The smashed car's alarm still blares. A porchlight comes on.

I ease my hands under Darroch's shoulders and lift. I can't lift much. 'I need to get you out of here,' I whisper, fully aware that the alarm will attract us an audience.

'The damage is done.' The god's voice is strained. 'My time has passed.'

'That's a bit dramatic. Come on, up you get.'

Darroch swats my hands away. He punches the road and his fist crumbles; his hand breaks off at the wrist and turns to dust. I notice his thigh is deteriorating too. He's right – he's dying.

'But you're a god.'

'Weakened by the—' Darroch coughs hard. 'Why didn't you let me pulverise the boy?'

'He didn't know what he was doing,' I say.

'He knew enough to do it.' His face softens. 'You are more compassionate than me.'

'Thanks?' It's all I can think of to say. I'm flustered. A god is *dying* right in front of me.

'You will protect Jivanta,' he croaks.

'I'm not sure how effective a protector I'll be,' I stammer.

'Swear it!'

'I swear it,' I vow.

His lips curl into a slight smile. 'You asked me earlier about commandments. I think I have one for you.' The god takes a staggered breath. 'I proffer this advice as someone who has fled for the better part of thousands of years . . . There is no peace in running. I see that now, at the end. A life spent running is not one lived.'

He then asks for his sword. It weighs an absolute ton. I drag it over, but honestly I don't know what use it'll be to him.

'I wish to die by your hand,' he says.

'Huh?' I hesitate. The request seems weird and unnecessary. 'I don't . . . want to kill you.'

'You would be granting me the dignity of knowing who slayed me.' He's smiling again, only now his lips are twitching. He's in pain.

I look into his eyes. They droop. They remind me of . . . 'I can't.'

'You must.'

My heart wrenches. 'This is so messed.'

He makes a sound, like a cough, only happy.

'Was that a laugh?' I ask.

He nods slightly. '*Messed*. The language is alive.'

I sniff. I don't know when I started crying. 'Okay,' I breathe.

I use my knee to seesaw the metal blade. The tip rises and connects with his torso. The blade slices through him and hits the bitumen. The stone around the fresh wound fractures and breaks away.

'That's it, then,' Darroch says.

He breaks into pieces. Those pieces crumble to dust.

Something else breaks. These tiny lightning cracks hang in the air around me, branching out. And then they vanish. Everything's normal.

Well, not *normal*. Darroch's gone. He's . . . dead. I killed him. I . . . killed a god.

'My car!' a man moans.

I look from Darroch's remains to the guy standing stunned on the nature strip, mourning his wrecked car. He's wearing a leather jacket over his striped pyjamas. I don't know what to tell him. We're watching each other and it's awkward. I try to push a sentence out. I stutter. It dawns on me that I'm holding a massive sword. There's no way standing here next to a wrecked car ends well for me.

I start jogging the way Sally drove.

'Oi!' the man shouts. 'Are you just . . . ? You can't just . . .' He pats his jacket pockets. 'I'll take a photo of you and show the police. I . . .' He curses.

He's left his phone inside. I'm thankful for the head start, but Darroch's sword is like an anchor. The blaring car alarm has attracted a host of neighbour witnesses. They're standing on their porches, watching me.

I jog faster. I'm getting used to the weight of the sword; it doesn't feel like it's ripping my arm out of its socket anymore. I don't even have to drag it. Must be adrenaline. My strides are longer. A lot longer. Like, I'm running. This isn't a second wind – it's a wind I never knew I had.

I navigate the backstreets, and all the while, I picture the owner of the wrecked car describing me to a police officer.

I have a feeling that 'teenager wielding sword' might pique their interest. I can't be in this neighbourhood if they start searching.

I rush down street after street, then down a graffiti-drenched laneway – *halfway* down a graffiti-drenched laneway. A mural of a smirking dolphin riding a motorcycle stops me in my tracks. I remember it. It's not the kind of mural you easily forget.

I've been here before. Mum used to fish the loose shrapnel out of her bag and send me off on walks. The coins would cover the cost of a hot chocolate and sometimes a muffin too. I'd sit under the bikie dolphin with my drink and sometimes-muffin.

I walk briskly. A couple wanders towards me, embracing tightly. I slip off my jacket and wrap the weapon. They don't notice. The laneway spits me out onto a main road. The rest is muscle memory. I pass the café and take a left. I hurry down the street until its line of houses is interrupted by the manicured front lawn of Sacred Heart Nursing Home.

# NINE

I watch the building.

Pappou's inside somewhere. Mum made sure I saw a lot of him growing up. He was a god to her and I think she wanted him to be the same for me. He knew everything. But he started to forget – small things at first, then he wasn't eating. He moved into the nursing home so there was someone to keep an eye on him. It wasn't long before he stopped speaking. Our visits were regular until they weren't. We've been busy.

Just being this close, my stomach is in knots. Pappou's been on my mind since Mum said that I should see him. And now I'm here, because apparently the world is the exactly the right size it needs to be to cause me emotional distress.

I can sneak in and see him. My foot hovers over the grass.

Or not. The next bus that goes anywhere near home isn't for forty minutes. I can roam the backstreets until then, even with the police potentially searching for somebody matching my description.

Okay, that's probably not wise.

Sacred Heart Nursing Home is a triple-storey fortress. It's the perfect place to hide. I can lock myself in the visitor bathroom. I don't even need to see him.

I should see him though.

A statue of a shrouded woman towers over a flowerbed in the centre of the lawn. I expect her to come to life as I pass, but she doesn't, because statues don't normally do that sort of thing.

I waltz past the front entrance. The side gate was always the best way to sneak out and back in during lengthy visits; if I yanked it hard enough, it usually popped open.

I yank the gate and it pops right off its hinges.

I take a step back with the gate literally in my hand. 'Right, I'm just going to . . .' I rest it against the wall and wander into the courtyard, weaving between the tables and potted plants. I open the door with a light touch. This one stays on its hinges. I slip inside and guide it shut behind me.

The temperature is controlled and the air smells aggressively clean. At the crossing of two corridors ahead, a cluster of ceiling lights illuminates the nurses' station. I tread lightly, the sound of my footsteps drowned out by the gentle murmur of whatever TV show they're streaming on the computer. I climb the closest staircase. I creep down the second-storey corridor and hope Pappou hasn't been moved since my last visit. As I near the room, I recognise his asthmatic wheezes. My breath catches in my throat.

I step inside. He lies with his back elevated, head turned slightly to face the door. I approach slowly and sink into his favourite lounge chair, the only piece of furniture he brought with him. Even in the dark, its fabric is golden.

I watch him sleep, features traced silver by the moonlight. His chest rises. His chest falls. His body sounds like eighty is more years than it was built for.

'Pappou,' I whisper. That's not enough to wake him and I'd feel guilty if it was.

I'm mad at myself for not keeping up regular visits. What kind of grandson am I if I only show up when he's dying?

*Dying.* The word summons an image of Darroch crumbling to dust. A god died in front of me today. He asked me to kill him, and I did. But I killed him before I even lifted his sword. I knew the Movement was bogus and I said nothing. Sally was endangering him, and I let her.

My heart cramps. I blink hard.

This is a lot. Too much. Pappou. Darroch. All of it.

I can't undo what happened to Darroch, and I can't take back the years I ignored Pappou. My heart is heavy and there's no way to lighten it.

I try. I cobble together some Greek from childhood memories. I struggle through three syllables and trip over my tongue. I don't know the words for what I want to say.

'I'm sorry I wasn't better,' I muster in English. 'I should have visited. I should have bothered to . . . I should have bothered. I'm sorry.'

My eyes are wet. I look away, down. The sword is balanced on my lap. I unwrap it and stare at my distorted reflection in the blade. I glance at Pappou, and I don't know if it's my imagination, but I see the features we have in common. The thick eyebrows. The deep crease that strikes through our foreheads. I wonder how similar we really are though. I wonder if he would like me.

The digits of his bedside clock tick over. It's ten.

His chest rises. His chest falls.

I sink deeper into the chair and let the time pass. They must allow residents to keep pets because after a short while, a bird chirps a simple melody a little way down the hall. It makes me smile. Another bird answers with a song of its own. They call and respond until they eventually meet in harmony. I let their duet wash over me – it's getting louder and louder as if they're getting closer and closer . . .

I lean over the armrest and peer back into the corridor. It's a shade of green that reminds me of the cracks in Jivanta's skin.

Jivanta. My heartbeat thumps in my ears and I default to panic. She's come looking for me. Does she know the Movement is bogus? Has she come to punish me?

I leap to the other side of the room and draw my sword over my sleeping grandfather. My hand is shaking and the tip of the blade is tracing little circles in the air. It's like I'm conducting an energetic symphony.

Jivanta floats into view. She stops whistling and the birdsong ends abruptly.

My imposing stance does nothing to rattle her. She enters and comes to rest in the golden lounge chair. 'What have you done, Darroch?' she asks under her breath.

He isn't here to answer her.

I swallow hard. 'How did you find me?'

She sighs and holds out her left hand. I notice that every finger has been broken off but one: the index. She twitches it, as if calling something to her, and then the grip of the sword squirms in my grasp. I release it. The weapon falls onto the edge of the bed. Pappou doesn't wake. His chest rises. His chest falls. The green grip unravels, and I realise it's a long, thin leaf. It slithers over the bed to Jivanta's fingertips. It wraps itself around her wrist.

'It was our way of finding each other without the Guardians, if the need ever arose,' she says.

I can't shake the image of Darroch crumbling to dust on the bitumen. My breathing wavers. 'He's dead.'

'I know.' She clasps the green wrapping on her wrist with the opposite hand. 'I don't presume killing him was your idea. I imagine he did not give you a choice.'

That's . . . eerily accurate. I wonder how she knows. Sally drove off before he started disintegrating.

'The Hound drove his car into Darroch and . . . he was wounded and . . .' I can't say that I killed him. Not aloud.

'Is the Hound still at large?' Jivanta asks.

'He is.' I hesitate. 'But it was strange. He wasn't acting like he was out to kill gods.'

'And yet, a god is dead.'

'He didn't even *know* you were gods though. He thought you were monsters. And he told me the Monuments attacked his grandfather, which makes no sense, because you've been hidden—'

Jivanta holds up a hand for silence. I shut up.

'We must discuss what will happen to you,' she says.

I didn't know that was something that needed to be discussed. 'I have to be home by midnight.'

Her brow furrows. She shifts to the edge of the seat. 'I don't want to alarm you,' she warns, alarming me, 'but you cannot go home tonight.'

'Why not?'

'You understand that Darroch possessed the strength to shape the world, yes?'

'He moulded the clay.'

That makes her smile. 'Yes, he did.' She locks eyes with me. 'We each had a hand in creating this world. Our powers are worth preserving, and we don't choose our heirs lightly.'

I scrunch my nose at her. 'Heirs?'

'We have the ability to pass on our powers.'

'But Darroch said you never did.'

She nods. 'Darroch chose you to take his place tonight.'

I laugh. 'No, he didn't.'

I search my recent history for some clue, some guidance he may have given me in those final moments. Before he died, he told me to protect Jivanta. Surely he didn't mean . . . 'No!'

The god shushes me. She points at my sleeping grandfather.

'But how?' I whisper.

'Our role is bigger than us. In the moment we expire, we surrender our powers to those who . . .' The pause is purposeful.

I gasp. 'That's why he wanted me to kill him? To take his power?'

'Darroch must have seen something in you. He wanted you to carry on his duty. It is why you can wield his sword with any efficiency – you have his strength.'

I look down at my hands. I make a fist with them. I don't feel any stronger. But the sword *did* feel a whole lot heavier when I first grabbed it, and I *did* yank a gate off its hinges.

I recall him brushing that car aside like it was nothing. 'I'm as strong as Darroch?' I ask.

'Not yet. As of now, you are a fresh bundle of potential. After thousands of years, you might even surpass him.'

I laugh. 'I think you overestimate how long humans last.'

'And I think *you think* you're human.'

I stammer. 'What?'

She smiles warmly, like a parent talking through the act of tying shoelaces to a toddler who isn't quite grasping the concept. 'You're a god, Connor,' she says. 'You will not age a single day and you will not naturally expire. Perhaps thousands of years is wishful thinking, but let's aspire to longevity.'

I'm a *god*.

I imagine strolling into Charlton Grammar tomorrow a god. I'll be the most popular guy on campus; I'll have *disciples*. Actually, why even go to school? One public miracle and I'll have wall-to-wall TV coverage by mid-afternoon. There'll be a bidding war for the holy text. I'll have more money than I'll know what to do with.

I'm a god. I'm not going to . . .

'Wait, did you say I'm not going to age a single day?'

Jivanta nods. 'Not a day.'

'I'll be super strong, but I'll look like puberty barely started then decided, *Stuff it, that'll do*?' I ask.

'You are a god. Aesthetics should not concern you.'

Easy for her to say. She *glows*. And she didn't grow up watching the movies I did. People who are bitten by radioactive spiders or injected with strength serum are supposed to grow pecs the size of traffic signs. I feel ripped off.

'If I'm going to look like this forever,' I try not to sound too ungrateful, 'what do I tell Mum?'

Jivanta's gaze softens as if she's been dreading the question. 'I think it is best if you consider this a rebirth.'

She's being vague. I don't like it. 'A rebirth?'

'In addition to his power, you have inherited the danger Darroch was in,' Jivanta says. 'As your power develops, I believe the Hounds will be able to sense you too. They will come for you.'

That's what she meant by considering this a rebirth – abandoning everything I know, everyone I care for. The idea feels terrifying and terrible. The full weight of it presses against my chest. The picture of my life made infinitely better by being a god is replaced with a picture of that life vanishing entirely. I'll be hidden in some underground sanctuary like the others forever. I can't breathe.

And I don't. I wait for my body to react, to gasp for air. Nothing happens.

'I don't need to breathe anymore?' I ask.

'Breathing is a habit, much like eating and drinking,' the god explains. 'You will adjust.'

I don't want to *adjust*. I take a laboured breath. I know it's pointless, but it's normal. I want normal.

I must look as shattered as I feel, because Jivanta says, 'You have been elevated to the status of a god, Connor. This is cause for celebration. I understand that it is disheartening, but you will come to lose interest in the life you lost.'

I don't know how she can say that with any certainty. She didn't abandon a life to become a god. She wasn't reborn. This is all she has ever known. And now it's all I'll ever know.

'You came to collect me for the Movement, didn't you?' I ask.

'I came to collect Darroch and I found you,' Jivanta says. 'We will leave together. Sally is waiting in her van outside.'

She's going to help find the other gods, then relocate us to some far-flung corner of the world. And before we're hidden in our underground sanctuaries, she's going to ask for her favour . . .

I speak up. 'There's something I need to tell you.'

The Monument raises an eyebrow. 'Oh?'

'Darroch made me promise to protect you.'

'His fixation with protecting me is the reason why he isn't here. He should never have left the van.'

'He should never have left his sanctuary,' I say. 'Sally is not his Guardian. She lied.'

Jivanta doesn't flinch. She doesn't even blink. 'I know.'

I'm flabbergasted. 'You know?'

She tilts her head forwards. 'I created the Guardians, do you honestly think I can't sense their presence? Sally is not the descendant of an understudy. It was likely Darroch's presence that opened my sanctuary, not hers,' Jivanta says. 'I expect she has been more forthright with you?'

I nod. In the seconds before I betray Sally's trust, I feel guilty. I barely know her, my life is effectively over because of her, and I'm bound to protect Jivanta, but I still feel guilty.

'The Movement was a convenient lie for Sally to find you. She wants you to resurrect her parents.'

'I see.'

I explain that Sally plans on asking Jivanta after helping find the other Monuments.

'How fortuitous. That will motivate her. We will keep up the ruse that she is Darroch's Guardian and—' Jivanta gasps. She stares at the wall dividing Pappou's room and another resident's. The tension snaps and her shoulders drop.

I think I know what happened. 'Did someone just . . . ?'

Jivanta nods.

'Can't you save them?'

She isn't looking at me when she says, 'No.' She takes a breath I'm certain she doesn't need. 'Darroch considered everything. He sculpted the earth with such care. He was an artist – but if he heard that, he would likely say that I was one too. He never could take sole ownership of a compliment. I created life, and the means for that life to sustain itself. I added colour, flourishes of green, skin of every hue, but whatever beauty exists in that is accidental. I did not set out to make art but rather to give his an audience – I made the eyes to marvel at his labours. I quickly learnt, however, that when life stretches on and on, it is easy to take things for granted. I couldn't destroy his art, so I destroyed mine. I gave life an expiry date, so humans were compelled to . . . notice.' She sighs and turns back to face me. 'There is an appreciation for all things that only comes with the knowledge that life will definitely end.'

'You're not going to resurrect her parents, are you?'

Jivanta shakes her head. 'We ought to leave.'

I don't want to. Once we leave, once we're in Sally's van, my life is over. I need more time.

'Give me a day to say goodbye,' I plead. 'Give me that at least.'

Jivanta doesn't say anything.

'The Hounds can't sense me yet. I'm not in any danger. One day. Please. I didn't ask for any of this. I don't want to be a god.' My voice cracks. 'Why didn't you all just pass on your powers to your understudies? They wanted this. They prepared for this. They were made to replace you. Why didn't you let them?'

'Sometimes,' Jivanta says, pushing off the lounge chair, 'it is best to pass on power to those who do not want it.' She lingers by the bed, running two fingers over the blade of Darroch's sword. When she touches its hilt, the wrapping around her wrist unfurls.

'This sucks.'

She doesn't try to convince me that it doesn't. 'I am sorry, Connor.'

What do I even say to that?

Nothing. I say nothing.

Jivanta glides over to the room's single window and parts its blinds. She guides the pane open. 'I will grant you one day,' she says without turning to face me. 'Farewell your loved ones. I will seek refuge and return for you at sunset.'

She drifts out into the night.

I watch her float across the lawn and into the back of Sally's van. They drive off. I close the window. It clicks loudly into place.

Tomorrow at sunset, I walk away from my life. It's been decided for me.

When I turn from the window, Pappou's staring at me. I go from god to grandson in a heartbeat. One resounding thump against my ribs.

I reach for the sword and say Pappou's name, my name. He was the man Mum measured me against. He's Constantine and I'm Connor, but when cousins would call out to a Con at family barbecues, we'd both turn. We're connected.

And now I need to say goodbye forever.

'S'agapo,' I say. It's the only Greek I know. It means, 'I love you.'

# TEN

I wake up with a start – doona bunched by my feet, fitted sheet drenched with sweat. The edges of the curtains glow. It's morning.

I let my upper body flop off the mattress and peer under the bed. Darroch's sword and the journal I swiped from the rotating sanctuary haven't been taken in the night.

Today is the final day of my human life. Well, technically yesterday was. Today is the coda, me tying its loose ends before surrendering to the Movement.

I can hear Mum in the kitchen. The kettle whirs. She's making coffee.

I have to say goodbye to her, and I don't know how. Do I tell her the truth? Keep it vague? Do I do it in person? Leave a note? And that's just the literal goodbye. How do I say goodbye to the only person I've known since before I was born? How do I live without the misspellings in her text messages, her rants about the petty feuds at work, her brownies?

Her brownies. There's nothing particularly special about them. They're made from the packet, but no one follows those instructions like my mother. And her laugh when she cuts me a piece . . . It shakes the earth.

At sunset, I lose her forever.

From the waist down, I'm still dressed for the debutante ball. I toss on something more casual, less stolen. I head down the hallway and then linger on the threshold. All the house from here onwards was added in the Great Extension of 2016 – a rustic kitchen that looks like it's been copy-pasted from a wood-cabin enthusiasts magazine, a small dining table and double doors that open out to a modestly sized garden.

Mum's squinting out the back like somebody who has extension regret. She often tells me she wishes we extended the house out further, or at least bothered to learn how to manage the garden. In the four-ish years since the landscaping, the greenery has overgrown its boundaries and now threatens the sundial centrepiece.

I watch her from the doorway for a bit. When she's still, Mum has the pointed edges of a cruel headmistress in a children's film, but in motion, she radiates the warmth of a kind teacher from the same movie. This is the last time I'll ever see her.

She turns and when she clocks me, her brow creases. She's surprised to see me. 'I thought I heard you leave early for school.'

I'm still very much here. 'Nope. Must've been the guy I snuck in.'

She points a finger. 'Not before I meet his parents.'

'That's a weird rule.' I sniff.

She shrugs. 'Try to break it, then.' She squints at me. 'You okay? Your eyes are watering.'

'They are?' I wipe them with the back of my hand. 'Hay fever.'

'You don't get hay fever.'

'I *could.*'

She takes up her coffee mug. 'Don't forget you have a driving lesson tonight.'

It's an opportunity to tell Mum I won't be here on account of the god fetching me at sunset, but I don't take it. Instead, I pretend this is any other day, when a mention of a driving lesson would elicit a groan.

I groan. 'I hate Janice.'

'Janice is doing me a service. If you're going to kill someone behind the wheel, I don't want it to be me.' She sips her drink and instantly regrets the joke. 'Please don't kill anyone.'

I picture the blade slicing through Darroch and hitting the bitumen. I banish the thought with a shake of my head.

'Thanks for last night,' she says.

Yeah, I imagine the night off from Connor duties was a hoot. She would've enjoyed watching her favourite reality TV shows without me sighing loudly at the clichés from the next room.

'Anytime.'

I slip past her to pop two slices of bread in the toaster. I might not need to eat, but I want to. I tap a percussion solo on the edge of the stone countertop – too hard. I chip off a wedge and catch it before it hits the ground. Darroch's strength. I'm a frantic mess trying to fix it back in place, before I panic and toss it in the cutlery drawer. Mum has her back to me. I relax. She checks her watch mid-sip, if only to make her reaction to how late she's running more pronounced. She sets down her mug and there's a brief comic skit where she's trying to get to her handbag by the toaster, and I'm trying to hide the destruction I've wrought.

She reaches past me and snatches up her bag. 'You're an odd one,' she says.

'I know.' She's almost out the back door when I add, 'I love you, Mum.'

She shakes her head. 'So odd.' She begins to close the door behind herself.

'And!'

She pauses. 'Yes?'

'I feel unwell!' It's the most unconvincing performance of my lifetime.

Mum weighs up whether or not to reward this lazy output with a day off school, and then, 'Okay, stay home.' The door slams shut.

I peel my body off the countertop. The chip somehow looks worse than before. I find some tape, fold it once over and sandwich it between the countertop and the broken piece. It's a fix. Not a good fix, but a fix nonetheless.

I plate up my breakfast – toast smothered in strawberry jam – and head back to my bedroom. I sit at my desk, dial Dad's number and put the phone on speaker. Two rings and I'm sent to voicemail. I end the call.

I have the whole day to get through to him. That's why I chucked the sickie. Well, partly why. I was woken at quarter-past three by an idea. Now, I'm not under the illusion that it's a particularly great idea – after all, I did have it at quarter-past three – but I am about to be forced to live underground for eternity, so all ideas are welcome at this point.

The gods are hidden away because they fear the Hounds. I met a Hound last night. He's not worth fearing. Sure, he wilfully drove his car into Darroch, but he was taught that gods are monsters. If I can find him before sunset and explain the truth, then he won't bother us again. Jivanta will see that the Hounds can be reasoned with. We won't need to be hidden away. I won't need to abandon my life.

Obviously, I'll still say goodbye to everyone in case this doesn't work, but it might.

How I'll manage it is where the idea gets dicey. Hounds can sense gods, so I'm thinking if I bring a Monument to the surface, I can use them as bait. Without Jivanta's scent to confuse him, the delivery guy will come to us. So, my plan hinges on finding a Monument that's been hidden for hundreds of years.

If that has any chance of happening, I'm going to need a Guardian. A real one this time.

I try social media, because if I've learnt anything from grown adults uploading five-minute videos about their bowel movements, it's that there's nothing humans won't share in the hope of going viral. Surely some loose-lipped protector of the gods is sharing secrets and using hashtags appropriately.

A search for *#Monument* returns a stream of tourist snap-shots in front of ancient ruins, while *#Guardian* inundates me with memes from a similarly titled movie. *#MonumentGuardian* returns no results.

And then: *Have you tried #MonumentGuardianSupport Group?*

I trust the algorithm and click on the suggestion. It feeds me seven posts, all from larpung43. The photos are filtered to within an inch of their lives: close-ups of smoothie cups, rock-climbing walls. I stalk her profile. Her bio says she's local, a first-year uni student and a liberal user of emoji. I scroll past pictures of spiral notebooks, legs on the beach, painted nails, nothing that really screams, 'I'm protecting a god hidden in Sydney!' It feels like a dead-end, but I climb into her DMs to be sure. I ask, *Is it just my sense of smell playing up, or has a Monument surfaced?*

I figure, if she's a real Guardian, she's smelt Darroch and Jivanta, and if she's not, then my message reads as nonsense.

I wait.

I spring up and pace the length of my bedroom, checking the screen intermittently. Eventually, a flashing ellipsis appears in the corner; larpung43 is typing a response. The ellipsis vanishes; larpung43 has stopped typing. The ellipsis flashes again, then a message appears.

*You sensed it too?*

I exhale and hunch over the keyboard. *Yeah.*

*Who are you?* she asks.

I conjure a believable backstory: I'm a newly minted Guardian looking to meet people like me. If she's part of a support group for Guardians, that should appeal.

The ellipsis flashes again. She replies with a string of colourful emoji and an invitation to meet her during her midmorning English lecture. She sends me the details.

She tells me to bring proof.

# ELEVEN

I'm late for the lecture, but it's not entirely my fault. larpung43 didn't give me much time, and the northern side of the university is a labyrinth of interconnected sandstone castles that all look the same. The theatre door is shut. There's a small window cut out of it. If I stand on my toes, I can see through. Tiered rows of wooden seats stretch to the ceiling, most of them filled. larpung43 is in there somewhere. I send her a direct message.

She responds. She's coming out now. There are so many people on their phones that I can't tell who she is until she stands up in the fifth row.

I step away from the door and hit a guy with my backpack on his way past. He stumbles and regains his footing. He has a mop of dirty blond hair and I think of—

He scowls at me. He's got a patchy beard and a nose ring. He's not who I'm thinking of. It never is.

'Sorry,' I say. 'I'm not good with bags.'

I'm only wearing one because of Darroch's sword. The

hilt sticks out the top, so I've draped a beach towel over it. No one's noticed yet.

larpung43 emerges from the lecture theatre. My first impression is that there's a lot of blue going on. She has blue earrings, a necklace to match, a blue denim skirt and bright blue kicks. She's a bit cagey until I flash her the leather-bound journal, then she relaxes. Her mother gave her a journal exactly like it.

'Larissa Pung,' she says, shaking my hand. 'I'm the founder and de facto leader of the Monument Guardian Support Group. I'm Finn's Guardian, and obviously a bit of a fangirl – hence the blue.'

Finn's the god of ice. Darroch mentioned he was calm and measured, a perfect candidate for the Monument to use as bait. Larissa knows where he is. She just needs to tell me.

Larissa asks me who my Monument is, and when I hesitate, she apologises. 'Tell me when you're ready,' she says.

We walk and talk. Well, she talks and I listen. I'm fascinated, sure, but I'm antsy. I can't spend all day with her. I need Finn aboveground. I've got the delivery guy and four other Hounds to lure.

Larissa doesn't know this, so she treats me to her life story. When she was fourteen, her mother told her about the Monuments and passed on to her the duty of guarding Finn. Her mother was very clear that the responsibility was hers and hers alone, but apparently stoic silence isn't really Larissa's jam. Last year, she decided to look for the descendants of the other Guardian families. She found Tash, Aiden's Guardian, and Bevan, Darroch's. The three of them now meet on the first Tuesday of every month – for smoothies on the beach or hikes or rock climbing.

When we come to a small garden nestled between two castles, Larissa sits on a bench. She's surprised I don't take the backpack off when I do the same. 'We have something serious to discuss,' she says.

Yes. Finn's exact whereabouts.

'Darroch has surfaced,' she continues. 'Bevan went to check on him yesterday and he was gone.'

Pang of guilt. 'Oh.'

'That explains what we've been sensing. Now, we don't know why Darroch's left his sanctuary, or if he was taken against his will. I really think it's our duty to investigate, you know, follow the scent in case—'

'No!' I snap. 'It could be dangerous,' I add, a little more calmly.

Larissa nods. 'That's what Bevan's dad says. Bevan will realise *he's* the Guardian at some point, but until then, he's going to do what his dad says. Tash is relieved. I think the prospect of more active guarding spooked her a bit. And I shouldn't follow the scent alone. I mean, if you . . .' Her eyes widen. She wants me to say I'll join her.

'Darroch isn't our Monument. I think we need to respect Bevan and his dad here.'

'You're right. You're right.' She spies the journal on my lap. 'Make sure you hold onto that. Bevan left his in the sanctuary and it disappeared along with Darroch.' She reaches out. 'Can I?'

'Sure.'

She opens to the back page. 'Same as mine.'

'What's that language?' I ask.

'Your dad never taught you Wren? Don't feel bad, I can only recognise key phrases.' She takes out a pen. 'Do you mind?' I shake my head again and she annotates. 'It's the language of the Guardians. Which family are you?'

I blink at her. I have no idea what she means.

'Guardian family,' she clarifies without glancing up.

My heart sinks and I worry this is some vital information I should know. Will not knowing it out me as a fake Guardian?

'We can find out for you, don't worry,' she adds. 'The Guardians who brought the Monuments to Australia were Cottle, McLean, Miller, Orwell and Tyrell. Jasper Orwell was my however-many-greats great-grandfather. He was the one who decided to put the Monuments under schools. He believed education could make gods of us all. Tash had to research her ancestry; she's a Cottle. Bevan's a Tyrell. That was easy because his surname is still Tyrell. You're either a Miller or a McLean. And you're the last Guardian.'

There are five Guardians, and if I really was one, I'd only be the fourth. I ask about the other one.

'Oh, there isn't one. My great-grandad shot their ancestor. Well, the person who would have been their ancestor.'

I gasp. It's involuntary. 'Do Guardians have a habit of shooting each other?'

'It was an accident. Collin Orwell was overly fond of his double-barrel shotgun.'

That's not as good an explanation as she thinks it is. She returns the journal. I tuck it into the back of my pants, because even with the backpack, that feels like the natural place for it.

'During a school break in 1937 – I remember because all the digits add up to twenty – Collin brought Finn to the surface to attract some . . . miscreants.'

'You mean, the Hounds?'

Larissa nods. 'There were fears they'd made their way to Australia, so he camped out for a week waiting for them. Four showed up and he made sure they had no children before . . .' She mimes Collin firing his weapon. 'Target practice. And then, unfortunately . . .'

'The fifth Guardian?'

She nods gravely. 'Collin was so excited that he'd found the final Hound that it slipped his mind that curious Guardians might also come looking. He returned Finn to the sanctuary pretty quickly and I don't think he ever went back.'

I'm stuck on an earlier detail. There's only one Hound. The delivery guy is the only Hound. He's the only threat to the Monuments. This is good. This is *great*.

And Larissa is sitting here, drenched in blue. Once she tells me where Finn's sanctuary is, I'll be able to bring him to the surface, lure the delivery guy . . . Too easy.

'Jivanta's my god, by the way,' I say.

'*Monument*,' Larissa corrects.

Oh, yeah. There's no one else in the garden, but I imagine discretion is still important. Whoops.

'But *life*, that's a sweet gig,' she says. 'Congrats.'

'Not sure I deserve congratulating, I didn't really do anything. Dad just told me she's over at Eden Ladies'—'

Larissa presses her hand so hard into me it's almost like a punch. Her eyes are wide. 'Don't! Guardians don't reveal where their Monuments are, not even to other Guardians.'

'Oh. Sorry.' My heart sinks. This is a hurdle I didn't anticipate.

'I like to avoid Finn's sanctuary. I don't want to run the risk of being followed. Bevan spent a lot of time in Darroch's and I don't think it's a coincidence that he's gone missing. I prefer to guard with some distance. Last night, when I was checking on Finn, the second I got underground, I could sense him. That's enough for me to know he's safe. Tash is the same. She checked on Aiden this morning. Once she could smell him, she was certain he was fine.'

I exhale. 'Right.'

Okay, now I know Finn's underground, that . . . isn't much help. All the Monuments are underground.

My phone vibrates. A preview invades the top quarter of my screen. I have a new message from a number I don't recognise. *Is that you in the garden?*

I look up and past Larissa. Locky, the most gorgeous guy to ever roam the earth, is standing in the window of the castle to our right. He waves a little, and all I manage is an expression of utter confusion.

My gaze snaps back to Larissa, who stresses that she doesn't want to sound like she's blaming Bevan, before sounding exactly like she's blaming Bevan.

'He took a photo on his phone in Darroch's sanctuary. Come on. Don't do that. Everyone knows photos are geotagged.'

I sneak another glance at Locky. He waves again. He's cute. It's distracting. I try to focus on the conversation I'm supposed to be having. 'Yeah. Everyone. Photos are geotagged.'

I'm so flustered that it takes a second to properly process what I've repeated back to her. Phones geotag our photos. Phones track where we go.

Larissa visited Finn's school last night.

I need to check her phone, but I can't just snatch it.

Locky mouths something at me, I don't have a clue what, then he points off to the side and vanishes. I'll text him as soon as I'm done with Larissa. Because I have his number. Because he gave me his phone and asked me to text myself.

He. Gave. Me. His. Phone.

I need to convince her to do the same. Honestly, it doesn't take much. I tell her I need to get going. She's disappointed, but she brightens when I suggest we exchange details. I offer to text myself from her phone and she hands it over. It has an aqua blue cover.

I'm not used to the operating system, but I manage to get Maps open. I navigate to her location history. A wormlike line stretches across Sydney; it's the path she's travelled today. She started in Miranda down south and came straight to the uni campus in the city. I find yesterday's worm. She started in the same spot, came to uni, but then took one hell of a detour out west on the way home. I zoom in.

Greater Western High School out in Blacktown.

'Texting yourself a novel?' she asks.

I close the app. 'Your keypad's giving me grief.' I surrender the phone. 'I'll DM you my details later.'

'That works.'

I need to get going before I forget the name. Greater Western High School. Greater Western High School.

We rush our goodbyes and I'm halfway around the castle when somebody momentarily grabs my hand. I turn around. It's Locky. He's grinning. 'I thought you were still in high school.'

'I am. I'm sixteen.' It occurs to me that he never told me what school he went to. 'You're a uni student?'

'Yeah. I'm eighteen.' He laughs. 'You didn't reply to my text.'

In the mess that was the rest of my night, replying to Locky completely slipped my mind. I own it. 'I usually wait a few days and let the guy descend into a spiral of self-doubt before I finally message back.'

'Is that how it is?' he asks.

My smile is crooked. 'Yeah. I feel like it's the healthiest way to start a relationship.'

'Obviously.' He rocks back on his heels. 'I know this spoils your plan, but I've got some free time, and since you're here, do you want to . . . ?'

'I can't,' I blurt out.

His shoulders drop and he looks wounded. 'Oh.'

He wants to hang out. I'm flattered, but I've got to get to Blacktown. I can't ignore all the god stuff just because the most gorgeous guy to ever roam the earth wants to hang out. It's not as if I can drag him along with me. On the other hand, this might just be the final day of my human life, why not spend it with him?

After all, Darroch's sanctuary was a two-person job.

'Want to come on an adventure?' I ask.

He's intrigued. 'What kind?'

I play the abridged version in my mind. It's ten-out-of-ten ridiculous. 'I have to warn you it'll be difficult to believe. It's the reason why I wasn't super forthright with you last night.'

He feigns shock. 'You weren't forthright? No!'

'Shut up.'

'Go on, then.'

I hesitate. I want to be honest with him, but I also don't want him to cackle, roll his eyes and saunter off because this random high-schooler he met last night just spouted a bunch of nonsense at him.

'I'm on a scavenger hunt – it's why I was at the debutante ball, it's why I'm here – but it's not your regular scavenger hunt.'

'That explains the sword,' Locky says.

'My what?' I peer over my shoulder. The beach towel has shifted to reveal the ornate hilt of Darroch's sword. I sort *that* out in a hurry. 'I'm on a quest to find a god.'

His face doesn't twist like I was worried it would. I wait for the cackle and the eyeroll that don't come. He raises an eyebrow. 'Is this one of those immersive role-playing, like-a-videogame-but-in-the-real-world sort of things?'

I consider telling him the truth.

'Ah.' He waves a finger at me. 'You wouldn't be able to tell me. That'd break the rules, huh?' He glances around. 'Are umpires watching? Is it like Olympic racewalking where judges pop out from behind bushes waving paddles when you're disqualified?'

I laugh nervously. 'You caught me.'

'Vi did a themed scavenger hunt in the summer holidays. They drove down to Canberra for it. There were people dressed as elves and trolls speaking in riddles and everything. When you mentioned an adventure, I thought you meant we'd like . . . go get gelato or something. But I'm totally game to join you on a little quest.'

He flashes a smile that makes my heart melt – and the crunch of the delivery guy's car colliding with Darroch rings in my ears. Suddenly, I feel guilty for playing down the seriousness of all this.

'It could be dangerous,' I stress.

He shrugs. 'I'm not worried either way. You've got a sword.'

I have a sword, yes, but I have no idea how to use it.

# TWELVE

Five minutes into the train ride, Locky asks if I skip school often.

I arch an eyebrow. 'Is that a first-date question that goes to my character?'

'Is this a first date?'

'I guess.'

'Well, in that case.' Locky reaches into his own bag and plucks out two roast chicken and avocado sandwiches. He hands me one. 'If we're calling this a date, we have to at least eat.'

I unwrap my sandwich. This is good. Actually, this is better than good. When we hopped onboard, I mistook the train carriage for the sort with reversible seats, pulled on one and popped its legs right out of the floor. Locky assumed the seat was already broken, so he has no idea I possess the strength of a god, and now I have a sandwich. This is an astounding recovery.

I'll be the first to admit I love the sound of my own voice. I'm always itching to say something, to fill in any silence with my cleverness. But it's different with Locky – I'm compelled to ask him questions and listen. I love the sound of his voice too.

I sketched a vague outline of him in my mind at Eden Ladies' College last night. This, our official first date, is all about colouring that vague outline in.

Lachlan Joy is a short-distance sprinter and one-time performance poet. I try to goad him into reciting a few lines, but he refuses. He's studying a degree in politics and international relations. He's the youngest of two boys; he shows me a photo – both awe-inspiringly handsome. They grew up in the country but moved to the city for their dad's job. His brother Hugo now lives on a small island off Thailand. He's a journalist who spends his time on a beach freelancing for online publications.

The carriage rocks as the train picks up speed, a baby cries, someone answers their phone – infrequent reminders that there's more to the world than Lachlan Joy.

'So, a degree in politics and international relations . . . Does that mean you're going to be a politician?'

'Hopefully, yeah. My brother's satisfied writing about what everyone's doing wrong, but I need to be in the thick of it, working to make things better. I can do that in politics.' He takes an ambitious bite and shakes the rest of his sandwich at me. 'This is such a pivotal moment and our leaders refuse to meet it.'

'Will there be a Prime Minister Locky one day?'

'That's the plan. What about you? What's your big dream?'

Mum's a consultant who helps businesses improve efficiency, and Dad's a property developer. Mum wants me to follow in her footsteps, and Dad, in his. Honestly, before yesterday I always figured one of them was right. But now that Darroch's thrown the *god* spanner in the works, I'm not sure what the future holds for me.

'I don't know who I want to be.'

'Well, I look at you,' Locky says, leaning in, 'and I know you're going to be someone incredible.'

I'm just trying to be someone who doesn't have to hide underground for eternity. 'Calm down, you've known me a minute.'

'Fine.' He sits back and shrugs. 'Prove me wrong.'

I'm biting back a smile. The guy's charming, I'll give him that.

'I don't think I have it in me to change the world,' I tell him. 'You'll make a great politician though. I'm feeling very inspired.'

There's a flash of doubt in his eyes. 'You think?'

'Yeah.'

'The dream is to be the first Aboriginal person to lead the country, but that's a depressing dream.'

'Why?' I scrunch my face. 'You can do it.'

'That's not what I mean.' He runs his free hand through his hair and sighs. 'For me to be the first, I'd have to be the *first*. No one who looks like me, who has a family like mine, can hold that office, not until I build experience, campaign, get elected, rise up in a political party, go grey, challenge for the leadership, fail, go greyer, work on the numbers, challenge a second time, win . . . It's depressing to want to be the first. I want to be the seventh. I want my being a Wiradjuri man to be unremarkable by the time I get there.'

He exhales. I watch him peel open his sandwich and pick at its contents.

'Well, I hope your dream doesn't come true, but that you become PM anyway,' I say.

Locky accepts it with a nod. 'Thanks.'

At the next stop, a station employee boards our carriage at a passenger's behest. He inspects the damaged seat, swears under his breath, which, thanks to a clear inability to modulate his speaking voice, is still quite loud, and then disembarks.

I'm petrified the employee's brief appearance will rekindle Locky's interest in the damaged seat, but it barely registers. He doesn't turn from me. He's *interested* and I can't help but feel wholly unworthy of the interest.

He's so . . . And I'm so . . .

'How would you change the world if you could?' he asks.

I'm caught off-guard. 'That's a very big question.'

He shrugs. 'It goes to your character.'

How would I change the world if I could? I know he means it in a big-picture political sense, but I can't push past my current predicament.

'I would stop the sun from setting so that today would last forever.'

# THIRTEEN

While some Greater Western High School students spend the final minutes of their lunchtime tossing footballs and whatnot, others hang by the fence and are surprisingly chatty when approached by strangers on the street.

Sally had months to research schools thoroughly. She'd narrowed the search field down before she even set foot on a campus. Without that luxury, Locky and I need to consult experts – in this case, Nina and Casey.

The legends I grew up hearing about Charlton Grammar turned out to be kind of true, so I ask if they've heard any rumours circulating about GWHS. Their answers run the gamut from, 'Like, about Mrs Wright and Mr Anderson?' to, 'Ms Foley killed a guy.'

'Any rumours about underground passageways?' I prompt.

'Oh. There's the crypt,' Nina says. 'But that's not a rumour, it's an actual place.'

'Your school has a crypt?' Locky asks.

'It was sealed off until a couple of years ago, then they reno-vated it for the theatre freaks,' Casey says, sparing no disdain.

I pull up a pixelated satellite image of GWHS on my phone. The school is bounded by a fence of black bars that are twice our height and just far enough apart that I can squeeze a hand holding a phone through. I angle the screen upwards and ask them to point out the crypt.

From above, the school resembles a snowflake on a concrete slab. There's a white building at its centre – the boarding school that became the public school – with demountable classrooms attached to accommodate growing enrolment numbers. They were probably intended to be temporary and now stretch the meaning of the word; their white paint has splintered and their supporting beams have rusted over.

'There,' Nina says, pointing to the backside of the white building. 'That's the entrance.'

I pull my phone between the bars, and Nina clicks her tongue against the roof of her mouth. She asks us why we care so much about the school. Before we can respond, she gasps. 'Are you St Pat's boys? Are you doing another prank?' She seems . . . excited by the prospect?

Locky grimaces. 'We're really not allowed to say.'

'Knew it!' Nina's smirking. In her mind, we're definitely St Pat's boys. 'You're going to get the teachers, right? And nothing with paint, because then they make us clean it.'

I regain control of the conversation. 'How will we know when we've found the crypt?'

There are signs, apparently.

They point us in the direction of a side entrance and wish us luck. On the way, I source two crimson jumpers that have been abandoned by the fence. I hand one to Locky. With the school shield on our chests, we look the part. Sort of.

A sign by the open gate instructs all visitors to report to administration. We ignore it and venture deeper into the school, camouflaged by the flurry of student activity around us. The staff on duty don't realise that from the waist down we're not wearing the proper uniform.

'Do you reckon they were following a script or just ad-libbing?' Locky asks.

'Who?'

'Nina and Casey,' he says. 'I know I'm supposed to suspend disbelief, but I'm fascinated by how it all works.'

Ah. The scavenger hunt.

'Best not to think about it,' I urge him, but I can tell he keeps thinking about it.

We arrive at a concrete staircase that sinks beneath the school. I descend first. When we reach the bottom, Locky's disappointed. With a name like the crypt, he'd expected it to feel like something out of a prestige cable fantasy drama. I have a vague idea of what he means and I'm not quite sure why he's unhappy. There's the smell of rising damp, the grand sandstone arches, the dramatic lighting.

'But they've spoiled it,' he whispers. He gestures to the shiny vinyl flooring, the wall-mounted air-conditioning unit that purrs, and the troupe of drama students knotted in a frozen tableau. Their heads turn to us in unison.

'Hi there!' The voice comes from inside the knot. 'Are you here for Drama Club?'

'No . . . We're on a scavenger hunt.'

'Cool.' That's a different disembodied voice.

'You spend a lot of time down here, don't you?' I ask the troupe.

'We *live* down here,' another voice replies.

The others laugh.

'Have you ever stumbled upon anything mysterious?'

'The critical success of the Year Eleven production of *Hamlet*, because that staging was appalling.'

Locky cracks up.

I persist. 'Anything in the actual space?'

'I mean, there's *that*.' A hand extends out of the mass to point at a narrow sandstone tunnel blocked by a single overturned bin. 'We're forbidden from heading down there.'

That sounds about right.

Locky and I leave them to finish whatever it is they're doing. We step over the bin and follow the tunnel to a door. Locky lights our way with his phone. The deeper we get, the more satisfied he becomes.

'Now *this* is giving me major prestige-cable-fantasy-drama vibes,' he says. 'I can see why the organisers chose this place.'

We've come about as far as we can without me telling him the truth. 'Locky?'

He doesn't look back. 'Hmm?'

'Hypothetically, how would you feel if we weren't on a scavenger hunt?' I ask.

'And what, we were randomly trespassing?'

'Not *randomly*. You know how I said—?'

'Oh my . . .'

We've reached the end of the tunnel: a chamber constructed out of contorted bodies. Not real, obviously. Rock. I lift my foot off a face carved into the floor. Locky runs the light over the scene: sculpted humans of every shape and size frozen in passion or locked in feuds, their limbs extending in odd ways to shield innocent eyes from offending downstairs bits. The chaos swallows us – the rock figures climb the walls and lie sprawled across the ceiling. They claw at each other.

'This is a bit much,' Locky says.

That's understating it. My skin's crawling.

'They didn't make this for a scavenger hunt, did they?' Locky asks.

I shake my head. As if on cue, my phone starts vibrating in my pocket. I ignore it. I remove my backpack and pull out the sword. 'This is an actual sword. Nina and Casey just go here. We're on a legit quest to find a god.'

Locky stares at me and I check my vibrating phone. It's Dad calling. Finally. I should probably answer, this potentially being the last chance I'll get to talk to him and all. Locky continues to stare. The one side of the conversation he hears goes exactly like this:

'Hi, Dad . . . Nothing's wrong . . . I understand how seven missed calls might give you that impression . . . Hello? Yeah, I'm underground, so the connection must be shoddy . . . I just realised I didn't properly thank you for the weekend . . . I get that I don't have to thank you, but I wanted to say that I love you . . . Hello? Can you hear me now? Okay, good . . . Yeah, that's it . . . I'm hanging up now, Dad. Bye. *Bye*. Love you.'

I exhale, pocket my phone and apologise.

Locky hasn't moved an inch. 'We're on a legit quest to find a god?' he asks, occasionally looking to the sword.

'Yes.'

He doesn't fake a bathroom emergency and sprint back the way we came, which is promising. He tells me he's going to need the backstory.

'And I'll give it soon, I promise, but before then, leap of faith.'

Every minute Finn isn't aboveground is a minute before sunset that I'm wasting. I can't walk Locky through the fine print, not yet.

'Okay. I'm leaping.'

I smile. 'If we've got the right place, this is a sanctuary that was designed to test us,' I explain.

We approach the wall to our right and examine its carvings. They remind me of Darroch's, only on a larger, more alarming scale. But where Darroch's work told a story, I don't quite understand what I'm being told here.

An anvil-chinned dude scowls, his arm flexed around a man's neck. A woman picks a flower from another woman's hair; they smile. A boy sleeping upright grips a candle. It's a tangled mess of bodies.

'I don't know where to look,' I say.

'Their eyes,' Locky says. 'My visual arts teacher always told me to follow the subjects' gazes. Here.' He passes me his phone and places his hands on my hips. My heart skips a beat. He gently guides me backwards. He points to the anvil-chinned dude, the choking man, the woman picking flowers, the other woman – no matter which way their heads tilt, their eyes all point to the boy with the candle. 'They're looking at the story.'

I instantly think of the cartoons I watched growing up, where pulling on a candlestick in a haunted castle would reveal a hidden passageway. I hand Locky back his phone and pull on the candle with my free hand. It doesn't budge. A hidden passageway doesn't materialise.

'Secret candlestick lever?' Locky asks. He'd been thinking the same thing.

'Yeah.' I inspect the candle closer. The details are incredible. There are little rivulets carved into the stone to give the appearance of melting wax and the candlewick is actual cotton.

Wait . . . Why?

I ask Locky if he has a lighter. He finds one in the bottom of his bag. I'm worried he smokes, but he assures me it's because this is the bag he takes camping. He hands it over. I hold the flame to the wick until it lights.

I watch the tiny flame flicker. It burns the entire wick and then is swallowed by the wall. But it doesn't extinguish. The rock glows red as the fire traces a path behind the carvings. I tug on Locky's jumper so he steps back. The fiery glow climbs, then charts a crooked course across and down. It returns to its origin and goes dark.

The traced segment of the wall fractures. The fissures spread from the outside in, and before long sizeable pieces of rock rain down to reveal a childlike figure standing in the narrow alcove. He has this reddish-brown crust that from the neck down is riddled with cracks. They have an orange intensity like his insides are on fire. He opens his eyes – same burning intensity.

Locky gasps.

I stare at the uncovered Monument and I realise something isn't right. I'm here for Finn, the calm, measured one, not . . .

'Aiden?' I ask.

The childlike figure nods. A quick glance at Locky's face confirms he's bursting at the seams with questions. The statue is *alive*. And I have questions of my own. Did Larissa lie to me? Or does she not know which Monument her family's actually guarding?

'Are you going to introduce yourselves?' Aiden asks with a lilt I don't expect, given his constitution.

'My name is Connor,' I say. 'This is Locky.'

Locky lowers his phone, mouth agape. 'Hi.'

'Is one of you my Guardian?' the Monument asks, gaze darting between us.

I shake my head. Locky asks what a Guardian is.

'To what do I owe this visit, then?' Aiden is holding a crossbow. One finger teases the trigger. There's a quiver of bolts strapped to his leg.

I can feel the warmth radiating off him.

Locky defers to me. There's the slightest tremor in his voice when he says, 'Connor, the talking statue—'

'God,' Aiden corrects.

'The . . . *god* wants to know why we're here.'

I clear my throat. 'A Movement began yesterday,' I say. 'Jivanta and Darroch were brought to the surface. There was a run-in with the sole surviving Hound and Darroch sustained an injury.' I gesture towards the sword in my hand.

'That's his sword?' Aiden asks the question like somebody who understands what my being able to wield it means. 'Did you—?'

'Darroch asked me to,' I interrupt. I killed Darroch and inherited his strength, but Locky doesn't need to know that on our first date. 'Jivanta is keen on resuming the Movement this evening. I'm hoping to avoid that, but I'll need your help.'

'If Movements were avoidable, I would have avoided one by now.'

A particular point bears repeating. 'Darroch was attacked by the *sole surviving Hound*,' I say. 'When that Hound is dealt with . . .' I let Aiden piece it together.

'No more hiding,' the god breathes, eyes wide. 'Imagine that.'

The grip of the sword twitches. I tighten my clasp. 'I can't be sensed.'

'But I can,' Aiden says. 'You're setting a trap.'

'Pretty much. We'll leave and find somewhere quiet to wait for the Hound. He'll come running when he senses you.'

'And Finn?' Aiden asks.

I don't understand the question. 'What about him?'

'We're twins. I'm not going to leave him behind.'

I glance around. 'Is he here?'

'He's close by. We are always interred near each other. We are rarely separated by more than a hundred paces.'

There's a second sanctuary on campus. That explains how following Finn's Guardian led me to Aiden.

'Come.' The god walks straight past us.

Locky's a little stunned, but I don't really have time to catch him up. I slip Darroch's sword back into my bag, thread my arms through its straps, toss the towel over the hilt and hurry after the Monument. The cracks in his crust illuminate the tunnel.

'Aiden!' I whisper-call.

He's going to get us caught.

The crypt is, thankfully, empty; lunch must be over. Aiden climbs to the surface and we follow him – me, trying to get the god under control, and Locky, just generally bewildered.

The demountable classrooms that branch out from the main building are elevated a metre off the ground. Aiden disappears under one – barely hunched over. Locky and I need to run the whole way around, and by the time we do, he's under the next. His strides are short, but he moves briskly. The soles of his feet spark with every step. We don't intercept him until he pauses in the middle of a handball court out the front of the school.

'This is the entrance to his sanctuary,' Aiden says.

I see no entrance. 'Here?' I ask.

The Monument points down at the concrete. 'There are stairs beneath us.'

I'm uneasy. We're exposed. All it'll take is one student to stare absentmindedly out a window and we'll be spotted. And as for the stairs, I feel like I'm explaining the obvious when I tell him, 'They're under concrete.'

Aiden tilts his head forwards. 'You wield Darroch's sword.'

'Right.' He wants me to use Darroch's strength. 'I don't think I—'

'You can.' The lilt in his voice is gone.

He wants me punch right through concrete in the middle of a first date. Not ideal. I glance at Locky. My hesitation must be obvious.

'You,' Aiden says to him. 'Give me some privacy.'

Locky glances around.

Aiden points to the demountable. 'Stand guard on the other side.'

Locky does as he's told and disappears from sight.

Aiden waits.

I clench my fist. I'm about to drive it into the concrete when I reconsider. I wrap the beach towel around my hand to protect my knuckles and *then* I drive it into the concrete. It breaks into pieces. I'm in awe.

'Quickly,' the Monument urges.

I've got to marvel at that feat of strength later. He's eager to visit Finn's sanctuary immediately. I lift a chunk of concrete and place it to the side, revealing—

'Where are the stairs?' Aiden asks.

I'm flustered. 'I don't know. Are you sure this is the right spot?'

'I'm *sure*,' he snaps.

There's only earth. I claw at it. Nothing.

I think of Larissa. She said she checked on Finn. She sensed him. He should be around here . . . Oh. She said she sensed *a* Monument. She's never been inside his sanctuary. She's been entering the crypt and sensing Aiden this whole time.

'Where's Finn?' He looks to me as if I have the answer. When he repeats the question, it's a little louder.

'I don't know,' I tell him. 'It's been hundreds of years, maybe they—'

'Destroyed the sanctuary?'

'They could have built him a new one and moved him to it.'

'He wouldn't have moved without me.' Aiden steps away from the split concrete. 'Finn?' he calls out.

Okay, less of that.

I follow him. He has to listen to me. 'Aiden, I don't think—'

'He *must* be here.' The fissures in his crust widen. The air around him ripples. 'They demolished his sanctuary.'

'We can come back, have a better look, but right now . . .' I trail off.

The concrete at his feet cracks. We're staring down at it when a hand made of knotted tree roots breaks through, grips him by the shin and pulls him to the ground. The hand recedes into the earth. I scan the surrounds and catch sight of Jivanta kneeling by the front entrance, her hand submerged.

My stomach drops. The concrete at my feet cracks and I know what's coming. I feel the grip on my leg before I feel the ground.

# FOURTEEN

Sally's van is held together by duct tape and prayers. Judging by the sounds it makes as we barrel down the highway, it isn't long for this earth.

Jivanta tracked me. She didn't trust me. At some point before leaving Pappou's room, she wrapped the green leaf around Darroch's sword. Now she's in the back, placating Aiden. He's ranting. The humans were supposed to keep Finn safe and close. Jivanta assures him that his twin will be found. He is adamant that nothing she says will put him at ease, but he gradually relaxes. In the rear-view mirror, I watch him lean into Jivanta's side. The splits in his surface shrink.

Sally glances at me intermittently. When she finally speaks, it's through a smile. 'Couldn't get enough, you had to have your own solo spinoff Movement?' she asks.

*Solo.* They think I acted alone. As she led me and Aiden out of the school, Jivanta didn't notice Locky poking his head out from behind the demountable. The last thing I did was shake my head in his direction, in case he considered following us.

If I don't avoid this Movement, I'll never see him again.

My phone vibrates. It's the fourth message from Locky. *Are you in trouble? Where are you going? What do you need?*

I ignore it like the rest.

'A bit quiet today,' Sally says. Her smile vanishes. 'Is it . . . because of Darroch? Were you there when it happened?'

It's a weird question. I say, 'Of course.'

Sally scrunches up her face like it's a weird answer, and I realise Jivanta hasn't told her I'm Darroch's heir. A pretty big detail to skip, if you ask me.

The deathtrap of a van makes a new disconcerting sound. The orange light on the dashboard pulls Sally's focus. We need petrol. And stat. The warning light only comes on when the situation's dire. Thankfully we're not far from the nearest service station.

Sally merges without indicating to reach the exit lane, because old habits die hard.

I volunteer to pump the petrol and Sally's happy to let me do the honours. As I climb down from the van, my foot catches on the beach towel. I drag it out with me, roll it into a ball and stuff it back beside my—

Sally's staring at my uncovered bag. The hilt of the sword is exposed. She understands the significance, I can tell.

Darroch chose me as his heir.

My heart thumps.

'Actually,' she says, 'I'm going to give you a hand.'

Filling up a vehicle isn't usually a two-person job, but the gods don't know that. Sally doesn't pretend it is either. She leans against the bowser and watches me work in silence. As soon as I've replaced the cap, she grips my arm and leads me into the store.

A pleasant chime alerts the employee behind the counter that we've arrived. He straightens up and acts like he wasn't just caught resting his head on the chocolate display.

Sally doesn't bother with a warm-up. 'We're killing gods now?' she asks.

'Not on purpose.' I reconsider my wording. 'It was on purpose, but he asked me to.'

She plucks up a random magazine and pretends to flick through as I elaborate. After the recount, she asks if I'm the reason why they went to the nursing home, so I recount some more. I mention the day I was given to say my goodbyes and . . . the fact that Jivanta knows about the plan.

'What plan?'

'Your plan. To resurrect your parents.'

Sally clears her throat. 'And how does she know that?'

I grit my teeth. 'Because I told her?'

She slowly slots the magazine back onto the display rack and takes a long breath.

'Darroch made me vow to protect Jivanta,' I explain. It doesn't feel like one of those situations where explaining helps, but I keep going. 'She's going to let you help find the other Monuments.'

She takes another long breath. 'And do you think there's a chance she'll still bring them back?'

I clear my throat. 'I don't, no.'

Sally grips the display and leans into it, defeated. 'That's it, then? It's over?' she mutters. 'Even after what happened to

Darroch, I convinced myself this'd still work. I slept with the fire poker in case Jivanta sensed the Hound and woke me. She didn't. We only needed to find three more Monuments. This morning, she mentioned someone who could help us, and I thought he's who we've spent the day stalking. Turns out, we've been following Darroch's sword all day, you're a god and you've betrayed me.'

'That's a strong word.'

She looks daggers at me. 'Is it the wrong word?'

I stammer and she's satisfied I have nothing else to say. She walks over to the counter. She pays and collects me on the way out. The pleasant chime sounds.

Sally's quiet for the entire ride back to McKenzie Street. In fact, the four of us are. Jivanta breaks the silence when we arrive. She would like a word with me in private. Sally covers Aiden with the blanket and leads him across the lawn. He burns enough holes in the wool that it's barely a disguise by the time they disappear from sight.

My phone vibrates. It's a notification from YouSnaps, an app everyone used to send selfies and short videos for about five minutes last year. I didn't realise I still had it on my phone. *SoUnlocky (Lachlan Joy) has added you as a contact.*

I only open YouSnaps long enough to add Locky back.

'How are you feeling?' Jivanta asks.

'About abandoning my life? Not great.'

'I didn't hurt you at the school, did I?' Jivanta asks. 'Aiden was worked up and reaching for people is an efficient way to—'

I twist around in my seat and assure her that she didn't

hurt me. She seems relieved. Apparently, she wasn't quite sure how much force to use.

'Aiden can be difficult to manage,' she says. 'What were you doing, bringing him to the surface without us?'

'The delivery guy is the only Hound left. I thought ... I hoped that if he sensed Aiden, I'd have a chance to reason with him and he wouldn't be a threat anymore. And the Movement wouldn't have to happen. And I wouldn't have to leave.'

'Mm.' That's all she gives me. Just that sound.

'But I'm right, right? If he doesn't hunt you, you don't have to hide.'

Jivanta sighs. 'I appreciate you making the effort, Connor, I really do. But it's not that simple.'

My brow furrows. From my end, it looks exactly that simple.

'We created your world,' she says. 'I created life. But life is not some static thing that is made and left alone – it constantly remakes itself. Life requires attention, nurturing. It was a job I believed I could delegate. I took three pieces of myself, buried them in the earth and from those mounds sprouted three new gods, sisters who could manipulate the whims of lifeforms. Under their influence, life evolved to what you know it to be. But the sisters rebelled. Their mandate to guide lifeforms warped into a desire to rule them. They commanded armies and the world was consumed by war.'

This all sounds familiar. I recall the evil sisters from Darroch's carvings. 'One of them died, didn't she?' I say.

Jivanta briefly lowers her gaze. 'She did. Her sisters continued to wreak havoc, so we were compelled to act. The rebel gods sat on their thrones and battled via the humans and animals under their influence; to fight them would be to fight all of those who live. We instead lured them to a parallel realm and sealed it off.'

Darroch depicted the gods as having broken off pieces of themselves to forge that seal. 'You were weakened, weren't you?' I ask Jivanta.

'I might not look it, Connor, but I am fragile,' she says. 'The two realms once overlapped. It was possible to leap from one to the other. To seal away the rebel gods, we separated the realms with our bare hands. We stood between them. We still do. Our bodies never left that space between realms, but we left our bodies. Upon our return to this realm, we wore the world as flesh, knowing full well that if anything were to happen to us, the bodies we left behind would cease to exist. We are all tethered to those bodies by the thinnest of threads, keeping them alive.'

'So, if anything happens to the Monuments the realms collide?' I ask.

Jivanta nods. 'Precisely,' she says. 'When Darroch perished, the tether between his form in this realm and his old body broke, and now, the wall between realms is weaker.'

I exhale and wonder what this all means for me. I ask if I'm expected to pick up Darroch's slack now that he's gone. 'You know,' I add, 'leave my body in the space between realms and wear the world as flesh.'

I picture a version of myself that looks more like the Monuments.

'That is beyond your capabilities.'

That's a relief. I'm not sure how being a sentient lump of stone might suit me. 'To clarify, if I die, it doesn't affect the wall?'

'Correct.'

'I don't need to hide then, right? We can move you and Aiden and the others, and I can stay. If I'm ever powerful enough for the delivery guy to sense me, all I have to do is explain all this to him. He won't kill me.'

Jivanta shakes her head slightly. 'The Hounds were our understudies, Connor. They were especially created to be loyal to us. Before imprisonment, the rebel gods corrupted them. They were twisted, made to lust for power. You might look at that one remaining Hound and see a problem to be fixed, but I see a symbol of the rebel gods' corrupting influence, a reason why we should never take any chances that could lead to their return.'

'And living my life is us taking a chance?' I ask.

'Even without antagonists who sense your strength, regular people will realise you don't age. You will be discovered. Darroch's strength will be discovered. Forget corrupted understudies, ordinary people will covet your power. They will strive to take it from you. And what if they are not satisfied? What if they seek *us* out? So long as you advertise our existence, you jeopardise the wall between realms. You must join the Movement.'

I swallow hard. It feels unavoidable. The remaining Monuments will be found and then the five of us will be whisked away.

I'm scared, upset, but mostly angry. Angry at myself. Today was the final day of my human life and I wasted it.

# FIFTEEN

I spend the next hour at Sally's dining table, staring at my phone. When I switch it off tonight, I'll be severing the connection to my entire life. The messages I type now, they're sacred. That's a lot of pressure. Too much pressure. I haven't typed a single word, or rather, I haven't typed a single word I haven't then immediately deleted.

Aiden sets his crossbow down on the table and slides onto the chair beside me. I'm surprised it doesn't catch alight. We both watch Sally and Jivanta, who are busy with the sprawling map of Sydney. There are dozens of schools marked in silver and no real way to narrow the search for Nuo's sanctuary, but Sally's trying. Journal in hand, she's reeling off everything that she knows about the campuses and assessing the likelihood that they might shelter a god.

I don't know why she's still so invested in the Movement. She knows Jivanta isn't going to bring her parents back. Maybe she's hoping the Monument will warm to her and reconsider . . .

Aiden finally speaks. 'They will begin their search for Nuo at nightfall.'

'What about us?' I ask.

'We will find Alek,' he says. 'He is the key to locating my brother.'

I furrow my brow. I haven't heard that name before. 'Who is—?'

There are two hard knocks at the door. Aiden reaches for his crossbow and I look to Jivanta. She shakes her head. She doesn't sense an understudy.

'Connor?' a voice calls from the other side of the door. I *know* that voice.

It's Locky. Sally recognises his voice too. She's looking at me like I blabbed.

'I didn't tell him where I am, I swear.'

Her eyebrows almost hit her hairline. 'How is he here, then?'

'I don't know.'

She comes over and asks for my phone. I surrender it. She taps the screen furiously.

'He texted me earlier, I ignored him,' I explain. 'He sent me a YouSnaps message and I ignored that too.'

Sally groans. 'Of course.'

'What?'

'You're on YouSnaps.'

'I literally haven't used it in yonks.'

'But you used it today.' She angles the screen at me. YouSnaps is open. She swipes down and a map of the city appears. It's peppered with little cartoon avatars. She pinches the screen to zoom. The cartoon Locky is standing next to the cartoon Connor on McKenzie Street.

I'm stunned. 'It automatically shares my location? I didn't tell it to do that.'

'YouSnaps' privacy controls are terrible,' Sally says. 'Everyone knows that. I live off the grid and I know that.'

Locky added me on YouSnaps so that I would share my location with him. He used my phone to spy on me, just like I used Larissa's to spy on her. I feel violated . . . and like we're soulmates.

'Connor?' Locky calls again.

'Go shoo him,' Sally hisses.

'All right, all right.' I snatch my phone out of her hand. YouSnaps is uninstalled before I reach the door. I grip the knob and peer back. Six eyes are trained on me. Aiden points his loaded crossbow. I tilt my head forwards and he gets the hint. He lowers the weapon onto the table.

I only open the door wide enough to slip through. I close it immediately and exhale. Locky is standing there, shock and relief etched into his face.

'You're okay,' he whispers, lunging forwards and wrapping his arms around me. He hugs me tightly.

'I am.' He's still hugging. 'What are you doing here?'

Locky releases me and retreats. He clears his throat and straightens up. 'I'm . . . here to save you.'

I bite back a smile. 'Save me?'

He relaxes. 'Don't make me feel bad for worrying. You were taken away by a floating woman and you weren't replying.'

I owe him a lengthy explanation, but I'm not going to give it standing right by the door. I lead him out of earshot – up the side of the house to the front lawn. I ask if he remembers the broken seat on the train.

Locky nods. 'It was a memorable moment.'

'It wasn't broken when we boarded. I broke it. I have godlike strength because I'm a god.'

He laughs. When I don't, his face drops. 'You're serious?' he asks.

'It's a relatively new development. Basically, if you kill a god, you become their heir and inherit—'

'You *killed a god*?' I've never seen someone blink so much in my life. 'Gods can die . . . and you've killed one?'

'He asked me to.'

'You're a god,' he whispers. 'I'm guessing the floating woman is . . .'

'Also a god, yeah,' I finish for him. 'She came to fetch me and Aiden because the gods have these Movements where they're carted off to distant places and hidden away.'

He scrunches up his face. 'Wait, you're leaving?'

'I don't really have a choice.'

'Don't you?' He glances down the street. 'We can piss-bolt to the bus stop right now.'

He's got a point. I'm outside, unsupervised. I don't have Darroch's sword; Jivanta can't track me. I can leave and avoid the Movement. But if I do that, I risk being found out, and that risks the other Monuments and the wall between realms.

'I can't, Locky,' I tell him. 'When you become a god's heir, you stop ageing. I'm going to look sixteen forever. How am I going to explain that to people?'

He's crestfallen. 'This is the last time I'll ever see you?'

I can't bring myself to answer him directly. 'If things were different, I would've really liked a second date.'

Locky sighs. 'Me too. Something more low-key though.'

I laugh. It hurts a little.

'Thanks for coming for me. That's the sweetest thing any guy has ever done.'

'I am pretty sweet.'

He takes two slow steps backwards. He isn't in any hurry to leave.

'If I left with you right now, you still would've dated me?' I ask. 'Even after all this?'

He kicks the grass softly and smiles at me. 'Yeah.'

There's nothing more to say, but neither of us wants the conversation to end. Thankfully Sally pops up out of nowhere. Leaning against the side of the house, she asks Locky if he wants to stay for dinner. 'Jivanta's asking,' she adds.

Locky's confused. He doesn't know who Jivanta is. I'm confused. I don't know why Jivanta . . .

It dawns on me. 'You could hear—'

'We could hear most of that,' Sally says, pointing to a small window that lets light into the basement.

Locky enthusiastically accepts the invitation, and when we enter, Jivanta lays claim to him. They sit on the couch and the god bombards him with questions. Locky answers them with a perfect balance of charm and sass. Jivanta laughs. I hear all the beauty of the world in her laugh.

Obviously, Locky has a ton of questions for her too. She indulges him.

I watch them from the other side of the basement, where Aiden attempts to regale me with stories from the early days of humankind – he was worshipped as the god of fire and it was marvellous. I'm only half-listening. Locky is difficult to take my eyes off.

Aiden notices.

'Movements are interesting times,' he tells me. 'Yes, every second we are aboveground, we are in danger, but we are also *alive*.'

Jivanta's gaze meets mine. She slowly nods her approval of Locky. If things were different . . .

'She's convinced you to abandon it all,' Aiden says. 'I wouldn't wish a life cooped up in a sanctuary on my enemy.'

I exhale. 'It isn't that bad, is it?'

He doesn't answer. Instead, he wanders off to bother Sally, who is thumbing through her journal and highlighting passages. They chat for a bit, but I can tell Sally isn't really invested in his stories of how things used to be. She keeps glancing at Jivanta and Locky – no prize for guessing which god she'd rather be speaking to. She excuses herself at the first opportunity and approaches Jivanta. She asks if they can speak in private. The god agrees and Sally leads her out to the backyard.

Aiden sets his sights on and immediately ensnares Locky, who doesn't seem to mind the rambling nostalgia. He even asks follow-up questions. I linger close.

Sally returns without Jivanta. She keeps her head down and walks briskly to the kitchen. She has her back to us, but I can tell she's upset. I've tried to hide my sads from enough people to recognise the signs. I wander over and she pretends to be intensely interested in the drawer of loose takeaway menus.

She sniffs.

'Where's Jivanta?' I ask.

'In the yard,' she says. 'Do we want Thai or Indian? Actually, Chinese is pretty good and the wait isn't usually long.'

I attempt to ask what happened. Her answer is vague, but it leaves me with a general idea. She asked about resurrecting her parents and Jivanta refused.

I tell her that I'm sorry and she waves me off.

'Chinese?' she asks.

'Sounds good.'

Sally borrows my phone. She's partway through ordering when Aiden steps out to get some fresh air. She asks him to be discreet. For obvious Hound-related reasons, Sally's a bit skittish about having food delivered. She tells the restaurant she'll pick the order up. When she eventually leaves, we hear her out the front, nervously encouraging Aiden to stargaze where fewer people might see him, like in the backyard.

'Wow, you really can hear everything through that window,' Locky says.

I sink onto the couch beside him. I expect a Q&A, but he must be all out of Qs, because he doesn't say a word. I listen to the sound of him breathing.

Sally returns with too much food. We spread the takeaway containers across the dining table and it's a free-for-all. I let Sally and Locky liberally heap lemon chicken, beef in black-bean sauce and fried rice into their bowls before I attack – it'd be wrong to hog it all when I don't actually need food.

We eat in relative silence.

Every so often, the floorboards above us creak.

Sally abandons her meal after a while and instead, thumbs the crossbow. Aiden left it on the table with a single bolt. She's absorbed in thought. Locky and I divvy up the remaining takeaway containers. I'm almost done with mine when the front door opens gently to reveal a hovering Jivanta. It's dark out. Her opal underlayer shimmers. 'Connor, come join us outside.'

She leads me to Aiden, who's crouching in the centre of a neglected garden. A tangled nest of branches lies in front of him, engulfed in flames. I sit on the grass opposite him.

Sally's upstairs neighbours are away on holiday. We have privacy, but my eyes play tricks on me. I see shadows moving in the darkened windows. Imagine how strange that'd be, looking out into your backyard to see two animated statues and a teenager huddled around a campfire.

Jivanta speaks first. 'Aiden has informed me that he does not wish to join the Movement,' she says.

'He has?' I ask, looking across at him.

'He will help us find Finn and Nuo, but he will not relocate,' she continues. 'I worry about what this means for the world we have worked so hard to preserve.'

Aiden doesn't flinch. 'I yearn to live, Jivanta. I refuse to believe that being stuffed in some dank sanctuary is my lot in life.'

'But in those dank sanctuaries, we are protected.'

'From who? The Hound? The *one* Hound?' He turns to me, his orange eye sockets glowing with a vivid intensity.

'You've met him, Connor. Do you think he would trouble the god of fire?'

'Oh, you will dispatch him, will you?' Jivanta asks. 'What then? Do you, the god of fire, waltz down the street and procure a job?'

'Don't tease.'

'Tell me, what is the place you see for yourself in this world? In my eyes, we do not fit. We gave the world to humans and they shaped it into something else. This is their world now. We belong in our sanctuaries, out of sight and ensuring that the wall between realms remains intact.'

'I do not want to live in a hole in the ground,' Aiden says. His chest expands and the cracks in his crust widen. 'I want more.'

Someone else speaks. 'I want . . .'

I look back. Sally's standing by the house, Aiden's crossbow raised in her hands. It's shaking a little.

'Sally?' I ask. 'What are you doing?'

She takes a deep breath and adjusts her grip on the weapon, no doubt hoping to look imposing. 'I want Jivanta to bring my parents back.'

Aiden stirs and Jivanta extends an arm to stop him. She doesn't turn to face Sally when she asks, 'Do you really intend to use that weapon?'

Sally swallows hard. 'Yes.' She's not really selling it. 'I can kill you and become your heir.'

'I am certain of that. I am weak. One bolt should do it. But know that even when your power matures, you will not be able to recreate your parents as they lived, only as you remember them. You would be giving bodies to memories.'

'Resurrect them, then.' Sally's voice trembles like she's on the verge of tears. 'Properly.'

'They are already here. Life is wondrous like that,' Jivanta says. 'You are your parents. You grew from them. You are every lesson they taught, every story they told and every secret they shared. Wherever you go, you carry them with you. But know that ultimately the path is yours. Do not let your attachment to them lead you somewhere you do not want to go.'

It must dawn on Sally that she's standing in her backyard with a crossbow pointed at a god, because her face cracks and she begins to sob. 'I'm so sorry. I just really want to see them again . . .'

'It's all right. Lower the weapon,' Jivanta coos. She can reach through the earth and pull Sally to the ground, but she doesn't. 'We will forget this ever happened.'

'I'm so sorry,' Sally repeats. 'I have to try.'

Jivanta braces herself and a bolt pierces her shoulder. It's like she knew it was coming.

Sally drops the crossbow, stammers another apology and flees.

The Monument squints down at the tip protruding from her front. I ask if she's okay. She doesn't respond. She clasps the bolt, pulls it all the way through her and tosses it onto to the ground. She prods the exit wound. Her rocky flesh has started to crumble around it. Her opal underlayer dims.

She is not okay.

Jivanta pushes herself up and staggers towards the house. She no longer floats. Where she steps, flowers grow, bloom and wither. She's following Sally.

Aiden shadows the wounded Monument, suggesting he be made her heir. When she rebuffs him, he stops in his tracks. 'Why not?' he asks.

The fissures in his crust widen and the air around him is suddenly thick and hot.

Jivanta ignores him.

The fire crackles. I turn to see the burning nest of branches unfurl and stand tall, assuming the frame of a man. It approaches Aiden and grips him from behind.

'You cannot be serious!' Aiden barks. 'After all I've done for you! Jivanta!'

I scramble past him and follow Jivanta into the basement apartment. She leaves a trail of rubble from the door to the kitchen, and her footprints have warped the floorboards. She rummages through the cutlery drawer. Her arm closest to the wound breaks off. She uses her other hand to grab a steak knife.

Sally isn't in here. Locky is. He's clearing the dining table, confused by the spectacle. 'What's going on?'

Jivanta stumbles over to him and thrusts the knife into his hands. 'We don't have long. I need you to end my life.'

She's choosing him as her heir.

Locky's bewildered. 'Sorry, what?'

'Kill me,' she urges.

There's confusion and then clarity. His eyes widen. He remembers our conversation. 'If I do . . . I become your heir,' he says. 'I inherit your power.'

Jivanta nods. 'Yes.'

Locky's flustered. 'Why?'

The god's knees buckle. 'I have seen your heart.' She reaches out to him with her arm, while the opposite half of her body turns to dust. 'Do it!'

I try to reel off all the terms and conditions, but Jivanta is deteriorating rapidly – far faster than Darroch did.

Locky asks, 'I just . . . stab you?'

Jivanta groans, 'Yes!'

And he does.

'Find my son,' she says, as her face begins to crumble. Four words are all that's left in her. 'I kept him close.'

# SIXTEEN

Locky's shell-shocked. I know exactly how he feels. A god can tell you to kill them, but it still isn't any less confronting when they actually die. Staring at Jivanta's remains, he mutters, 'She fell apart.'

I'm rattled too. Deep, shimmering cracks decorate the space around us. They're more intense than last time. Locky's too engrossed by the fallen Monument to notice them before they're gone.

'And her son?' Locky asks.

I'm as mystified as he is.

Outside, Aiden bellows Jivanta's name. 'I will rip your power from whichever human husk you hide it in!' he shouts.

Locky blinks at me. 'He'll do what?'

'Apparently, he's not taking being passed over for Jivanta's heir well,' I say. 'We need to get you out of here.'

I grab the sword with one hand and pull Locky out the door with the other. Jivanta's fiery man has been reduced to a heap of smoking branches. Aiden kneels to retrieve his crossbow, and I pull Locky back inside. We cross the room and there's nowhere to go. There's just wall.

But I have Darroch's strength.

I release Locky and make a fist. I punch straight through to the air outside. The wall fissures and crumbles. We now have an escape route.

Locky's impressed. He follows me through the plume of rising dust. We rush down the side of the house. I stumble over a potted plant, but quickly recover my footing. When we get to the backyard, Locky offers me a leg-up over the fence dividing 71 from 73 McKenzie Street.

A flaming bolt whizzes past my ear. I glance back – Aiden is standing by the hole in the house.

Locky has meshed his fingers together so I have somewhere to step. 'Hurry.'

I charge at the fence instead. There's an explosion of timber fragments. I sprint across the lawn, apologising profusely to the bewildered couple who were, until very recently, enjoying a wind-down wine on their back porch. I charge through the opposite fence. This next yard is littered with decorative paraphernalia. I dodge a plastic pink flamingo. Locky trips on a garden gnome. He hits the ground, avoiding the fiery arrow that would have otherwise pierced his back.

I stop and turn. Aiden is standing in the bewildered couple's yard. He lowers his weapon. 'Give me Jivanta's power,' he says.

'No.'

My heartbeat pounds in my ears, thumping louder and louder.

What would Darroch do? Um. He shaped the earth.

I look down. There's a lot of earth.

I toss the sword aside. The blade clangs against a gnome. I kneel. The grass is wet. I think strong, godly thoughts and drive my hands into the soil. The earth splits open. I'm kneeling in a crater as deep and wide as I am tall.

All right, I wasn't expecting that. I'm getting stronger quicker than I anticipated.

'Are you okay?' Aiden calls. 'I can take Darroch's power too if it's troubling you.' He cackles.

I can't see out of the hole, so I punch the wall of soil ahead of me with alternating fists. The crater widens. The disturbed soil flows and buries my calves. My control melts away. I beat the earth like a kid trying to swim for the first time. Every impact leaves a mark. I experiment with more force, slapping the soil. The earth quakes and I don't stop, landing hit after hit until the ground fissures. I pull my hands back.

I can't hear any laughter.

I claw at the walls of the pit to pull myself up, but every time my hand connects with earth, the crater widens. I try a lighter touch; the earth doesn't dent. I climb out.

Only when I'm standing above it is the full extent of the damage clear. A trench has opened up across several backyards.

My chest rises. My chest falls. I did *that*. I'm a little proud.

Aiden's struggling to get out. The crevice is deeper than he is tall. He spits, 'I will end you both!'

Locky takes my hand. 'Come on.'

I pick up Darroch's sword and follow him down the side of the house and over the front fence. We're sprinting along the street. We take the next turn and keep running. Locky's impressed I can match his pace.

He hollers when he sees a bus. We reach it just as it begins to pull away from the kerb. He slaps his hand against the side and the bus jerks to a halt. The doors reopen. We rush to the front and hop aboard. It takes us too long to fish our travel cards from our wallets. The driver stares at us . . . and then the sword.

We head down the aisle. The fluorescent light is harsh. There are rows of empty seats. Locky has his pick of anywhere, but he sits next to me and rests his head on my shoulder. His hair grazes my neck. I exhale.

I ask him where we're headed.

'To the end of the line,' he replies.

Sounds perfect. I want as much of Sydney between us and Aiden as possible.

'That was intense,' he says.

'We almost died.'

'Silver lining, we didn't.'

We're quiet for a short while. I keep replaying the night back, over and over. The bolt piercing Jivanta. Her rapid deterioration. Aiden chasing us. His cruel laugh.

Locky's chest expands and contracts with each breath. 'Did you feel any different after you became a god?' he asks eventually.

'Not really.'

'So, I'm the same, only I can create life now, is that the deal?'

'It's a gradual thing. You're not instantly Jivanta.'

'Right.'

I try to take stock of our situation. Darroch is dead. Sally is MIA after firing a crossbow at Jivanta for refusing to resurrect her family. Finn is missing. Aiden, in a bid to prove that Darroch calling him fiery was the understatement of the year, just tried to kill us. Jivanta wants us to find her son. Nuo is hidden in a sanctuary under one of dozens of schools. We need to find her too because there's supposed to be a Movement. And to make it all spicier, the delivery guy is still out there. I know he's not much of a Hound, but he *is* a Hound, and he's already mortally wounded one god. We don't know when he'll be able to sense us and what he might do when he can.

I open my mouth and everything tumbles out. When I'm done, Locky simply rests a hand on my thigh.

'Let's not talk about the scary stuff for a little bit,' he says.

'Okay.' I don't know what else to talk about though.

'Tell me everything you know about pineapples,' Locky suggests.

I laugh, but he's serious. I endeavour to tell him everything I know about pineapples, which is . . . not very much. When I'm done, I go quiet. He doesn't quiz me about another fruit.

The bus route makes little sense on its own, but I'm sure it's vital in the broader sense of the city's transport network. When we arrive at the north side of the harbour, the driver calls last stop. He watches us in his mirror until we amble off the bus. From where he's dropped us, we can see the Harbour Bridge, all lit up in its tourist-attracting splendour, and the city behind it. I know the area a little. Olly lives in one of the hyper-exclusive apartment buildings by the water. When we were younger, his dad would send us down to the shops with thirty dollars and strict orders not to return until we'd spent it. There's this great gelato place nearby. One summer, we ate our way through their entire menu.

It isn't too late to go on the adventure Locky expected. In the interests of not talking about the scary stuff, I push down the still-way-too-fresh memory of Aiden shooting fiery bolts at us and lead Locky through the Burton Street Tunnel that passes under the highway. There's a strip of shops on the other side. We both order two scoops of gelato, mine in a cup with a useless little spoon and his in a waffle cone. We then dawdle back to the tunnel.

Olly first brought me here. We were like ten. We'd spent the last of our thirty dollars on a packet of chocolate-coated almonds. He walked me to the middle of the tunnel and, looking crafty, told me to stand against the wall. He ran across and stood with his back against the same wall as it curved down to the pavement. We faced each other. He reached into his pocket and extracted an almond. 'You ready?' he whispered, and I heard it like he was whispering in my ear. He explained that it had something to do with sound waves and the curvature of the arch. I remember being so impressed.

I stand Locky against the wall and cross over to where Olly once stood. And like him, I whisper, 'You ready?'

The closeness of my voice startles him. 'How did you do that?' he calls.

'Speak softer and into the wall,' I instruct.

'How did you do that?' he asks quietly. I hear it right in my ear.

I tell him to talk, to just send the first thing that comes to his mind across the curve. He mentions his brief stint as a performance poet, and asks if I want to hear his piece. I do. It'll be a perfect distraction. 'Tough,' he says, but he tells me about standing on the café's makeshift stage – a sturdy coffee table – and the terror of forgetting his lines.

And as the archway carries his voice to my ears I'm transported back to the times Olly and I spent here. We were close, but we were always closest with some distance between us. There was nothing we were afraid to say in the tunnel. I told Olly that I was gay here. It was two years ago. We were in Year Eight. I'd known it for a while, but dreaded saying it aloud. I pressed my hands against the wall to steady them so my voice wouldn't shake. It shook anyway.

Goosebumps prick my skin as I recall the silence that came after. I blink back tears.

I want to say Olly did something wrong – it'd make us not being friends anymore so much easier – but it was perfect. He asked if I was sure, and when I nodded he offered me the rest of the chocolate-coated almonds he was hoarding in his pocket. He was fine. We were fine.

I will never come here and not think of Olly. He was the first person I ever told, and this place is that moment played on loop. I can say the memory is spoiled by the fact he doesn't want me in his life anymore, but it's not. And after the upheaval of the past two days, it's comforting being here. It's like he's with me.

I wonder what he'd think about all this.

About me being the heir to a god. About Locky. About us needing to find Jivanta's son. About Aiden seeming pretty keen on killing us.

I imagine Olly standing beside Locky. I imagine his smile.

# SEVENTEEN

I invite Locky to spend the night at mine – I know, without
Mum meeting his parents. Such a rebel.

My thinking is, we have to find Jivanta's son tomorrow, it'll
be easier if we start from the same spot. And we're probably
safer from Aiden if we stick together. Yeah. That's why I want
him to come home with me. For efficiency and safety. It has
absolutely nothing to do with wanting to spend more time
with him before the fire god ends us both.

Home is two trains and a bus from the Burton Street
Tunnel, but it takes less than an hour. Locky waits outside
my bedroom window with the sword, while I wander around
the front. I'm barely through the door when Mum calls, 'That
was a long lesson,' from her bedroom.

She thinks I've been out driving with Janice. I'm not
going to correct her. I rush straight to my room, mumbling
something about wanting to get to sleep. Through the door,
Mum asks if I'm feeling any better. It's the same door I'm in
the process of blocking with my bedside table.

'What do you mean?' I ask, one nanosecond before I remember I chucked a sickie today. 'Oh. A little bit. Sleep should fix me up.'

'I can make you some chicken soup.'

'Honestly, I think sleep will do the trick.'

She lists a number of other easy-to-digest foods.

'Night, Mum.'

I lean my weight against the bedside table and stare at the door. If she tries to barge in and realises she can't, I don't know how I'm going to explain it . . .

'Night, Con,' she says.

I hear footsteps down the hallway. I wait until I'm certain she's gone back to her room, then I wait a little longer, and *then* I open the window for Locky. He attempts to lift the sword, but he can barely get it off the ground. After a series of difficult-to-decipher hand gestures, he realises I want him to leave it. The sword isn't going anywhere. He climbs in without a sound.

Within seconds, we're on the bed, the light's off and most importantly, Mum doesn't know I've invited a guy over.

My phone vibrates. One new message. My stomach drops. I fear it's Mum, I fear she knows. I check the screen . . . The message *is* from Mum, but it's another list of meals she's happy to prepare.

*Go to sleep, Mum.*

I toss her a second message that's just a load of Xs.

She replies with an incoherent emoji sequence: cowboy, prayer, applying polish to fingernails, koala, rainbow. It's her way of saying that she loves me and that newfangled ways to communicate confuse her.

I leave my phone on the floor. I'm lying with my back to Locky. I can hear him breathing we're that close. When you're sharing a single bed, you have to try really hard not to touch the other person. Tonight's especially difficult for . . . reasons.

'Do we actually need sleep?' he whispers.

'Um.' I want to answer boldly – tell him we don't, so we can stay up the whole night talking. The truth is, I don't know. 'I'm certain we don't need food or air, but I like it when I eat and breathe, so I imagine sleeping is the same?'

'Okay.' He goes quiet and I suspect he's resisting the urge to breathe. He lasts a while before inhaling. 'That felt wrong.'

'Exactly.'

He yawns. 'Good night, doofus.' He traces a small circle on my back with one finger. The skin beneath my shirt tingles.

'Sleep well . . . doofus.'

'You haven't earned the right to call me that.'

The laugh escapes before I can smother it with my hand. 'Stop it,' I hiss.

'Not my fault you can't control yourself.'

He goes quiet. He's drifting to sleep and I'm staring wide-eyed at the opposite wall. The most gorgeous guy to ever roam the earth is in my bed. I feel myself smiling.

Long after I've assumed he's fallen asleep, he asks what kind of music I like.

'Pop.' People are usually dismissive when I tell them that, like I'm lazy for enjoying stuff that's popular. Locky isn't.

'Nice. I'm a sucker for a good remix.'

'Clubby stuff?'

'Sometimes. I'm more into when they take a song you love and change its DNA by adding something or accentuating an element you never noticed.'

'When I'm down, I . . . Actually, never mind.'

'Nah, you started it.'

'You know when you start speaking and then you realise what you're about to say is incredibly cringe-y, so you decide not to?'

'You're not convincing me not to want to hear this.'

I groan. 'But you have to promise not to judge.'

'I'm not promising that.'

I sigh and surrender. 'I have this knack for finding sadness in songs. It could be the biggest bop ever, but if I'm feeling a bit low I can find a line to twist to match my mood.'

'Right.'

'When I'm down, I'll play a song at seventy-five per cent speed to really bring out the feels.'

'You slow down fun pop songs to cry at them?'

'I don't *cry*.'

'I get that though. The song changes. That's the promise of a remix. When an MC shouts, "Remix!" at the top of a track, you realise nothing is set in stone. Any song can be taken and reworked. Sometimes I wish life was like that, you know? There's so much I would do over.'

'Like?'

I hear him smack his lips together as he considers it. 'I probably wouldn't have taken so long to come out. People think I didn't – I told my family when I was fifteen – but I had a feeling way before then. Everyone else did too. Mum would warn me to keep my wrists from going limp, before I understood what she meant. Dad would lecture me about being private, and I didn't even know what I was supposed to be hiding. And when I did, all I noticed were my wrists. I kept them strong and I kept quiet. I wasted too much time thinking there was a part of me I couldn't telegraph, that I shouldn't share. I would rework that.'

'Just rock up to primary school wearing pink?'

'Hell yeah, you know I'd make it work.'

He laughs. We both do. I catch myself and shush him.

'But . . .' Locky lets it linger. 'But I probably wouldn't be here right now if I'd reworked that. I focused so hard on seeming strong that I became strong. I focused on sports. I met Vi at track. I asked her out because that's what guys do, they ask out the hot girl. We went to the movies. I was nervous. The backs of our hands touched. I was petrified. And I snapped before the film even started. A guy got shirtless in a trailer and I turned to her like, "Nope. I'm gay." And my nerves evaporated. We had the best time. We're so close now. I wouldn't have gone to the debutante ball with her if we weren't. And I wouldn't have chased after you. And I wouldn't have . . . We have *powers*, Connor.'

I turn around so we're facing each other. Locky moves one hand to cover the opposite forearm, striking a pose for me.

'Jivanta has a son, however that works,' he whispers. 'We're going to find him tomorrow. He'll sort all of this out and we can focus on what's next.'

I ask him what he means.

'The gods built the world and now we have the power to change it,' he says. 'Think of all the injustices we can set right and the inequalities we can repair. People will listen to us. We're gods.'

I can't shake what Jivanta warned me about in the van. Say Locky and I do reveal we're gods. How long will we have before people try to kill us to become gods themselves?

'Maybe we shouldn't tell anyone what we are,' I say.

Locky blinks at me. 'After that speech before, you don't want me to come out? That was your takeaway?'

I playfully slap him on the shoulder. 'Shut up.'

He's laughing again, quietly though. He settles down. 'If we come out and it goes badly for us, I'd rather that than not coming out at all.'

'But it's not just about us.'

His face creases and I realise he doesn't know about the rebel gods and the wall between realms. I pass on everything I know. As I describe Jivanta breaking off three fingers and burying them in the earth, I remember the missing fourth she never explained. She must've buried it like the others and created another god – her son.

'So,' Locky says when he's up to speed, 'Jivanta believed that if people discovered you were a god, it'd risk the hidden Monuments?'

'Yup. Which is why she wanted me to join the Movement, and why now, I think she'd want you to as well.'

Locky ruminates on it. 'Interesting.' He ruminates on it some more. 'I mean, I'm not doing that.'

'You're so certain.'

'I'm certain I don't want to hide any part of me,' he says. 'Not again.'

'So, what do we do?' I ask.

'We honour Jivanta's dying wish and find her son. He can rein in Aiden and find the other Monuments. They can do whatever. You and I have to figure out our own ways to be gods.'

I like the sound of that. My world can keep spinning while I decide what kind of god I want to be. There'll be school and assignments, sure, but there'll also be nights Mum and I eat a whole tray of brownies.

And there'll be Locky.

I grab him by the front of his crimson jumper. I pull him closer and we kiss. My heart skips a beat.

We pull apart. He rests his forehead against mine. 'Took you long enough,' he whispers.

# EIGHTEEN

It's pushing six o'clock when I wake. I stretch across the full width of my bed and feel something press against the small of my back. I reach behind and realise I fell asleep with the leather-bound journal still tucked into my pants. And then I remember I didn't fall asleep alone. I sit up. The guy I kissed is gone. The window's open. I leap to it and Darroch's sword is still there. I double-check my room, in case he's here and I just missed him.

He isn't and I didn't. I reach for my phone and there's a message from Locky. *Woke early. Chilling outside. Didn't want you getting in trouble.*

I swoon. Every time I think he's reached peak perfect, he finds a way to shift the summit a little higher.

I carefully move the bedside table back and open the door. If I'm going to get away with a second sickie in a row, yesterday's half-arsed attempt won't fly. Mum's going to demand evidence. Orange juice mixed with milk does the trick. I chug it down and well . . . I doubt you really need specifics. I'm cleaning the specifics out of the sink when Mum comes in for her coffee at quarter-past. She orders me back to bed.

I head to the bathroom to freshen up first. Convincing Mum I'm sick and Locky I'm cute are on different ends of the spectrum. I need a shower and a lot of mint-flavoured mouthwash to swing me from one to the other.

I wait in bed for Mum to leave. She'll duck in on her way out, so I need to be here for that. I text Locky to let him know I won't be out until a little after seven. He's cool with waiting. That's when Violet's picking us up anyway.

*Why?* I ask.

*Jivanta said she kept her son close. Eden Ladies' College.*

It makes sense. In fact, I can't think of anything else Jivanta might have meant. There's a second god hidden somewhere on the campus. But we can't exactly just stroll onto the grounds.

My phone vibrates.

*Vi's bringing disguises*, Locky says.

I needle him for details and he remains coy. Apparently all I need to know is, we'll find Jivanta's son and we'll look fabulous doing it.

He adds, *Aiden could walk right past and not recognise us.*

My stomach drops at the mere mention of the Monument. Last night, he seemed pretty unstable and I'm gripped by this intense, immediate dread. Maybe his tantrum escalated while we slept. I do a quick search for recent news articles about a malevolent fire god terrorising the city and come up with nothing.

I exhale, relieved. Not completely relieved, but the sort of relieved you are when you get the best outcome in the worst situation. I have time to set this right.

I awakened a god I shouldn't have and now I need to stop him before he hurts anyone. I have no idea how to do that. I hope Jivanta's son does.

I'm not going to say it's up to me to save humanity, but I'm not going to say it's *not* either.

Locky sends a selfie. *How could anyone want to end this face?*

I'm smirking at my phone when Mum ducks in wearing the yellow jacket that almost hits her ears. A cashier at a boutique clothes shop told her shoulder pads were making a comeback. Mum didn't believe her, but she wears this jacket every so often to hedge her bets.

'Phone down,' she says, snatching the device from my hands and placing it on my bedside table. She checks my forehead with the back of her hand and tells me to keep hydrated.

The moment the front door closes, the sheets are off. I tuck the leather-bound journal into the back of my shorts and slip on my shoes. I snatch the towel that's drying over my door and hop out the window. I wrap the towel around the sharp bits of the sword and set off.

I find Locky in the park across the road. He's staring at a rose and that makes me stare at him staring at a rose. He asks if it looks right.

'It?' I ask. 'Oh! The rose.'

He made it. *He made it.* At his feet, there's proof of his process: numerous attempted roses that were close but not quite right, ripped from the earth in frustration. This one, the last rose standing, looks real. I graze its petals. It *is* real.

'I was inspired by your feats of strength last night. Wanted to test out the ol' . . .' Locky wiggles his fingers. 'Pretty cool, huh?'

I try not to seem too interested. 'I mean, it isn't split-the-earth-across-several-backyards cool, but it's okay.'

He scrunches his face at me and I assure him that it's very cool, just as a black, apartment-sized car pulls up close by. After two short horn bursts the tinted passenger window lowers.

'Hurry up,' Violet says. 'Traffic's atrocious and I don't want to miss first period.'

We hop into the car. It's a high-end model, the sort that comes with all the space-age features included as standard. If somebody told me there was a spa and sauna, I'd think it was a bit much, but I wouldn't immediately disbelieve them. It's an adjustment after Sally's van, let me tell you. And Violet indicates before leaving the kerb too. Radical.

She's virtually unrecognisable out of the debutante ball get-up – less ready to be married off and more like her best friend woke her at the crack of dawn and insisted she drive across Sydney to fetch him. Her hair is roughly braided down one side and a massive pimple dominates a chunk of forehead above her right eyebrow.

'Let me just . . .' Locky reaches out and Violet swats his hand away while she drives.

'Try it again and you'll be in the back with your boyfriend.' She glances at me in the mirror. 'I didn't get too good a look at you on Monday night, but I think the junior uniform might be a better fit for you. Are you cool with wearing a skirt?'

'He has the calves for it,' Locky says.

'What now?' I ask.

Violet draws my attention to the two stacks of folded clothes beside me. ELC uniforms. I know Locky mentioned disguises, but I hadn't given any thought to what they might be. And now I know. We'll be sneaking onto campus dressed as students.

'You can wear the tracksuit. It's a bigger size,' she tells Locky.

'Did you bring *the thing that we discussed*?' he asks.

She pops open the glove compartment. Locky gasps and removes a platinum blonde wig. When we're stopped at the next set of traffic lights, she helps him secure it on his head. He checks himself out in the mirror.

'I am stunning.' He pouts.

Violet groans. 'Connor should worry. You'll never be into anyone as much as you're into yourself.'

He checks himself from another angle. 'Fair.'

She glances at the rear-view mirror again. 'I don't have a wig for you,' she says, 'but if you look under my seat, there's a hat.'

There is a wide-brimmed hat.

'How's Fake Taylor?' Violet asks.

I have no idea. The last I saw of her, she was fleeing, thinking she'd killed a god. 'Yeah, she's good,' I say.

'And you?' Violet asks. Before I can answer, she adds, 'I see you've brought along a sword.'

Okay, wrapping a towel around the blade doesn't make it less obvious. I know for next time.

'We're on a scavenger hunt,' Locky explains.

'Yeah, you said that in the text, but I doubt there's one happening on campus without me knowing.'

'It's a secret scavenger hunt,' he adds.

I see her roll her eyes in the rear-view mirror. 'Anyway, I thought about what you asked, and there's only one statue on campus. It's the one of the school's founder in the study dungeon.'

Locky curls his lip. 'They make you study in a dungeon?'

'It was the cellar a hundred years ago, then they converted it into a library, but when they built the Vickers Memorial Library, they turned it into a study area for seniors,' Violet says. 'It's underground so we call it that.'

Locky turns so he can tilt his head at me. An underground statue, that's ticking some boxes. 'Is the statue a dude?' he asks Violet.

'Yes, Daniel McLean is a dude.'

The name sounds familiar, but I don't know why. I must have seen it on a plaque in the manor on the night of the debutante ball.

'And you reckon we can walk in?' Locky asks.

'I'll need to swipe my card,' she says.

It seems easy enough.

Violet doesn't like the idea of us taking off our seatbelts while she's driving, so she only lets us change in bursts whenever she stops at a red light or the traffic's at a standstill. It means I have to undress and re-dress in segments so that if the car starts moving, I'm not left flashing too much skin.

My disguise is the more complicated one – a white blouse, a tartan skirt and a green blazer. Locky's ELC-branded tracksuit takes seconds to put on.

I open the internet browser on my phone and search for recent news articles about a rampaging child whose insides are on fire. Still no results.

We drive through the school's side entrance and share the road with the students walking from the nearest train station. I shield my face; Locky plays with his wig hair.

The student carpark on the eastern side of the campus is a capital-M Mess. The lines that divide the spaces are treated as mere suggestions rather than strict boundaries. When I hop out of the apartment with wheels, Violet immediately vetoes the sword.

'Absolutely not,' she adds.

I want to tell her I have it so I can defend myself, but she doesn't know that a god tried to kill us last night. Who needs a weapon on a scavenger hunt? I hide the sword under the car. It'll still be there when we're done because no one else is strong enough to wield it.

We follow Violet down a pathway girded by manicured hedges. We keep our heads down so that we don't catch anyone's attention, but to be honest Locky's hair is about seven shades too bold. We weave between clusters of students. I watch them from the corner of my eye, expecting them to notice that we don't belong.

'Love you, Vi,' Locky whispers.

'You'd better,' she replies.

Bar the moment Violet shoves Locky into the hedges to avoid a severe-looking teacher walking towards us, we arrive at the study dungeon entrance without incident. It's a glass door at the base of a large stone building. Through it, I see the top of a wooden staircase and not much else. Violet holds her school ID card to the sensor and the door slides open.

'If anyone catches you,' she warns, 'I don't know you.'

She scurries down the path and we head inside. We rush down the stairs. There are strip lights under each of the steps to give the illusion that they're floating. We reach the bottom, and to be honest, Violet undersold it when she called it a study dungeon. It's not as oppressive as I imagined. Tall stone pillars stretch up to grand vaulted ceilings, and light pours down from the surface-level windows. There are rows and rows of long tables, each peppered with students either diligently powering through last night's homework or reading.

Locky and I make a beeline for the elevated statue watching over us: Daniel McLean, ELC's founder, rendered in stone, elevated and draped in fairy lights. He's dressed like a wealthy guy in a Jane Austen adaptation, with one arm pressing a bundle of books to his chest. Our faces are in line with his feet. We stare up at him.

'Do you reckon that's Jivanta's son?' Locky asks. 'Hiding in plain sight as the founder is pretty clever. No matter how many times they reno this place, they're never going to chuck him in the bin.'

My eyes are drawn to the plaque. I'm impressed by how much praise for Daniel McLean they've managed to squeeze into so few sentences.

I lean closer to his left shoe. 'Hi, excuse me,' I whisper. 'I bet students don't usually talk to you, but your mum sent us. We've got an Aiden situation and we could definitely do with some help.'

Daniel McLean is unmoved.

I persist. 'Jivanta sent us to find you.'

Locky peers back at the rows of desks and asks, 'Have we considered what happens when everyone in this room sees a statue come to life?'

'That's it!' I say too loudly. A couple of students look up. I continue more softly, 'You have Jivanta's power. You bring things to life.' I mime laying a hand on the statue.

He raises one eyebrow. 'Just one problem at a time, then?'

'Pretty much.'

Locky grips Daniel McLean's boot. We wait. 'Didn't the others require some puzzle-solving?' he asks.

'But he's not a Monument, is he?'

'How would I know?'

He has a point. I produce the leather-bound journal from the back of my skirt. He has questions but I shush him. I open to the back – Larissa's only circled and annotated the names of five Monuments. Unless there's a mention she didn't translate, then the Guardians didn't know about Jivanta's son. They didn't build him a sanctuary. Jivanta kept him close, presumably to wake him herself.

'Are you sure you're doing it right?' I ask.

'Jivanta didn't leave a manual, did she?' Locky asks. He releases the boot, then tries again. 'Maybe my power isn't advanced enough?'

'Put some force into it.' I mime what I mean and . . . put too much force into it. I slap the pillar Daniel McLean is perched on and it fissures. The top half, statue included, topples over and shatters on impact.

Locky and I blink down at the rubble spread across the chequered floor, then up at each other. We contemplate the ramifications of accidentally killing the god we came here to find before we, in unison, remember we have an audience. The girls in the study dungeon are staring at us, their tasks truly interrupted. One of them asks if we're boys.

Locky looks like he's cooking up some elaborate excuse, but then he abandons it and shouts, 'Run!'

He doesn't need to tell me twice. We bolt down the aisle and up the well-lit stairs. I slam my palm against the little green button to release the door. Oops – too hard. I've punched through the wall. The door opens though.

That sets Locky off. We're sprinting towards the carpark, our feet slapping the pavement, hearts thumping, and he's *laughing*.

'It's not funny.' But I'm laughing too.

We turn a corner and almost collide with an adult. We blink at him, in our unconvincing disguises, and he blinks at us.

He has a trimmed brown beard with a ginger tinge and wears a buttoned flannel shirt that treads the fine line between lumberjack and hipster barista.

Wait . . . I've made that joke to myself before. It takes me a moment to place him – he was the guy with the clipboard at the debutante ball.

'Daniel McLean?' Locky asks.

Come to think of it, he does bear an eerie resemblance to the school's founder.

'Can I help you, gentlemen?' he asks, straight-faced.

Locky and I hesitate. Neither of us knows how to play this.

'How about we head to my office, and I give you all the time you need to come up with an answer?' he continues.

We hesitate some more.

'I'm quite happy to call security and the police instead.'

That cures our hesitation in an instant.

The path to his office reminds me of Charlton Grammar's service corridors, like he's purposefully taking a route everyone else has forgotten exists. Not everyone. A teacher turns into our corridor up ahead, but before she gets close enough to realise Locky and I are in drag, we're led up a narrow staircase on our left.

The office doesn't have a name on the door. The lumberjack hipster barista struggles to get around his desk. Yes, the room was likely once just a broom closet, but the towers of stacked books and random trinkets aren't helping matters. He can't be more than five years out of uni, but his collection looks like it's been cultivated by generations of hoarders.

He eases onto his swivel chair and promptly swivels a bit. According to his coffee-stained mug, he's a history teacher and the sort of person who buys a customised mug to tell people that.

He motions for us to sit in the two chairs facing his desk. We do. He then slides a pad of paper closer and reaches for a pen. He asks us to tell him everything.

Locky and I exchange glances. We still don't have a strategy. We're silent.

'All right, different tack,' he says. 'What's the date?' Before we can answer, he checks his watch and makes a note of it in the margin. 'Your names?'

We stay quiet. He tilts his head forwards to gently remind us we've been caught trespassing. 'We take that very seriously here at Eden Ladies' College,' he says gravely.

I know, I've seen the fancy sign.

I introduce myself, first name only. He doesn't ask for a second, jotting it down and looking to Locky, who seems less willing to volunteer the information. But he does, eventually.

'How is it that you find yourselves here this morning?' he asks.

Locky shifts in his seat and peels off his wig. 'Well, we took a wrong turn and—'

The lumberjack hipster barista says, 'You'll have to excuse the interruption.'

It's ... strange. Locky furrows his brow. He tosses me a look. 'Okay.'

The door opens and a man steps in. He has a trimmed brown beard with a ginger tinge and wears a buttoned—

I look between the guy who burst into the room and the carbon copy sitting at the desk.

'They're here, impersonating students,' the lumberjack hipster barista behind the desk tells his doppelganger. 'Pop back fifteen minutes and you'll catch them between D and E blocks.'

The intruder nods, retreats and closes the door in his wake.

The lumberjack hipster barista consults his brief notes and prompts Locky. 'You took a wrong turn *and*?'

I'm still stuck on the interruption. I haven't excused it.

Locky's eyes are wide. 'Was that—? Did we just see time travel?'

'Evidence of it, yes. I told myself to go fetch you,' he says, like it's nothing.

And the shoe drops. Jivanta never said the gods she created resembled the others. We came here looking for another statue, when all she told us was that she kept her son close.

'You're Jivanta's son,' I say.

He nods. 'I am Alektos. I prefer Alek.'

Locky says, 'Jivanta sent us to find you before she . . .'

Alek nods. He already knows she's gone. 'What is it that she needs from me?' he asks.

I tell him she didn't say.

'But Aiden's loose and . . . angry,' Locky says.

'Right. First, I'll need to know everything,' Alek says, hovering the pen over the pad.

'Everything?'

'Yes, spare no detail. Let's start with how you first became involved with the Monuments and work from there. Are you Guardians?' he asks.

I shake my head. 'No, but do we really have the—?'

'Time? Don't worry, Connor, that's never in short supply around me.'

Oh, right.

I tell him everything, and I mean *everything*. Anytime I try to skate past by only divulging some things, he interrupts me with probing questions. Locky hasn't heard a lot of this stuff. He sits with his head resting against one hand, absorbing it. Alek keeps writing long after the recount ends.

I survey the artefacts piled in the space while I wait for him to finish. The extensiveness of the collection makes more sense now. He's been here a while.

'Hasn't anyone noticed you don't age or die?' I ask.

'At the moment, I'm Lucas Bentley Jones, fledgling history teacher.' Without looking from the page, he briefly taps the mug.

'Hyphenated?' Locky asks.

Alek pauses and glances at him, the picture of confusion. 'No, why?'

'It's an ELC thing,' I explain.

He resumes his notetaking. 'I've only been Lucas a couple of years. Before that, I was a caterer, and before that, a groundskeeper. I dabbled in teaching mathematics once – that was a low point. But yes, I've been here since the school's inception and I've always found it's easy to get lost on a campus this size.'

'And the Hounds haven't come after you in all that time?' I ask.

'I'm not powerful enough for them to sense me.'

It's pretty remarkable that he's been around so long – since the school's inception – without his secret being discovered. 'You were Daniel McLean, yeah?'

He sighs. 'In one of many past lives,' he says. 'I really

wish the school never commissioned that statue. It makes concealing myself so much more difficult.'

Locky's smirking. 'Trust us, that bad boy won't be causing you any more grief.'

Alek scrunches his face and I decide it's not worth explaining. He takes a couple more minutes to finish his notes and then sets down his pen. 'All right, we will drive to,' he consults his page, 'McKenzie Street.'

'You don't think Aiden's still going to be there, do you?' I ask, right before it dawns on me. 'You're going back to last night, aren't you?'

Alek doesn't give me an answer and it occurs to me that he might go back even further. He could confront Sally before she ever burst into my life, undoing all of this. No Monuments, no heirs, no trapping me in the body of a sixteen-year-old . . .

No Locky.

Alek removes a ball of clothes from his desk drawer; there's a lot of flannel. 'I tend to spill lunch all over myself, so this is my emergency stash. Find something that works better than those uniforms.' He tears the sheets from the pad and folds them in half. He tucks them under one arm and manoeuvres out of the office.

The door clicks shut and Locky turns to me. 'This is pretty neat, huh?'

It hasn't occurred to him that Alek has the power to make sure we never met. I don't have the guts to tell him. I watch as he says a heartfelt goodbye to his wig. I'm smiling. I have to make sure, whatever Alek does, I don't lose Locky.

He strips down to his underwear. Ah, to have the confidence of a track athlete. And the body of one. I don't begin undressing until I've separated my outfit from the ball on the desk. I make sure only half of my body is exposed at any one time, and even then, I change with my back to him. I shrink into myself.

While I dress, Locky entertains himself by raiding Alek's drawers. I'm tucking the leather-bound journal into the back of my pants when he says, 'Oh, this is trippy.' He raises a stack of lined pages. The ink has faded and the paper has yellowed. There's a crease through the middle where the sheets have been folded.

They're the notes Alek left the office holding. 'He gave them to himself, his past self,' Locky says. 'He's known we've been coming for a while.'

When we step out into the corridor, Alek's waiting for us against the opposite wall. His arms are crossed and he no longer has the notes.

Also, we look like triplets in matching flannel shirts. Any other day, I would have been embarrassed. Alek leads us out of the building the way we came and waits with Locky while I fetch the sword from under Violet's car. We then head across campus. The day's classes have already begun, so it's a little less awkward carrying a barely concealed weapon.

We arrive at the staff carpark, where people are only slightly better at parking their vehicles. Alek's car doesn't have much in common with Violet's. The body rattles when the engine starts, but as he says, it more than gets the job done.

We drive out of the school gates. Alek founded this place to protect Jivanta's sanctuary. He watched over her for hundreds of years.

'Were you her Guardian?' I ask.

He takes a moment to answer. 'Yes.' He says it like he's disappointed in himself. 'But I can make this right.'

# NINETEEN

I picture what awaits us at McKenzie Street. Last night, Sally would have returned to a partially demolished house and Jivanta's remains spread from the kitchen to the dining table. I wonder if she retraced our steps and saw the signs of struggle in the damage that stretched from her yard to her neighbours'. Does she think we're dead? Is she overcome with grief and guilt? I imagine how she'll react when we appear on her doorstep.

I play out a scenario in my head. Sally opens the door and she's surprised, relieved. She embraces us and apologises. She never intended for any of this to happen. Her finger slipped.

When we park across from Sally's house, we lower our windows and encounter something different. The house is one of several cordoned off by the police. People have congregated by the tape, seemingly to exchange third-hand gossip and wild theories. Two police officers emerge from Sally's basement apartment and stride over the lawn.

Of course, the police were called. Last night occurred in the real world.

'What now?' Locky asks.

Alek's looking the other way. He has his eyes on a tree in front of 74 McKenzie Street. 'Come.' He opens his door and tells me to leave Darroch's sword. 'You won't need it.'

We wander over to 74 McKenzie Street as a flannel-clad trio. Alek unlatches the gate and waltzes on through it. Locky leaps over the fence like it's a track hurdle. I have a go and end up clipping the fence with my leg. The whole thing topples down. Nobody across the street notices, but Locky does.

'Close,' he says reassuringly.

Alek is waiting for us under the tree. 'You are both comfortable with the idea of travelling back in time?' he asks.

'Very,' Locky says.

I'm not as enthusiastic. We're here to *make this right*. That means stopping Sally from ever visiting Charlton Grammar. That means us never rotating the chamber and awakening Darroch. That means never meeting Locky at the debutante ball.

Alek asks how many hours ago Jivanta died.

Locky counts the hours with his fingers and gives him a rough approximation. Alek nods, pinches at nothing with both hands and pulls like he's opening a packet of crisps. Only he's tearing open the fabric of time to reveal the same streetscape at night. He stretches the tear until it's big enough for him to climb through, and then he does.

Locky and I both marvel at the window to the past. It hangs in the air like a thin sheet. Whichever way we look through it, we see the world, only darker. It's last night.

'Why aren't we going back a couple of days?' I ask. 'I get he probably wants to save Jivanta, but we can save Darroch too.'

Locky raises an eyebrow at me.

'What?' I ask.

'You did see him talk to himself, right?'

I'm not sure why he's bringing it up. 'Yeah?'

'There's only one timeline. Alek entered his office one day and saw us sitting with himself. He then went back in time, fetched us and dragged us up to his office. He became the Alek he saw us sitting with. Everything he does in the past has already been done. Whatever we do when we step through, we've already done.'

'Okay.'

'Do you get it?'

'Sort of.'

'You've never read spec-fic, have you?'

I shake my head. 'Why are we here then, if not to fix everything?'

Locky shrugs and slips through the portal first. I follow him. On the other side, the air is colder and the sky is a deep purple canvas awash with stars.

Alek's waiting on the footpath, but I'm uneasy about leaving the portal in someone's garden. 'Aren't we . . . going to close that?'

'It's hidden enough. We'll need it to get back,' the god says. 'I can only create openings to the past.'

'Why?' I ask.

'Because the future doesn't exist yet.'

Locky leaps over the fence again but I use the gate this time, bitterly aware of my athletic limitations. Alek's car is gone, replaced by an orange hatchback covered with learner stickers. It's parked in front of a car whose front has been totalled.

'That lesson's going well,' Locky jokes.

We're at Sally's brick fence when a childlike figure emerges from the side entrance. He's coming towards us, flaming cracks splitting his crusted exterior. I crouch and pull Locky down with me. Alek drops too.

I peek over the barrier. Aiden is standing in the middle of the garden, staring up at the moon. He launches into some kind of Shakespearean soliloquy about missing the night.

'My mother?' Alek whispers.

She's in the backyard. To get to her, we'll have to pass Aiden. We can risk crawling and hope he doesn't look away from the moon, or . . . The fences on either side of the house are tall. We can head down the neighbour's property and then climb into the backyard unseen.

'Follow me,' I whisper into Locky's ear.

I crawl over to 69 McKenzie Street and hop into the front garden. Locky and Alek do the same. We're careful to tread lightly as we hurry down the side of the house. When we arrive in the backyard, Locky gives me a boost and I can see over the top of the fence.

Jivanta's standing beside a knot of branches. She has her back to me. She's alive. Like Aiden, she's looking up at the starry night, but she's quiet. Her chest expands as she takes a breath; she exhales and watches the heat of her body escape in plumes.

'Go on,' Locky urges. He gives me another boost and I flop over the fence.

Jivanta turns as Locky and Alek land with a lot more grace. She gasps. 'Alektos.' She opens her arms and accepts him in a tight embrace.

Locky helps me up, but when I go to walk closer, he pulls my arm and shakes his head. 'Let them . . .'

The hug ends, and we watch Alek tell his mother that she will die tonight. She barely reacts, accepting her fate with a nod. It occurs to me that if this all happened before I was invited out into the backyard, she knew she was going to die, and when she told us to seek out her son, she knew we would find him.

'How does it happen?' She's looking at us now. 'Is it the Hound? I sense him near.'

'You do?' I ask.

'It was Sally. She threatens you with Aiden's crossbow and fires it when you refuse to resurrect her parents,' Alek says, very matter-of-factly.

Jivanta doesn't seem shocked. 'That is no surprise, I have just denied her first request.' Her brow creases. 'And my heir?'

Locky raises his hand.

'Ah. Lovely.' She seems way too cheerful considering the subject matter. 'How are you finding it?'

'I'm okay,' he says. 'I made a rose.'

Alek interjects. He relays everything I told him about Aiden not wanting to join the Movement and his overreaction to her choice of heir. When he's done, he admits he's at a loss. That's why we're here. He's after guidance. He wants to know what to do next. 'I'm sorry, Mother.'

Jivanta smiles and reaches out to touch his cheek with her palm. 'My Guardian. My son.' I hear all the world's joy in her voice. 'When the understudies were corrupted, they killed the young woman who would have been my first

Guardian,' she adds for our benefit. 'Alek stepped up and I am so, so proud of him.'

'But I . . .'

'You will find Finn in the past,' she says. 'He has always had a calming influence. Aiden will listen to him and understand why he must be interred once more. You will then find Nuo and complete the Movement – five gods hidden in the earth. You will be their sole Guardian.'

My stomach drops. Locky and I had fooled ourselves into believing that finding Alek would free us of our obligations, but it's only cemented them. We won't get the chance to figure out our own ways to be gods. We will seek out Finn and Nuo, placate Aiden and relocate with Alek as our sole Guardian.

Jivanta glances back at the house. 'You should leave before you're seen.'

She embraces her son one last time and motions us towards a ladder of entwined vines that has sprouted up the fence. I'm the last to climb it so Locky can help me down from the other side. I hear the ladder recede into the earth.

I can see Jivanta between the fence pales. I remember her deteriorating, crumbling. And then I remember the deep cracks that split the air when she died. I ask her what they were.

Jivanta approaches. 'Someone in the other realm is trying to break through,' she says. 'The wall between realms is holding, for now. It is vital that the Monuments endure.'

We retrace our steps. On the other side of the fence, the basement door opens and within seconds, we hear Sally nervously encourage Aiden to stargaze where fewer people might see him, like in the backyard. When he's gone, she mutters, 'It's like herding cats.' She jumps into the van; she's going to pick up our Chinese food. We wait for her to drive off before climbing out of the neighbours' yard.

We cross the street in silence, then slip through the portal behind the tree and into daylight. Alek repairs the opening by encouraging the torn edges back together.

'Do you have to do that every time?' Locky asks.

'Yes, or they remain open until I die.'

'Oh.'

We walk over the wrecked fence of 74 McKenzie Street. No one's noticed it, still. We hop in Alek's car and wait for him to start the engine. He doesn't. He's staring at Sally's house.

'I knew this was coming, but that doesn't make it any easier to accept now that it's here,' he says, voice filled with sorrow. 'While you two dressed, I opened a small window in time and slid the notes from our meeting under my door, delivering them to myself on the day I claimed that office half a century ago. I'm a creature of habit. When Jivanta created me, she envisaged a god less restricted by time, who could act as her messenger. I would send dispatches from the future, without hesitation and without delay . . . I neglected to tell her that she would die when I received those notes. I could have woken her to warn her, but I didn't. I was ashamed – those notes were proof that I would fail her. She had entrusted me to be her Guardian. It was my duty to keep her safe and I didn't.'

He starts the car. 'I failed her, and I will not fail her again.'

# TWENTY

Look, it's easy to romanticise the idea of time travel, but if we boil it down to its essence, what is it? One minute you're standing between two commercial dumpsters behind a discount chemist, relishing the heady aromas of bin juice and decaying meat products, and the next you're still in an alleyway, the smells are still weird, only now it's 1938.

Oh, who am I kidding? It's unreal. Absolutely pinch-me-I'm-dreaming unreal. Five stars.

Alek mends the hole behind us and disappears from sight. Given he's unable to tear an opening into the future, and leaving a portal to the 1930s unattended is too big a risk, he's opted to remain in the present. He'll create another portal when we've had enough time to collect Finn – hours on our end, mere seconds on his.

Locky told him we'd need eight hours.

'We could've done it in two,' I say.

'Yeah, but you heard Jivanta,' Locky says. 'She's instructed Alek to complete the Movement – five gods hidden in the earth, you and me included. We need time to hash out our strategy.'

'Our strategy?' I ask.

'We can accept this is our fate, do some sightseeing, find Finn, escort him to the present, spend eternity in hiding. I'm not too wild on that option.'

'What's the alternative?'

'We can flee right now. We have an eighty-two-year head start. We can go anywhere we like, they won't find us,' he says.

I wince. It's definitely doable, but it feels wrong. We were the ones who awakened Aiden in the first place, we should at least rectify that. I tell him so.

'You want to escort Finn to the present and then flee?' he asks.

'Before they take Finn to see Aiden, yeah.'

Locky scrunches his face. 'That's a small window.'

'It's a car ride. We'll make it work,' I say, trying to speak confidence into existence. 'I think it's the right balance between assuaging our consciences and saving our skins.'

He accepts it with a nod. 'All right. Let's find ourselves a god in vintage Sydney.'

Finn was brought to the surface in 1937 – I remember because all the digits add up to twenty. He was returned to the sanctuary after the Guardian was shot, and I doubt Larissa's great-grandfather was particularly eager to disturb him again. So, we've returned to 1938 to disturb him ourselves.

Locky waltzes towards the high street. I watch him, a little bit mesmerised that he's with me. He's funny and charming, and that shirt clings to his muscular frame like—

'Wait, have flannel shirts been invented yet?' I ask.

He shrugs and grips the hem. 'If this freaks people out, wait till they see my phone.'

I glare at him and he grins.

'Don't even joke about that,' I warn.

We step out of the lane. It feels strange, like we're wandering through an early sketch after having spent our entire lives in the completed illustration. The streets are less cluttered, the buildings less interested in touching the sky. There are two blocks between the discreet portal location and Greater Western High School. As we walk, something shifts within me; I stop looking for what's missing and instead appreciate what's different. All the men seem dressed for an important dinner, even though it's the middle of the afternoon and the sun is sitting high in the sky. The specials are written in white paint across the windows of the corner store, and I don't recognise the currency or half the brand names that smother its exterior. The cars look like they've been driven straight off the set of a retro mobster movie. I tell Locky. He agrees.

The street slopes down to GWHS, which has been stripped back to its humble core, a lone building. Its bricks are exposed, not painted white. There's a lot of dirt and greenery, the campus hasn't yet fallen victim to an ambitious concreter.

Alek assured us he'd send us to a Saturday, so we should have the whole school to ourselves. We climb over the modest wooden fence. Where Aiden said the entrance to Finn's sanctuary was, there's a circular wading pool.

'Is this it?' Locky asks.

It looks like a regular wading pool. 'I don't know.'

'If it's not, we should have a swim before we leave.'

'Sure.' There is no way I'm getting in that pool.

While he kneels down to test the water temperature, I survey the area. I kick at the ground. Aiden expected to find stairs. There must be some sort of . . . I kick, the dirt shifts, and I see wood. A trapdoor. That seems about right.

I call Locky over and sweep the dirt aside. He peers over my shoulder. 'They could've buried it a little more,' he says.

'There's a padlock, no one's getting in.'

Locky raises an eyebrow. 'Aren't they?'

He has a point.

I thread my fingers through the latch and pull the door off its hinges. I toss it to the side, and there are the stairs Aiden was looking for. We descend them into the darkness. The musty smell hits my nostrils immediately. I retch.

I shine my phone's flashlight when we reach the bottom. We're in a narrow tunnel. Locky's teeth chatter. 'It's freezing down here,' he whispers.

I guess that means we're in the right place.

We walk for a couple of minutes before we reach the chamber at the end. The light from my phone immediately hits two sparkling sapphire eyes.

'Hello,' the childlike statue says.

I scream a short, very manly scream.

Locky's fighting the urge to laugh. 'Finn?' he asks.

The Monument nods. Even though he and Aiden have the identical shape, the way he controls his features gives him a certain softness his twin lacks – it also helps that his insides aren't on fire. He has a light blue crust, covered in years of accumulated scratches. When he moves, the crust cracks to reveal his glowing icy interior.

There isn't a crossbow in sight.

He asks our names and then extends a hand for us both to shake. He's so cold, the brief contact numbs my palm.

'You're the god of ice?' Locky asks.

'I've been called that in the past, but if I'm being pedantic, my brother and I are the gods of regulating temperature – while I remove heat, he generates it.'

Locky laughs. 'He's the god of heat and you're the god of cool.'

'And you two are?' Finn's eyes settle on me. 'You're not my new Guardian are you? Collin's boy?'

'No. Jivanta sent us from the future,' I explain. 'Aiden is a little volatile at the moment.'

Finn nods. 'He has always been fiery.'

I grit my teeth. 'He tried to kill us.'

'Jivanta thinks you can calm him down,' Locky adds.

'Aiden tends to get anxious when we separate,' Finn admits. 'That was my biggest fear when Collin awakened me – the fool of a man – but to his credit, he put me back and sealed the exit.'

I glance around the room. It's as if they used up all the sanctuary budget on Aiden's. There's no elaborately carved mural. The walls are bare. In fact, the only defining feature is a rectangular opening in the floor.

Finn catches me looking. 'There was a time when this entire chamber was filled with water,' he explains. 'Collin swam to me to prove his worth.'

'The entire way?' I ask.

The Monument nods. 'He then dislodged the stone that sealed the chamber. The water drained, falling on my resting place in the cavern below.'

Locky's peering back down the tunnel, clearly estimating the distance. 'I could've done that.'

'Alas, the sanctuary's puzzle can only be solved once,' Finn says.

'We can pretend you did it,' I say.

Locky sighs, disappointed. 'It's not the same.'

The Monument eyes us expectantly. 'Shall we be off?' he asks.

There's the matter of the seven-and-a-bit hours we have to fill. Group consensus is that it's too risky to explore Blacktown with Finn in tow, so we decide to hang at GWHS. Finn is content with roaming the grounds by himself, and Locky is intent on going swimming.

'Isn't it funny,' he says, unbuttoning his shirt, 'that we came here because Aiden has separation anxiety, but when you think about it, us taking Finn is what gives him separation anxiety.'

'You're serious about swimming?' I ask, fixing the trapdoor back in place and covering it with dirt.

Locky throws off his shirt. 'Very serious.' He strips down to his underwear and dive-bombs into the pool. The splash is loud. He resurfaces, flicks his hair off his face and grins.

Adorable, but we need a voice of reason.

'We should try to be quiet,' I say.

'Whoops,' he mouths, wiping his face with his wet hand, which . . . I don't think has the desired effect. When he speaks again, he whispers. 'I've been thinking, we need a couple name.'

'Like when they merge celebrities' names together because they're dating?' I ask.

'Yeah.'

I slam our names together in my head. 'Nope. Not a good idea.'

He looks wounded. 'What's wrong with Lonnor?' He curls his lip. 'Actually, never mind.'

'Figured it out?'

He quickly changes the subject. He asks if I've noticed that he's in the pool but I'm not.

I sigh. 'Five minutes.' I start unbuttoning my shirt and Locky makes no attempt to disguise the fact he's watching me. He's treading water, smile crooked, pecs twitching with every circular stroke.

Yeah. Nope. I'm buttoning my shirt back up.

'What gives?' he asks.

He looks like the guys on the packaging for underwear value packs and I look like a skinny soft serve that's a little melted. It doesn't feel like *he* should be looking at *me*.

I tell him I'm not getting in. I lie and say I'm not a confident swimmer, and he says it doesn't matter because we don't need to breathe. I still resist.

He swims up to the edge of the wading pool and folds his arms over the sandstone. 'I may be totally misreading this, so feel free to interrupt me, but I get it. We all have hang-ups.

Like this.' He lifts one arm out of the water and points to his forearm with his nose. I don't see anything. 'The dark circle. No? Well.' He lets his hand drop. 'When I was a kid, I scratched and scratched at a mosquito bite until it became infected. Gross, I know. I kept scratching. It left a scar. It's nothing. I'm literally all brown, but this one browner spot irks me. I'm *aware* of it. Even if I'm wearing a long sleeve, my instinct is to cover it with my other hand.'

'That's bizarre.'

'I know. I keep doing it anyway. It's a hang-up.'

'Yeah, but no one else can actually see what makes you self-conscious.'

He raises his eyebrows. 'You want me to repeat that back to you, or ... ?'

'I meant *you* specifically. It wasn't a general remark ... Look, shut up.'

He smirks. 'I like you, Connor. I liked you before a god tried to kill us, but I have a hunch that brought us closer.'

I laugh. It's hard not to.

'Nothing under your shirt will make me like you less,' he continues.

Forget a little melted, I'm a puddle on the floor.

'I like you too, Lachlan Joy,' I say.

He cringes. 'Don't full-name me.' He kicks off the side of the pool. 'By all means, jump in fully clothed. You can wear my gear while yours dries.'

'No, I can ...' I peel off my shirt. He wolf-whistles. I tell him he's pushing his luck, but we're both laughing. When I'm down to my briefs, I gently ease into the water. I swim up to him and motion for his forearm. He holds it out to me and I inspect his soaked skin. I still see nothing. I swat it away.

'It's there,' he says, 'I swear.'

And for a moment I forget we've been thrust almost a century into the past. That isn't what's special about this – it's Locky. It's the way he looks at me, the way he makes me feel. He wraps an arm around my waist and pulls me against his body. We kiss.

It's unreal. Absolutely pinch-me-I'm-dreaming unreal. Five stars.

We lie at the bottom of the pool until it loses its novelty. We resurface, dry ourselves and dress. We chill under a tree close by. I shut my eyes, just for a second . . .

I wake up with my head on Locky's chest. I sit up. He's snoring lightly. He is every bit as adorable when he sleeps. I look up at the sky. The sun has set, and it's like the entire galaxy is out to greet me. I've never seen a smattering of stars like it.

'Connor!' My name is hissed as though this isn't the speaker's first attempt at catching my attention.

I didn't wake up, I was *woken*. Finn is hiding in the fork of a nearby tree.

'What's up?' I ask.

The Monument points over towards the bushland past the western edge of the grounds. I can make out the glow of a lantern and the vague shape of the man holding it. He emerges from the trees and steps over the school's fence.

He's coming towards us.

I shake Locky awake. The sight of our surprise guest cures his post-nap grogginess almost immediately. I scramble, looking for Darroch's sword, before I remember I don't have it. I didn't bring it with me. It's in Alek's car.

The man stops on the other side of the pool and raises his lantern. I'd say he's slightly older than Locky; his beard has grown in patches. He, like the men on the high street, seems dressed for a fancy dinner: white shirt, pants and suspenders. He checks over his shoulder, and I get the impression that maybe he isn't supposed to be here either.

The exchange that follows is stilted and awkward. The man insists we know what he wants from us. We don't, so we deny everything.

He sniffs the air like he smells something I don't. 'I know there's one here,' he says, extracting a knife from his pocket. He takes another step. The weapon's blade gleams in the lantern light. Another step.

He's here for Finn. He could be one of the other Guardians, here to protect him. He could be the one Hound that that Collin didn't kill, here to hurt him. We can't let either happen – Finn must return to the present with us. We can't reason with Aiden without him.

I speak. 'Actually—'

A fist-shaped root punches through the soil beneath the man. Branches extend like fingers to clasp his calf. He struggles against the restraint. He kicks his leg; the hand maintains its grip.

Locky grunts behind me. I glance back. He's lying on his front, one forearm deep in the earth. His face is all creases of effort as he tries to pull the man to the ground the same way Jivanta would. He struggles. He sinks deeper, the soil swallowing him to the shoulder.

Locky's root releases the man's calf, extends and strikes the back of his knee. The man's leg goes limp and he falls backwards. His knife-wielding arm swings. There's a delay between the slice and the scream. He drops the lantern and clutches his face, writhing and sobbing. He's slashed himself.

Locky pulls his arm from the earth and rises, his mouth agape. He steps closer to the man. 'Are you okay?'

The man holds out his hand and shuffles backwards, his shrieks shattering the night. Blood is smeared across the right side of his face. His palm is stained red.

Locky tries to get closer to help. 'Let me just . . .'

'No!' the man barks, struggling to stand. He leaves the lantern where it lies and flees back to the bushland, stumbling over himself to get away.

My mind is a mess as I try to make sense of what's just happened. The man was sniffing aggressively – he could sense Finn. But who was he?

Something clicks in my brain and I remember the night of the debutante ball . . .

'We have to see if he's okay,' Locky says through shallow breaths.

I grab his arm and hold him back. 'The man's fine.'

'What do you mean?' Locky asks. 'He's clearly not.'

'The delivery guy who attacked Darroch said his grandfather sought out a Monument,' I tell him. 'He had his cheek slashed, but he survived. This was that.'

'We can't leave him,' Locky insists, fighting against my grip. I let go. 'We can get him help.' He raises the fallen lantern from the ground.

'You said it yourself, there's only one timeline. Everything we do in the past has already been done,' I say. 'He's going to tell his grandson that you're a monster. He wouldn't say that if you helped him now.'

Locky's staring at the bushland. 'But that doesn't mean I *am* a monster.' He sets off after the man. Finn and I follow him.

We search for some time. Eventually it sinks in that we're fighting against a future that's set in stone. No matter how much he wants to, Locky won't be able to make amends.

# TWENTY-ONE

Alek and Finn are in the front of the car, exchanging anecdotes about ancient civilisations. It's a reunion between two very, very old friends. Locky and I are in the back – our thighs are touching but we're miles apart. He's silent and withdrawn, like he's left a part of himself in 1938. He can still hear the man's screams. I'm sure of it. They're ringing in my ears too.

This is our small window, the car ride between finding Finn and confronting Aiden, but he's shaken. If we're going to flee the Movement, I'm going to have to be the one that makes it happen.

I try the door at the next red light. It's locked. I was kind of hoping it would be that easy.

There's a natural lull in Alek and Finn's conversation. I speak up. 'This looks like a nice spot to let us out.'

'What do you mean?' Alek asks.

It might be sunny, but inside the car, the air is icy. I have to remind myself not to be unnerved. That's just what Finn does.

'Locky and I aren't part of the Movement,' I tell him. 'We've fetched Finn for you, but we're ready to call it a wrap.'

Alek glances at me in the rear-view mirror, and I can tell I'm not going to like what he has to say. 'We're going to McKenzie Street, the four of us. Finn will calm Aiden. I will then visit the Guardians of the 1788 Movement, learn Nuo's whereabouts and seek her out. I imagine we'll then begin the process of resettling you.'

'But we pass for human,' I say. 'We don't need to be resettled.'

Alek says, 'There's never been a Movement where *all* the gods didn't *move*.'

'If an exception is made for you two, then Aiden might expect one for himself,' Finn adds.

'But I—'

Alek is firm. 'I'm your Guardian. My word is final.'

Locky opens his mouth to speak, but there's no point arguing. I place my hand on his thigh and squeeze. He remains quiet. Alek doesn't want to fail Jivanta, so he's not taking any chances. If we're going to get away, we're going to need to be smart.

'All right,' I say.

After a suitably uncomfortable silence, Finn launches into another anecdote. He asks Alek if he remembers the time when . . . and Alek doesn't remember the time, until partway through the retelling, when he slaps the steering wheel, nods and wow, reunions are the worst.

In a whisper, Locky asks what the strategy is. I tell him to trust me, but the truth is, I have no idea.

We slow as we near Sally's house. It's now pushing midday and the crowd has mostly dispersed. Across the road, the occupants of number 74 survey the damage to their fence. It's safe to say we can't use their tree again. At the next intersection, we turn left, and then left again into the driveway of a block of units. We park at the rear.

Alek's the first one out of the car. Locky and I leave with far less enthusiasm. Finn's quick to remind me that I've left the sword behind. I go back for it.

The sight of the blade makes Locky uncomfortable.

Alek surveys the small yard. 'This should provide ample cover for the portal,' he says, turning back to us. 'We will confront Aiden last night, immediately after he chased the two of you. He will see Finn, that will put him at ease. And the sight of three other gods will remind him to *remain* at ease.'

I raise both eyebrows. 'You want us to intimidate Aiden?'

'That sounds . . .' Alek trails off. 'Think of it like you're reminding him you have a sword.'

Aiden isn't going to feel threatened by me or Locky. This is a bad idea. *Good*. If I can convince him of that, then Locky and I can stay behind. We'll get away while Alek and Finn do whatever in the past.

'I had a sword before and he was still pretty keen on ending us,' I say. 'We're not intimidating because we're gods. He wants our powers.'

'I can't imagine that's right,' Alek says, tearing open time between the clothes line and the apartment block.

'I don't need to imagine anything, Alek. He *told* us.' My voice is shaking. Alek's not picturing the worst-case scenario – Aiden making good on his threat to end us. One shot to my chest and it's all over. I'm dead and Aiden has Darroch's power. But Alek thinks I'll be fine because I have a sword.

'Locky doesn't have a sword!' I blurt out.

Alek looks to me, a circle of night behind him. 'Yes?'

It might be too much to convince him to let us both stay behind, but he's loyal to Jivanta. He'll want to protect her power. I can exploit that. I can give Locky a chance to escape.

'Jivanta made Locky her heir,' I say. 'She specifically didn't want Aiden to inherit her power. If Aiden attacks Locky, swordless Locky . . .' My heart is pounding. I'm determined to save at least one of us. 'If that happens, then we don't honour Jivanta's choice of heir.'

Alek bites his lip. My argument's working. 'What do you propose?' he asks.

'Let Locky man the portal, make sure nobody else wanders through,' I say. 'We'll go ourselves.'

Alek asks Locky if he's comfortable watching over the portal alone, and either Locky doesn't understand what I'm doing or he's the most dependable kissing partner I've ever had, because he says he wants to come with us.

'No, Connor's right,' Alek says. 'You should stay.'

Locky insists and then . . . abruptly stops. He's realised I've orchestrated his escape. 'I'd feel safer if you guarded the portal too,' he says to me.

I don't want to push my luck. The others might catch on.

My mouth says, 'We'll be back before you know it.'

My eyes add, 'So, you better *run*.'

If I don't escape, I won't see Locky again. Either Aiden will make good on his threat to end me, or he won't, we'll return, Locky will be gone and I'll be whisked away with the gods.

I don't want to stretch out our goodbye. I'm first through the portal and into the night. Alek and Finn soon follow.

I resist looking back until the very last possible moment. Our eyes meet. Locky covers his forearm with the opposite hand, catches himself, and then lowers the hand back by his side. His face twists a little. I feel my eyes begin to water, but I keep it together. I force a smile and then set off around the block of units, behind Alek and Finn.

I never pegged myself for the type to make grand sacrificial gestures, and yet here I am, grandly sacrificing.

I need my own way out of this now, because I'm pretty sure Darroch's sword is not going to be much help if Aiden lashes out.

We turn onto McKenzie Street just as Sally's van drives by. She doesn't spot us. It gives me a sense of when we are – she's on her way to collect our Chinese takeaway. We're too early to confront Aiden. We'll need somewhere to wait.

I remember that Sally's upstairs neighbours are on holiday. I'm fully prepared to rip the door to 71 McKenzie Street off its hinges, but the lock's missing. One nudge and the door opens wide. My stomach churns. Jivanta told us she could sense the Hound. He's here.

I whisper, 'Hello?'

No one responds.

I take one step and the floorboards let out a mighty creak. I'm more careful with my second. I tell the others to wait in the hallway, just by the door. Probably shouldn't risk the delivery guy meeting another Monument.

The house is dark. I shine my phone's flashlight. I check the first bedroom, the second, and find someone squeezed between two bookshelves in the study. Blue earrings, necklace to match. She squints at the light.

'Larissa?'

She's the understudy descendant that Jivanta sensed.

'Connor!' she gasps. 'You followed the scent too!'

'Um.'

'Your Monument's here,' she says. 'Jivanta is in the backyard with Aiden. I can't believe I've seen two . . . *gods*.' The way she says it, you'd think she'd never said the word aloud before.

She can't be here when Aiden cracks it. I don't even want to be here when Aiden cracks it. She needs to leave so that I can, but she has so many questions.

'Larissa, look at me. I'm holding a sword. You can't stay for what's about to happen. I need you to go. I promise, if I miraculously survive the night, I will find a way to answer all of your questions.'

'Oh my god,' she says.

There's a crispness to the air that I recognise.

'My god,' Larissa whispers. 'The god I'm guarding. He's here.'

I turn around. Alek and Finn are standing in the doorway. I handle the introductions.

'Hi,' she says when I'm done.

Finn plays it cool, pun mostly unintended. He extends a hand for her to shake and Larissa's practically giddy. She's having a fangirl moment, which I totally get. Throw me in front of a popstar at a meet-and-greet and I'm a gushing mess.

Finn thanks her for her family's service and then politely recommends that she leaves.

'All right,' she says, nodding down at him.

'Get as far away from here as you can,' he says.

'As far away,' she repeats.

Finn smiles. 'Perfect.'

I wrap my free arm around Larissa's shoulders and steer her towards the study window. She sits on the sill and glances back, like she's soaking in every detail. When it gets a bit tedious, I give her a gentle shove and close the window behind her.

Finn's smile fades. 'That was a Guardian? No wonder we're in strife.'

That's a bit unfair. If he'd seen Larissa the day we met, annotating the journal entry, he'd think differently. Then again, she did freely surrender a lot of Monument-related information to me and I'm not a Guardian. Also, her family's job was to guard Finn and nobody realised he was missing.

We exit the study. The hallway is decorated with framed photographs I can't make out. We follow it to the end and settle in the living room, which looks out onto the garden. Finn sprawls across the couch, the cushions sagging under his weight. I can see ice crystals forming on the fabric. Alek stands a fair distance from the window, watching the Monuments in the backyard. I stand with him.

Eventually he says, 'I'm surprised I'm not here.'

It takes me a moment to realise he means a different him, a slightly older him who's returned to this exact spot with a warning.

'I'm so used to running into myself and learning what comes next,' he continues. 'But I have no idea how tonight will unfold.'

Is he saying what I think he is? That he believes he might not survive this?

I can't ask him directly, so instead, I ask if not knowing scares him.

He sighs. 'I'm worried. I've never been worried before. Everyone else lives with this uncertainty, but the future has never eluded me. This is the closest I've ever come to experiencing time as others do. It's fascinating.' He exhales. 'Terrifying too. I admit, I'm relieved I can't pass on my power. I don't need to worry about selecting an heir.'

Yeah. He thinks he might die. And if he dies, that doesn't bode well for me.

I need to get out of here.

Jivanta disappears down the side of the house. I glance at Alek and then take what I think are subtle steps backwards. Without turning from the backyard, Alek tells me to stay close.

Busted.

'Okay.' I step forwards, look outside and realise why he didn't want me leaving his side. From here, there's a clear view of Jivanta leading me to the burning nest of branches. I gasp.

'It's a bit like that the first time,' Alek says.

Watching myself from this vantage point, it's clear just how out of place I am among the Monuments. Jivanta is majestic, her insides sparkle green and blue, and Aiden is a creature ripped from Hell, a tiny crusted fireball. They're these ancient creatures who wear the world as flesh . . . and I'm not. I look like a boy who wandered into the wrong backyard. I refuse to believe that the gods don't see that too.

'Are you actually okay with sending me off on the Movement?' I ask.

Alek doesn't turn from the meeting unfolding below us. 'It doesn't matter how I feel,' he answers. 'What Jivanta says, goes.'

'But you know it's wrong.'

He doesn't respond. His expression's blank.

I appeal to his fledgling teacher alter-ego. 'Imagine one of Lucas Bentley Jones's Year Ten students being whisked away to live in isolation forever,' I say. 'That's what you're doing.'

'It would be the right thing to do if that Year Ten student was a god.'

'That Year Ten student didn't choose to be a god.'

Alek's jaw tightens. 'It doesn't matter.'

'You don't really think that, do you?'

He takes a short while to respond. It's getting to him. 'It doesn't matter what I think,' he says. 'This Movement is happening.'

I needle him. 'Will you come visit me?' I ask. 'I'll probably get lonely, what with abandoning my loved ones and all.'

'Stop it.'

'You'll have to make sure my sanctuary is super deep so that no one on the surface can hear my muffled sobs.'

Alek turns to me. 'I don't have a choice, all right?' he hisses. 'I'm not going to fail her again.'

I pull back. His eyes are wide and wet with tears. He doesn't want to do this any more than I do.

I hear myself ask Sally what she's doing.

Alek's attention returns to the scene unfolding in the backyard. We gave him the crib notes; he knows what's coming. His mother is about to die.

'You probably shouldn't watch this part,' I remind him.

He ignores me.

Sally pleads for the Monument to resurrect her parents. I hear the anguish in her voice. She sounds like she's been pushed to the brink.

Jivanta's voice wafts across the unkempt garden. 'You are your parents,' she says. 'You grew from them. You are every lesson they taught, every story they told and every secret they shared. Wherever you go, you carry them with you. But know that ultimately the path is yours. Do not let your attachment to them lead you somewhere you do not want to go.'

It's almost too perfect, like Jivanta isn't just talking to Sally. I can't prove it's any more than a coincidence though.

I feel Alek watching me. He has a choice now. And I have a chance.

I meet his gaze and he speaks. 'You and Locky don't have to join the Movement.'

Finn peels himself off the couch and approaches the window. Alek keeps his eyes on me. The commotion outside escalates. Jivanta has been shot.

'Thank you,' I stammer.

'The Monuments will endure,' he says, 'just not in the exact way my mother dictated.'

It's like a weight has been lifted off my shoulders.

'I do have a favour to ask,' he says. 'Will you stay for this?'

I nod.

'If something happens to me, protect Finn.'

I hear Jivanta's muffled voice from beneath the floorboards urging Locky to kill her. And then she goes quiet. Deep, shimmering cracks decorate the space around us for a moment.

'The wall between realms is stressed,' Alek says, 'but it will hold so long as one Monument remains alive.'

Aiden wrestles free of Jivanta's fiery wooden man and stomps him into the ground until the flames extinguish. He seizes his weapon and strides into the basement. The house quakes. The light fittings rattle.

My heart is racing.

The fence explodes, and the ruckus bleeds onto the neighbouring property.

'It's almost time,' I say, unlocking the back door.

We step out onto the porch. I watch myself wield Darroch's strength. I feel the earth shake and see the outcome: a crack in the ground that runs the full length of the yard and extends past broken fences into others.

'I will end you both!' Aiden's struggling to climb out of the crevice. He manages to, eventually. He stands tall and picks at something caught in his chest crust. Finn calls his name and he looks up. His expression softens as he wanders over. 'You're here, brother,' he says.

Finn nods. 'I am,' he replies.

Aiden acknowledges Alek with a nod and then his gaze lands on me. My stomach drops. I expect his expression to sour, but it doesn't. Maybe Finn really does have a power over him. It's like his body is mending. His fissures are still there, but they're thinner.

'I've heard you've gotten a little carried away,' Finn says.

Aiden bites back a smirk. 'What? Me?' He rests the crossbow by his side. 'I will admit, I have been passionate in your absence. Without your words in my ear, I have felt so intensely, and I've come to learn exactly what it is I want.'

'You have?' his brother asks.

'I have.' Aiden raises the crossbow and fires.

Finn cries out. He angles his body towards us and we see the bolt lodged in his chest. 'What the heck, Aiden?' he shrieks, poking at his wound. 'You shot me.'

'And with the last bolt too.' Aiden tosses the weapon aside.

Alek pinches the air and tears a portal in front of the three of us. Aiden vanishes behind it. I'm staring into Sally's garden on a stormy afternoon. Rain beats down. Thunder claps. Alek tries to pick up Finn – no, he's too heavy. He looks at me.

I cradle the childlike Monument in my arms, but Alek stops me stepping through the portal.

'It's a shield,' he whispers.

I carry Finn through the house, the dwindling icy glow beneath his crust lighting our way in bursts. Alek drags Darroch's sword along the hardwood floor behind him.

I can feel Finn coming apart in my hands. 'Put me down,' he urges.

I lay him on the floor. He's crumbling from the inside. I can see through the gaping hole in his torso. He doesn't have long. Alek abandons the sword and sinks to his knees. I give them some space.

'I'm dying,' Finn tells him.

'No, you're not,' Alek insists. He tries to lift him. 'Hold on.'

Finn breaks apart. He hits the floor and the room darkens.

Alek clutches at Finn's remains, as if attempting to reassemble him. 'No ... No ... You can't. The Monuments must endure.'

Alek's skin has an orange tint. I twist to see Aiden standing at the end of the hallway, his insides glowing red-hot. Between us, the space is fractured like glass that has shattered but remains intact.

'You killed your brother!' My voice is shaking.

Aiden shrugs. 'Finn has this way of talking me into things and I am so over being talked into things. I want to live again and be worshipped like I used to. He would talk that want right out of my mind.'

I glance at Alek. He's absorbed by Finn's remains.

'But what about ... ?' I gesture at the cracks that have split the hallway into pieces, but I'm careful not to touch any. 'You've weakened the wall between realms.'

Aiden rolls his eyes. 'I'm so tired of having that waved at me like a stick to keep me in line.' He takes one step through a shimmering crack. The floorboards creak and he's unharmed. 'Watch.'

As if on cue, the cracks dissolve.

'How did you do that?' I ask.

'You really don't know much, eh? I didn't *do* anything. The benefit of having a wall that is alive is that it adjusts when weakened,' he says. 'When one body in the space between realms ceases to exist, another picks up the slack. A single Monument can keep the realms apart, but we were convinced to act together. I diminished myself to contain the infamous rebel gods that Jivanta created. And what was my thanks? When it came time to choose someone worthy of her power, she looked elsewhere.'

Darroch's sword is just out of my reach. I shuffle towards it . . . in case.

'Tell me, would you want me to be your heir?'

'I don't intend on dying any time soon.'

He's amused. 'Don't you?'

I grip Darroch's sword and raise it.

He takes a step. The floorboards creak.

'You're an infant,' he says.

Another step, another creak.

He reaches out and swats the blade aside. The heat of his touch travels up – I drop the weapon and retreat.

Aiden steps over the sword. We're barely an arm's length apart. The air is sweltering. 'Give up the pretence of being able to fight me,' he says. 'Surrender Darroch's strength with some dignity.' He lunges at me, grabs my wrist and squeezes. His touch burns. I gasp.

And then . . . his palm cools. His brow creases and I land one clean punch to his face. It cracks like a painted egg at Easter. He recoils. His cheek drops to the floor.

I encourage Alek to his feet and we rush towards the entrance. I open the front door . . . People are on the street, gravitating towards the disturbance. I close the door again and Alek pulls me back to make room for a fresh portal. He climbs through and reopens the front door, which now has a working lock. He rushes to the lawn and I follow him. It's early morning; the sky is marble swirls of purple and pink.

On the other side of the portal, Aiden plucks up the dislodged piece of face from the floor. It ignites in his hand and then extinguishes. He's flustered.

He's inherited Finn's power. He both generates and removes heat – he must be cancelling himself out.

'I will deal the blow that mortally wounds him,' Alek says, breathless.

'So, you know what's going to happen next?' I ask.

'No, that was confidence, not foresight. We will step back through the portal and close it, trapping him here to die.'

'Okay.' Sounds like a long shot but I'm game.

Aiden flicks his wrist. The chunk of face in his hand bursts into flames and remains lit. He turns to us.

'Steel yourself,' Alek says.

Aiden charges down the hallway and through the portal. He's coming for me, the flaming face-chunk raised. Alek pushes me aside and intercepts him. I'm on the ground; they are too, struggling against each other. Aiden gets on top. He prepares to strike with his makeshift weapon. Alek tears time open between them and catches the Monument's arm inside. He closes the portal, slicing the fire god's arm off at the elbow.

Aiden howls, and then that howl evolves into a cackle. 'Is that how it is?'

'It is.'

Aiden delivers one hard punch under Alek's pec. I hear the crack. Alek cries out and fights for breath.

'No!' I shout.

Aiden smirks and rises to his feet. 'If I die, you die. It's only fair.' He turns his little orange eyes to me. 'Jivanta modelled him after humans.'

With every step he takes, I shuffle back an equal distance – which would all be well and good if I wasn't running out of lawn.

'A cracked rib has punctured his liver,' Aiden tells me. 'That gives him five minutes of excruciating pain before it's lights out. Look at him.'

Feeble, Alek pulls himself across the lawn to the front of the house, then up the first step and the second. He disappears inside and I picture him crawling through the portal and closing it like we'd planned – trapping me with Aiden until he dies.

'Pathetic.' The Monument turns back to me. 'Would you care for the same?' he asks. 'Jivanta was always against harming humans, whereas I . . . Well, let's just say I am very well versed in the ways you can die.'

A large piece of his arm breaks off, but he doesn't seem particularly fussed. He's closer to me now. He kicks at my shoe.

'Hurry up and die,' I say.

'Not before I rip you limb from—'

He takes a shovel to the side of the head. The impact reduces him to a mound of reddish-brown dust. I stare wide-eyed at the charred remains, and then up at the woman wielding the shovel.

# TWENTY-TWO

Sally's upstairs neighbour Grace doesn't work on Mondays. She still sets an alarm though. She likes to spend the morning in the backyard, tending to her garden – it's really coming along apparently. This morning, she was digging a hole to plant her convolvulus when she heard the commotion out front. She ventured around the side of the house to find a crusty, fiery child threatening to rip me limb from limb. She was holding a shovel, so she took action.

Now, I'm sitting on a high stool at the breakfast bar in her kitchen with a mug of chamomile tea. I owe her an explanation.

I ask if she believes in the supernatural.

'I'm a science teacher,' she answers bluntly.

'Yeah,' I say, 'but like, how married are you to observable facts on a scale from one to ten, one being monogamous and ten being, "I have crystals that clean my energy"?'

Grace adds another teaspoon of sugar to her tea and stirs. She doesn't know that right now, the powers of two gods are mingling in her system. 'I . . . don't believe crystals can clean energy, no.'

'Are you religious?'

'Not in the slightest.'

All right. This is going to be a tough crowd. I come out with it. 'That fiery demon child who wanted to kill me was a god.'

'A god?'

'Yes. There were five main creator gods, the Monuments,' I explain, pulling the leather-bound journal out of the back of my pants and opening to the last page. 'Nuo bound—'

'Are you an actor?' she asks, head tilted to one side. 'Did Harriet pay you to visit?'

'I don't know a Harriet.'

A man in a suit ducks in. 'Hello, wife,' he says, pecking her cheek. He looks at me. 'Hello, random teenager.'

'I told Harriet I wanted to do one of those dinner parties where you eat with actors and one of them plays dead and you have to figure out who killed them,' Grace says. 'She's sent me an actor. He was on the lawn, cornered by a rock creature, I had to save him.'

'I don't know a Harriet,' I stress.

'How did you make the creature move?' she asks.

I blink. 'It was real.'

The man in the suit's convinced by my performance. 'Very good.' He shakes my hand and introduces himself. He's a Travis. 'Is this all-ages? Should I wake the possessed one?'

Grace shakes her head. 'Let her sleep a bit more. She was sick all night.'

Travis leaves. I'm annoyed I'm not being taken seriously . . . but I'm also curious. 'Possessed one?' I ask.

'Daughter, she ate something that didn't agree with her. Projectile vomited all over the bathroom.'

'Gross.'

'Yes.' She waves me on. 'Continue.'

I sigh. She's not going to believe me without evidence. My job would be a lot easier if the air had fractured when she pulverised Aiden with the shovel, but it hadn't. I think I saw a couple of fleeting silver marks, not enough to convince anyone of anything . . . I tear out the first page of the journal. I dangle the sheet between us and tell her to touch it for me. She pinches the page between her thumb and forefinger.

All she needs to do now is use a power she doesn't know she has.

'Um. I want you to think of heat, the flame of a Bunsen burner, the—'

The edge of the page catches alight before I run out of prompts.

She pulls her fingers away. 'How did you do that?' she asks, marvelling at what she thinks are the special effects of a dramatic performance.

'I didn't do anything. Pinch the page again, in the same spot.'

The same spot is still on fire, so she's – shockingly – against the idea. I promise her she won't be hurt. With some light encouragement she reaches for, hesitates, and then pinches the page like before.

'Does that hurt?' I ask.

Her brow creases. 'I can feel the heat, but you're right, it doesn't hurt.'

'Now, I want you to think of the absence of heat, the inside of your freezer, the—'

Again, it happens before I've exhausted my list of prompts – only this time the flame is smothered as the page freezes over.

Grace releases the paper and gasps. 'I did that?'

'I'm going to tell you some things. Your instinct will be to doubt me, but this will be a whole lot easier for us both if you believe me. Harriet has not sent me. Gods, plural, are real. They each have different abilities that helped them create this world. If you kill a god, you absorb their power. You become their heir. There was a god of fire. He could generate heat. He killed the god of ice, who could remove heat, and absorbed that power. Then you killed him with a shovel, so now you are the god of fire and ice.'

'I can manipulate the kinetic energy of atoms?' she asks.

'I fail science tests regularly, but if that means you can heat and cool stuff, yes.'

'That crusted creature outside was a god?' Her voice shakes a little like she's finally taking me seriously.

I nod.

She continues, 'And this is . . . ?'

'Not a performance, no.'

Grace sinks into a stool and asks me to tell her everything. That's . . . ambitious, so I instead opt to start with the bare bones and elaborate whenever she has a follow-up question. I name each of the Monuments and explain their role in shaping the world. Grace has no questions. I tell her the world was consumed by war thousands of years ago. I keep my explanation simple – the rebel gods are just sisters. Still no questions. I say the Monuments succeeded in containing the sisters but were left weakened. They entrusted themselves to a handful of humans called Guardians. They were pursued by Hounds.

'Dogs?' The first follow-up question.

'Humans who can sense gods. They will sense you as your powers develop.'

'Oh.'

'To keep the Hounds from finding them, the gods were hidden underground and regularly moved for thousands of years. They now reside in sanctuaries under the oldest schools in Sydney, designed to test people.' I stress that only the worthy are capable of discovering the secrets of their deepest chambers, without spoiling the fact that I've actually discovered the secrets of four.

Grace mulls it all over. She tries to make sense of everything I've told her using science and honestly, half of the words she says sound like gibberish. Mr Sim threatened that I'd live to regret not listening in class, and I'm shocked to have lived to see that day.

'What are gods expected to do?' she asks me eventually.

'There are no rules,' I say. 'You can be whatever kind of god you like. This is uncharted territory. There have never been heirs before. I mean, you can even ignore the fact you're a god, but remember you won't age or die of natural causes, so people will definitely have questions at some point.'

'I won't die?'

I think of Darroch. 'Unless you get hit by a car or something.'

'Oh.'

'On the flipside, you can tell everyone you're a god, but I'm not sure how people will take you setting things on fire with a touch.'

Grace cringes. 'I can't imagine they'd respond well.'

'And if you tell people, someone could murder you for your power.'

'Oh. I suppose they could.' She relaxes. 'I don't think I'll do *that*, then. I'll ... pretend I'm not a god, for now. I have enough on my plate,' she says. 'I recently applied for a head of department position and that's full-time. I've got Travis, who's a man and a child, and an actual child, and we've got the mortgage.'

'That's a lot.' Then something occurs to me. 'Did you say you have a mortgage?'

'Only a year left on the place,' Grace says, glancing around.

That's not right. 'No, you rent.'

She forces a laugh. 'No, I don't.'

'But you have an exchange student living downstairs, right?'

'No?'

My brain throbs. 'That's ... Um.'

She owns this house.

She has a daughter.

Oh no.

No. No.

I'm not in the present. Of course not. Sally's upstairs neighbours are on holiday.

I'm sitting in Sally's kitchen with her mum. She's alive. She knows about the Monuments because I told her.

The air hadn't fractured severely when she pulverised Aiden with the shovel because he was the first Monument to die.

'What year is it?' I ask.

Grace looks at me like that's the most preposterous thing I've said in the short time we've known each other, and I've said some pretty preposterous things.

She tells me the date: 31 March 2014.

It's six years ago.

# TWENTY-THREE

I swipe fifty dollars from the kitchen counter when Grace isn't looking. To make it feel less like stealing, I offer her the leather-bound journal on my way out. She says I don't need to give her anything. I insist.

My phone doesn't have a data plan in 2014, so I can't ask it to plan my public transport journey. I walk in the general direction of the closest train station and end up on a bus. There's nowhere to tap my travel card and the driver can't break a fifty, so I ride for free.

Grace is a god. Sally's deceased mother is a god. What will happen to her? How will she die? Will she grow powerful enough that the delivery guy senses her and . . . ? No, when he encountered Darroch, that was certainly his first god encounter.

The knowledge of Grace's impending death weighs on me. Alek is the only one in the world who knows how this burden feels. I need to warn Grace about what happens to her, and he can tell me how.

The loose pebbles of Eden Ladies' College's main drive swim beneath my feet. Everyone must be in class, because the campus is barren-wasteland levels of empty. I only spot one groundskeeper tending to a flowerbed between the gate and the tiny administration cottage next to the manor.

I'm barely through the door when one of two ladies at the desk asks how she can help.

I approach. 'I'm looking for Mr Jones,' I tell her. 'He's not expecting me. I'm his . . . younger brother.'

She smiles warmly and consults her computer. 'Mr Jones. Mr Jones.' There's the clacking of keys. She squints at her screen and then at me. 'Is he a member of staff?'

'He's a history teacher,' I elaborate.

She consults the screen again and smacks her lips. 'I'm sorry, no Mr Jones in our system.'

'He works here, I . . .' Alek must not have adopted that alias yet. 'Maybe he works in the cafeteria.'

'He would be in our system.'

'Oh, he'd be under a different name. I know how he looks if that's any help.' I regret it as soon as I've said it.

The two ladies behind the counter glance at each other like they don't believe I'm the younger brother of a staff member. They communicate without words. One reaches for the phone and begins to dial. 'If you just take a seat,' she says, 'we'll find someone to help you.'

They're calling security.

'I'm good, actually. Bye.'

I rush out of the cottage and back the way I came. I pass the groundskeeper tending to the flowerbed. I catch a glimpse of his face. Alek's face. It's obscured by a mop of sandy hair and a goatee, but it's definitely his face. I pause.

My heart cramps. He's dead in the future. If I start a conversation about Grace, I'm going to have to divulge that detail too. I'll have to watch him react to the news that his life is almost over. I don't want to do that. I can't.

And come to think of it, it's not the sort of thing he can do either. Right now, he knows about Jivanta and can't bring himself to tell her. He doesn't know how to deliver this news. It's undeliverable.

Alek catches me lingering. He furrows his brow and unplugs his earphones. 'Can I help you, dude?' he asks.

What do I gain if I tell him? Peace of mind? For me, maybe. I ruin the remainder of his life. Me telling him or Grace won't keep them alive. It won't alter their fates.

I feel like Locky must have after 1938 – trapped between an accident in the past and an unchangeable future.

'Is the exit this way?' I ask, pointing towards the gate.

He nods, plugs in his earphones and returns to his labour. He won't remember this tomorrow, let alone in six years.

Six years. I'm trapped in the past for six years.

What can I do? Where can I go?

I start with home. Mum's house. It's 2014, so it isn't called that yet – my parents are still together, it's *their* house. They're both at work and a ten-year-old version of me is at school.

When I try my key, it doesn't fit. It's confusing until I remember the locks changed in the divorce, not because of any drama, but because the lawyers kept saying, 'Common practice.' There's a loose terracotta tile with the spare key underneath. I unlock the door and return the key.

I step over the threshold and the layout's completely different. The Great Furniture Halving of 2015 and the Great Extension of 2016 haven't happened yet, so there's more crammed in to less space. The old kitchen is tucked in the corner where Mum's ergonomic workstation is set up in 2020.

I feel like an archaeologist examining the perfectly preserved artefacts of my childhood. I piece the visual clues together – the unfinished board game on the floor in the living area, the milkshake stain on the rug – and I begin to recall what it was like to be ten.

My bedroom is *definitely* the bedroom of a ten-year-old. An embarrassing number of posters cover the walls and figurines litter the floor.

I sit on my swivel chair and adjust it for a taller Connor. I tap the computer mouse and the screen blinks to life. I open my music library and play a random selection at seventy-five per cent speed.

I give the internet from 2014 a whirl (spoiler: it's mostly the same, some websites aren't as cool as you remember). I work my way through the browsing history and I can't believe how much of the stuff I used to care about I've forgotten in the years since.

I sink deeper into the chair. One track ends, another begins. An MC shouts, 'Remix!' and it reminds me of Locky. I won't see him for six years. I care for him now – a lot – but will I feel the same way when I see him again? I want to.

I rewind the track and reset the playback speed. The MC shouts, 'Remix!' a little faster.

Locky wished he could remix parts of his life, do them over and make them better. Here I am, in the past and I can't change a thing. There's only one timeline and all of my experiences are set in stone.

What am I supposed to do for six whole years?

I turn the music up and make a beeline for the fridge. I'm not hungry but it's a habit. I help myself to some fruit salad and peruse the trove of papers stuck to the front with magnets. Hidden beneath the electricity bill is a welcome letter from Sacred Heart Nursing Home.

Pappou's just moved in. The letter encourages families to visit regularly, and it's a punch in the gut to read it and know the future. The letter is months old. I doubt ten-year-old Connor is even visiting weekly anymore.

Staring at the paper, something dawns on me. Only my experiences are set in stone. I can change anything outside of those experiences. If ten-year-old, eleven-year-old, whatever-year-old Connor don't visit Pappou, then I can now . . .

I pull a duffle bag from the top shelf in my parents' walk-in and fill it with Dad's best clothes, but *best* is depressingly relative. I'm basically stockpiling the shirts without holes. I swipe fifty dollars from his sock drawer.

In the original track, Pappou lives alone, avoided and forgotten. This is the remix, where I take two buses across Sydney and cross the manicured front lawn of Sacred Heart Nursing Home, duffle bag over my shoulder. I burst into

Pappou's suite, saviour grandchild triumphant – but the suite's empty. I set down my bag and search.

I find him in the dining room. A nurse is helping him eat some soup. Pappou doesn't recognise me when I greet him but, to be fair, I was a lot younger the last time he saw me. I tell the nurse I'm family and he asks if I'd like to take over.

I would. I accept the spoon and feed Pappou in silence.

He asks me a question. It's Greek noise. I reply in English and he blinks at me. Zero comprehension.

'Right,' I tell myself.

I sigh and look at my feet, and then past them at the spotted vinyl floor. Darroch told me language lives in the earth. If the earth could speak to him, maybe it can speak to me.

I listen. The floors of the nursing home squeak with every step. I listen deeper, to the soil beneath the foundations. I hear whispers, languages spoken in unison, overlapping. I snap back into myself.

Pappou leans towards the spoon. I remember I'm supposed to be feeding him and raise it to his lips. The cutlery clacks against his dentures.

Determined, I focus harder on the earth, past the foundations, deeper into the soil. I wade through all the words the ground is feeding me, past the French, the Spanish, the whatever *that* language is . . . and then I say it.

'Pes mou pós eísai.' Tell me how you are.

Pappou replies and the earth tells me what he means.

My hand trembles. I set down the spoon and have a brief emotional moment, before I suck it up and have the first conversation I've had with my grandfather without Mum as an intermediary.

At the end, he asks my name.

'Con,' I tell him.

He points three fingers to his chest. His name's Con too.

I become an unofficial resident of Sacred Heart Nursing Home. I use the duffle bag as a pillow and sleep on Pappou's floor. Whenever his hand slides off the bed, I grip it.

I'm almost caught three times in the first week. I don't like my odds of remaining unnoticed, so while I continue to spend my days with Pappou, at night, I go to ground. I start with a modest cavern dug behind a cupboard in the basement – furnishings courtesy of the nursing home lounge room. I get a hang of Darroch's power over time, and that cavern evolves into a complex network of tunnels.

I keep my distance when Mum visits, but sometimes, I tempt fate. I creep up close just to hear her voice again.

The days melt together. I feel Pappou slipping away. His lucid moments are fewer and farther between. I sit with him. I sit with him. I wait for him to speak to me. And when he does, I reach past the foundations of the building to find words to say back.

# TWENTY-FOUR

I sit in Pappou's golden lounge chair and watch the digits of his bedside clock tick over to midnight. I recline and exhale like a weight has been lifted. It's Monday, 30 March 2020. Again.

The pages in my lap have torn at the creases. Years of folding and unfolding will do that. I wrote it all down, from my discovery of the trapdoor to Aiden's death. I didn't want to forget a single thing – not meeting Sally in the sanctuary, not pulling Locky by the jumper and kissing him, none of it.

Connor, aged sixteen, is scrawled across those pages.

I drift to sleep. I feel it like a blink. One minute it's dark, and the next, sunlight pours through the window.

I get dressed in Pappou's bathroom. I stole a Charlton Grammar uniform from Dad's clothes line. It's the uniform Mum used to say he tossed in the bin to avoid washing. It's been six years since I last wore it and it fits perfectly.

I'm still Connor, aged sixteen.

I sling the duffle bag over my shoulder. On the way out, I tell Pappou I've swiped his dress shoes, but not loudly enough to actually wake him. The nurse at the front desk is confused to see a school student leaving before visiting hours have even started. I wave.

From Sacred Heart Nursing Home, it's five minutes to a bus that gets me within walking distance of Charlton Grammar. The moment I step through the front gate, the campus sprawls ahead of me. A paved path that's intended for pedestrians, but that's wide enough to accommodate the occasional vehicle, weaves between buildings and ends at Founders Block.

The flags on the rooftop have been raised. Another me is up there, waiting for Olly.

After spending most of the past six years inside or in bespoke tunnels beneath a three-storey compound, this all feels surreal. I want to pause and soak in every sight and sound and smell, but the constant stream of arriving students makes moments of stationary introspection impossible. I keep moving. All the while, it's like I'm rediscovering a favourite song that's been culled from my regular playlist. Everything's familiar, but surprising at the same time.

'Oi, Connor.' I recognise the voice. I turn. I'm walking alongside a guy decked out in rugby gear. I know his name. It's on the tip of my tongue. Starts with A. Adam? No. Alex? No.

'Andrew Ilieff!' I practically shout. 'Is your name,' I add. I like to think it's a graceful recovery.

He blinks. 'Joshie's got a totally true story to share.'

I remember Joshie immediately: Joshua Parks, famed improv scene partner and noted exaggerator.

'He reckons some chick paid his brother forty bucks for his uniform at the train station on Friday afternoon,' Andrew says.

Joshua's indignant. 'It's *true*.'

'You're full of it.'

I bite back a smirk. Joshua's telling the truth, but I let them bicker until they wander off to sit with their friends. The stream of students thins the deeper into the school it courses, until there's only a handful of us heading towards our lockers.

We near the jacaranda to the side of Founders Block. Mr Wilson stands beneath it, waving students over and demanding they tidy themselves. He doesn't single me out, but he's already amassed a small crowd. There's one guy aggressively tucking in his shirt. He has dirty blond hair. He could be Olly, but I don't wait for him to turn.

I continue walking.

It was early on that I realised getting stuck in the past meant I had a chance to hang out with Olly again just like we used to. I waited years for the sweet spot – after I looked the right age and before the friend divorce. I dropped by his dad's place. Olly and I ended up on opposite sides of the Burton Street Tunnel. For him, it'd only been days since we last saw each other. For me, it'd been an eternity. I had waited for that reunion for so long that when it finally came . . . I didn't need it anymore.

When I arrive for first period, it doesn't hurt to pass the books he's stacked on my old seat so I can't sit there.

At the end of the day, I accept the keys from Ms Rowsey. Before I lower the flags on the rooftop, I shut the trapdoor and arrange the loose stones over the top.

I'm home well before midnight. 'Hello?' I ask, stepping inside.

No one responds, but it's still early. Mum hasn't finished work yet.

I plant myself on the couch and watch the door. I've missed Mum. A lot. I hear her scramble with her keys before I see her silhouette through the frosted glass. I straighten up. She tries a key in the lock and it's the wrong one. She swears at it and my eyes sting. I blink hard.

I'm smiling.

As soon as the door opens and she barges in with too many canvas shopping bags in each hand, I feel a rush. And *I* rush. I clear the distance between us and throw my arms around her, eyes wet.

She's startled by the naked display of emotion. She tries to complete the hug on her end, but the shopping bags are making it impossible.

'My wrists, Con.'

I squeeze tighter and then release. I carry the bags into the kitchen and start unpacking them. That's when Mum gets suspicious. She asks, 'Aren't you going to the movies?'

I shake my head. 'Felt like staying in.'

'Well, I'm not in the mood to cook anything fancy, but . . .' She plucks a box of packet-mix brownies out of the closest bag and shakes it at me; I give her the thumbs up.

We sprawl on the couch and eat the entire tray for dinner. I usually evacuate the room to avoid her Monday reality TV binges, but I want to be around her tonight.

Mum mutes an especially boring subplot on tonight's *Rich White Women Throwing Wine* (she has alternate titles for all her favourites). 'I hate Stacey,' she says. 'Never throws wine.'

I help myself to the last corner piece of brownie. Tastes exactly as amazing as I remember.

We watch the silent footage of Stacey not throwing any wine for a bit and then Mum speaks up. 'You need to see your grandfather,' she says.

Mum visited him on Saturday afternoon. I'd gone to fetch an ice-cream sandwich from the vending machine and when I came back, she was sitting on the edge of his bed. I waited by the door and eavesdropped. Her voice cracked with sadness. His condition has been gradually deteriorating for some time now, but with so long between visits, the decline was shocking for Mum.

'I know.'

She swallows hard. 'I keep thinking about him spending his days all alone,' she almost whispers. 'I should've been there more.'

I'm busting to come clean and tell her I'm a god. I've been living with Pappou. He hasn't been alone.

Mum sighs. 'When my yiayia was on her way out, my mum urged me not to see her. She said I'd want to remember my yiayia at her best. It worked. I have no memories of her in hospital. I didn't want your lasting memories of your pappou to be bad ones, so I kept you away.'

All this time, I thought we just forgot about him. We were too busy. That's not the truth – we stopped visiting on purpose. He was a god to Mum and that's how she wanted to remember him, how she wanted me to remember him. But the memories I've made these past six years aren't bad. Sure, Pappou's changed a lot since I was a kid, but he's still my grandfather. And nobody deserves to be ignored because they might be painful to remember. Pappou was there when I entered this world and I should try my hardest to be there when he leaves.

'I think your mum was wrong,' I tell her.

'I do too. But there's a nagging voice in my head that says she'll be pissed if I don't listen to her.'

Yiayia's been gone a while.

'At some point you'll need to do what you want, not what she does,' I say.

Mum squints at me. 'Which shirtless model on social media had that as their caption?' she asks suspiciously.

I act offended. 'I'll have you know, I learnt that from my own lived experiences.'

She nods and purses her lips like a duck. 'Of course.'

'I think I've done a lot of growing up over the past six years.'

She blinks at me. 'In January, you got your arm stuck in a supermarket trolley,' she says flatly.

'Hey! They shouldn't have made it so easy for people to squeeze their elbows through.'

'Sure, it's their fault.' Mum turns back to the TV, gasps and plucks up the remote. She unmutes the show. Beatrice and Collette are feuding and there's glassware close by. I have to admit, the scene is pretty entertaining.

When the episode ends, I realise it's almost eleven o'clock. I need to dash before another version of myself comes through the door. I ask Mum if I can use the final hour of my curfew to go for a jog. She isn't thrilled by the idea of me heading out so late, but I technically already have permission to be out until midnight, and by revoking it, she'd be a bad parent.

Her agreement comes with conditions. She relays them in dribs and drabs. I can't venture out of the suburb; I can't talk to strangers; I can't cross the road with music playing in my ears.

'And also, Con.' I brace for more conditions. 'Are you and Olly all right?'

I tell her the truth. 'We're not friends anymore.'

'And you're okay with that?'

'I am.'

'Well, if he gives you any grief, you let me know.'

I catch myself smiling. 'Thanks, Mum.'

'His dad's hit on me a few times, so I can always become his new mum and make his life misery.'

'And you ruined it.'

She laughs. It shakes the earth.

# TWENTY-FIVE

I find a used mattress earmarked for hard-waste collection and propped up against a garage door. I spend a night under the stars; not to oversell it though – I can't see many.

I unfold the torn pages. I can make out the writing thanks to a nearby streetlight, but it's an effort. My pocket sweat has smudged the ink.

I persevere. I re-read the parts about Locky until I fall asleep.

Now, I don't really strike myself as the sort of person who'll write a self-help book in middle age, but here's some free advice I'll give anyone who'll listen: if you find a used mattress earmarked for collection and propped up against a garage door, move it off the driveway before you lay it flat and go to sleep. If you don't, there's a chance you'll wake to the sound of that garage door opening and the sight of a needlessly large all-terrain vehicle about to accelerate over you.

It's Tuesday, 31 March 2020. Again.

I wander home and forget I'm supposed to wait for Mum and other-Connor to leave before entering. I hear the sound of talkback radio coming from the master bedroom, freeze and then dart out of the house. I wait across the road until they're gone.

I sloth on the couch. Every so often, my mind drifts to what's unfolding elsewhere. Other-Connor meets Larissa. He boards the train with Locky. They venture deeper and deeper into the crypt . . .

Tonight, Sally will shoot Jivanta and flee. She'll realise she is not Jivanta's heir. She won't be able to resurrect her parents. I don't want her to be alone when it dawns on her.

I'm going to follow her.

The plan is to borrow Mum's car and hope the police don't pull me over on the way. I'm not legally allowed to drive a car without an adult present, and I'm not technically competent enough to drive across Sydney unsupervised, but hey, drastic times, meet measures.

Dinner's plated the moment Mum arrives – pasta with a ready-made pumpkin sauce – so she's on the couch and distracted when I need to make my escape. I throw the duffle bag over my shoulder and creep across the living room like a—

'You're walking weird, stop it,' Mum says, barely turning from the TV. Tonight's back-to-back episodes of her favourite period drama. There are lots of gowns and accents. 'Have you done the dishes?'

I pause. I rush to the kitchen, rinse everything and then creep across—

'Did you wash them *properly*?'

She's going to make me late. I return to the kitchen, soak and scrub everything and creep across the living room, past the couch and out of her line of sight. I'm about to snatch her car key from the bowl of loose change and lollies when the doorbell rings. I pull back my hand.

Mum never invites people over when *Posh People in Castles* is on. She can't make sense of the accents when someone else is speaking too. I open the door. It's Janice from Janice's Driving School, which is less of a school and more of an orange car with stickers all over it. For six years, I've thought of Tuesday, 31 March 2020 as the night when everything happens – Sally flees, Jivanta dies, Finn dies, Aiden tries to kill us – completely forgetting it's also the night of my monthly scheduled driving lesson.

'Are you ready to hit the road?' Janice asks.

'Ah, actually . . .'

'I've already paid,' Mum calls from the couch.

Mum hired Janice for her seemingly boundless enthusiasm. She said anyone who taught me to drive would probably need it. That might sound a bit harsh considering Mum had never seen me drive, but she had been there for my first attempts to catch a tennis ball, try out for a rugby team, do a flip on a neighbour's trampoline and well . . . there was a pattern.

Janice has a spring in her step as she walks me to the car. Meanwhile, I'm the very picture of reluctance. I'm dragging my feet.

But a car's a car, I suppose. And I do need to get to McKenzie Street.

'That's a big bag,' Janice says. It's as close as she'll come to asking me why I've packed a duffle bag for a driving lesson.

I toss it in the back. It never hurts to be prepared.

When we're buckled up, Janice encourages me to take it slow. She wants me to check my seat and mirrors, then get comfortable. She suggests a breathing exercise, but I'm in a hurry. I don't want to miss Sally. I immediately start the engine and pull away from the kerb.

'Indicator,' she reminds me. 'But that's okay. Now, we're going to turn right.'

I take the first left. Janice responds to my insubordination with positive reinforcement: I'm taking ownership of my drive, and that's lovely. I've basically reduced the principal of a driving school (it's a car) to someone who meekly reminds me to check over my shoulder before I merge . . . every time I merge.

I park in front of 74 McKenzie Street and roll down my window. Sally's van is still here. I check the time and consult my record of folded pages. She's either about to go fetch dinner, or she's already returned.

Janice is worried we won't get back in time for the end of our lesson.

'Do you have another student tonight?' I ask.

She shakes her head.

'Then we can make this a double and you don't have to come next month.'

'I was hoping to—'

'I just feel really inspired, like I'm making great progress. I mean, I barely scraped the kerb when I parked. You're a wonderful teacher.'

This works a charm. Janice agrees to extend the lesson, and when she suggests I continue driving, I start fiddling with my mirrors – for safety. This is like driving instructor catnip. She's frothing. I adjust the rear-view mirror and catch a better look at the car behind us. It's smashed up. For a second I'm worried I reversed into it while I was parking, but then I notice the bumper bar is held in place by a liberal use of duct tape. It's a pre-existing condition.

'Ready to go?' Janice asks.

I look past her and notice a man in a flannel shirt on the footpath. He's looking back at number 74. Two other figures in matching shirts emerge from behind the tree. One of them is me.

'Get down!' I hiss, folding forwards.

'What?'

'Please!'

Confused, Janice follows my lead. For a moment, all I can hear is her breathing.

Then someone says, 'That lesson's going well.'

Locky.

There was a communal computer at the nursing home. It's amazing how many friends you can make on social media with a platinum blonde wig and photos that obscure your face. Mostly guys from Charlton Grammar. But also Violet Olsen-Smythe.

She tagged herself at the track every Wednesday after school. I sat in the stands one night. I made out her squad performing drills, but I couldn't spot Locky. I was disappointed . . . and then mortified when he climbed the steps, leaning against a single crutch. One ankle was bandaged. My platinum blonde wig was made for stalking from afar, not for seeing up close. I panicked, but I couldn't leap over the side of the tiered structure without attracting more attention. I tried to play it cool. He didn't know who I was. And I figured the odds of him sitting nearby were slim to none.

He sank onto the bench below mine and without turning, he complimented my hair. I disguised my voice when I told him the wig was for Halloween. He glanced back and smiled. My chest tightened.

Just as it tightens now.

I unfold a fraction to peek through the window and watch him cross the street. He's so dreamy, but I have to focus. Tonight's about Sally. I can't get side-tracked.

I know when we are. Time Travelling Group #1 (consisting of Alek, Locky and me) has arrived to speak to Jivanta. Aiden will come out onto the front lawn. Sally will nervously encourage him to head out the back on her way to pick up dinner. Time Travelling Group #1 will leave as Time Travelling Group #2 (consisting of Alek, Finn and a different me) turns onto the street.

'This is overwhelmingly uncomfortable,' Janice says. She's still doubled over.

I sigh. 'Okay, sit up.'

Aiden emerges from the basement apartment. I grit my teeth. Time Travelling Group #1 slips over the neighbours' fence to avoid him. Aiden gazes up at the stars. He seems utterly transfixed, but I don't know; I've seen 1938's starry night and 2020's doesn't really compare.

A door opens. I check the rear-view mirror again. Some guy flops out the back of the busted-up car and his long face is familiar. The delivery guy's returned. This time, he's wearing a shirt that fits and he's got a knife. He's sensed the surfaced Monuments and now he's going to try to vanquish them, starting with a volatile fire god. Great. This will end well for him.

I recognise the energetic symphony he's conducting with the knife. He doesn't have it in him to stab a god.

Before I can leap out to stop him, he loses his nerve. He retreats. He's back in the car. Aiden's still staring up at the sky, none the wiser, his cracks opening and closing like they're breathing.

I'm here for Sally; I can't get side-tracked.

Okay, maybe I need to get a little side-tracked.

'Wait here,' I tell Janice. I pull the key from the ignition, pocket it and slip out of the car, careful to cover my face in case Aiden looks over.

The delivery guy is staring down at his lap when I let myself into the passenger side. I grab the knife off the dashboard and drop it behind us before he can reach for it.

'I come in peace. Promise.'

'You're the guy from last night,' he says.

'I am. Connor.'

'Pete.'

'Hi, Pete. How are you?'

He sniffs. 'Rubbish. This smell is driving me up the wall and it's only getting worse and I'm supposed to kill them to make it stop and *look at him*.' He gestures too wide and hits the window. 'He's a volcano.'

I have no idea how to play this. Do I tell him a kissing partner and I are largely responsible for slashing his grandfather's face? No, that doesn't seem like it'll calm him down. It'll probably do the opposite.

'I just want to know why this is happening to me,' he says.

Oh, I can help with that.

'You're gifted, Pete.'

He raises an eyebrow. 'What?'

'You can sense powerful creatures like that flaming turd-child over there.'

He glances at Aiden as if to confirm, yes, that is a flaming turd-child.

'He's one of five creator gods,' I continue. 'You are one of . . . four – if my maths is right – people alive today who can sense them.'

Pete's eyes widen. 'They're hunting them too?'

'Great question. No.'

'No?'

'Basically, there are two factions, Guardians and Hounds. Guardians protect gods; Hounds hunt them. The other three are Guardians.'

He frowns. 'Why am I a Hound?'

'Because your however-many-greats great-grandparent was one,' I say. 'And they taught their first-born to be one, and they taught their first-born . . . and so on.'

'Can I switch sides?' he asks.

I don't think that's ever happened before, but we are in uncharted territory. I'm a god and I'm lacking in the Guardian department. He can be mine. But that means telling him that I'm a god, and he's a virtual stranger. Then again, the two other people I told were Sally and Locky, and we barely knew each other when I did.

Right. I'm going to tell him. 'Pete, I'm a god.'

'You are?' He looks between me and Aiden, in all his molten-rock splendour. 'But you're so . . .'

I grin through it. It is an effective, if not completely unintentional burn. 'How would you like to be my Guardian?' I ask.

He sniffs. 'But you don't smell.'

'I'm a god,' I insist.

'Will I have to kill anyone?'

'No killing.'

'What will I have to do?'

I haven't thought that far ahead. I mean, it's not as if I'm going to bury myself any time soon. 'Be my friend, I suppose.'

Pete hesitates. 'Okay. But you're definitely a god?' He doesn't believe me, and to be fair, I haven't made the most convincing pitch.

I ask him if he has a pen and paper. He has a pen and the owner's manual for his car. It'll do. I scrawl a message and hand it back.

*IOU 1 × godly feat – Connor*

I open the passenger door. I'm almost out when he asks, 'If we're friends, how will I find you?'

I'm half-tempted to tell him to project my silhouette into the sky with a spotlight. 'I'm Connor Giannopoulos. Two Ns in both names. I'm on social media. Message whenever.'

I hurry back into the driver's seat of Janice's orange hatchback. Aiden is still blissfully unaware that I'm across the street. I apologise to Janice, but she has reclined her seat all the way and is reading a novel with a shirtless farmer on the cover. She flicks the page. 'So long as your mum's paying by the hour.'

My god, I broke Janice.

Pete's car starts. The headlights fill my rear-view mirror until he pulls away from the kerb. He honks his horn when he passes. Aiden turns to face the street and I recline my seat way back like Janice's. I don't think he saw me.

'Would you like a book?' she asks. 'I have a bunch in the back.'

'No.' It sounds a bit abrupt. 'Thanks though.'

'Suit yourself.'

I hear a voice I haven't heard in years. Sally's. She nervously encourages Aiden to head out the back. The chastising ceases. Then the van's engine starts.

'Are those books any good?' I ask Janice.

'Wouldn't have bought a bunch if they weren't.'

I laugh. She turns the page. I straighten up a little. Aiden is gone, Sally's van is just two red lights in the distance and Time Travelling Group #1 is crossing the street.

I lie back and shield my face as they pass the car. My heart thumps.

When I check out the window again, Time Travelling Group #2 is nearby. I watch myself nudging open the door to 71 McKenzie Street.

I lie back. My heartbeat is still racing.

'Actually, I wouldn't mind—'

Janice slaps one of the books into my chest, like she had it ready for me. I'm ten pages in before I recognise the persistent rattle of Sally's van. I spy through the window. Sally parks outside her place and heads inside. The door shuts.

'Not long now,' I mutter, tossing my book on the back seat. Janice's head is buried behind hers. 'Take your time.'

'Can you text Mum and tell her we're having a double lesson?' I ask.

She raises her phone. Without looking away from the book, she types the message to Mum.

I straighten my seat and put the key in the ignition. I start the engine and roll the car forwards to get a clearer look down the side of the house. Janice mumbles something about it being unsafe to drive while a passenger seat is reclined. She turns another page.

I wait for Sally to reappear. I wait. I wait. And then I see her lingering by the basement door holding the crossbow. She's summoning the courage to act.

She summons it.

'Okay, get up,' I tell Janice. 'We're leaving in a sec.'

Her chair snaps upright and she tosses the book on the back seat. 'What are we waiting for?'

Sally runs down the side of the house and jumps in the van. The engine sputters to life. She sets off down the street.

'*That*,' I say.

I count to three and tail the van.

# TWENTY-SIX

There's a small park tucked between two near-identical houses, like a third one was bulldozed to make way for it. With some play equipment, a single wooden bench and a patch of grass barely larger than your average nature strip, it's a park that's doing the absolute least. Sally has ignored the bench in favour of the grass. She sits with her knees hugged into her chest.

When Janice reaches for her naughty farmer book, I know I've been waiting too long. I tell her the lesson's over and hop out. She asks if I'm okay to get home on my own. I am. I watch her disappear around the next bend and then turn to Sally, who has her back to the road. She hasn't budged.

I approach with caution. The last thing she did was try to murder a god, but she appears to have gotten that out of her system. I set down the duffle bag and sit beside her.

'I can't believe I did that.' Her voice is stripped of all its varnish. It's barely a croak.

I remain silent.

'I only meant to threaten her. After lying then coming clean, it was my only move left. It didn't work. I threatened her and it didn't work, and I was standing there with a crossbow. I had to take the shot.' There's a sharp intake of breath. 'Is Jivanta dead?'

'She is.' I don't wait for the inevitable follow-up question. 'She chose Locky as her heir.'

Sally absorbs the news like a physical blow. 'That's it, then. It's over. I'm never seeing them again. They're gone.'

I reach into the duffle bag and hand over the envelopes. They're held together by a single rubber band.

'What are these?' Sally asks, straightening up.

'Have a read.'

She keeps one envelope and drops the rest to the side. She extracts a letter and unfolds. She gasps. 'Her handwriting.' The more she reads, the deeper her brow lines become. She checks the front of the envelope and asks, 'Why was Mum sending you letters at a nursing home?'

I kept in contact with Grace. I knew her address, so I sent her snail-mail letters. I signed them with Pappou's full name, so when she posted her replies to the nursing home, they found their way to his bedside. I couldn't change Grace's future, but I could brighten her daughter's. In our correspondence, we would occasionally veer off the subject of gods – I made sure of it. I asked Grace about her family history, how she met her husband, her aspirations for her daughter. With thirty-seven letters, Grace recorded pieces of herself I could pass on.

'How is this even possible?' Sally asks.

I tell her everything, from seeking out Alek to becoming her mother's penpal. It takes a while.

'You've lived the past six years twice?'

'It wasn't too rough,' I say. 'I spent time with my grandfather, and I had your mum's letters to look forward to.'

Sally removes a folded page from a different envelope. She checks the date in the corner. 'When did they stop?'

'A year ago.'

She nods. 'When Dad got sick.' She sets down the letter and takes a long breath. 'My parents downplayed it. It was nothing, it was nothing, and then he was in the ICU. He died last year and Mum packed our bags. Dad had always wanted to see Europe, so we took his ashes. It was cold over there, but she'd reheat our drinks with a touch. We tried to enjoy the trip for him. Mum wanted it to be a celebration. As it went on, I would wake to the sound of her crying in the next room. She stopped reheating our drinks. Her powers were a reminder that she wouldn't age, she wouldn't get sick ... She watched her husband die and one day, she'd have to watch me die too. And that ... broke her.' Sally's struggling to speak now, tears welling.

Goosebumps prick my skin. 'Sally, you don't have to ...'

She wipes her eyes with the back of one hand. 'Mum felt cursed, but she was determined to make the most of it. There's a celebrity everything, so she figured she'd become a celebrity god. She'd perform miracles on morning TV or something, make enough money for us to have the best life. She scored a meeting with an agent. She took the day off work and let me skip school to come with her. We were on the way when a truck ran off the road and hit seven pedestrians. It missed me. People were screaming, scrambling. I found Mum ... And she knew it was over. She *knew*.'

Sally turns the empty envelope over in her hand. 'When she first told me about being a god, I was eleven. She said two gods chose her as their heir. But by the time of the accident, she'd told me the truth, that she'd killed a god with a shovel to protect a kid. That was how she got her powers. She didn't have any say,' Sally continues. 'I could tell by the look in her eyes she didn't want to pass on her powers to someone who didn't know exactly what they were in for. She asked if I could bear it. I understood what she wanted me to do. I had to do it. I had a steel nail file on me. I pressed it into her arm just hard enough to break the skin, to inflict the last bit of pain before she . . .'

The empty envelope catches alight. Its shape distorts as it burns.

I can't believe what I'm seeing. 'You're a god.'

'I kept it secret because I didn't know how the Monuments would react,' she says, extinguishing the envelope with a shake. 'When you found Aiden, I didn't understand. Mum had inherited his power and given it to me. I didn't know about Alek. If I did, I would've done everything very differently.' She swallows hard. 'Half a year . . . I devoted half a year to bringing my parents back. I cut myself off from the entire world to do it. I have nothing else.'

She lost both parents, and now that she can't resurrect them, it's like she's lost them again. I can't even begin to imagine what that feels like, and I tell her so.

'I'm not going to pretend like what I'm about to say will make it hurt any less,' I add, 'but you have me. You're not alone.'

That makes her smile. It fades too fast though. 'But what do I do now?' she asks.

I push myself up off the grass. 'Come. I want to take you somewhere. Well, that's misleading. I want to direct you to drive somewhere.'

She's wary, but she agrees. When we end up outside the imposing brick fence of Worthington College, an exclusive private school in the heart of the business district, she understands. I've found the sole surviving Monument.

Larissa Pung's great-grandfather shot Nuo's Guardian, so I had to create a shortlist of potential schools and search them one by one. There was a lot of trespassing, mostly at night. I might have accidentally smashed open a mausoleum at Fairmount College for Girls, but in my defence, it did look like a sanctuary for a god. Worthington College was the seventh school I tried.

I lead Sally to a gate that doesn't look like it'll be too expensive to repair. I rip it out of the wall and lay it flat. We keep to the shadows and arrive at a spot by the grassed quadrangle where the trees hang low. Their branches all bend towards the ground, like it has an especially strong gravitational pull.

'You remember those warring sisters from Darroch's carvings?' I ask. 'They're gods. Jivanta made them to influence humans and they rebelled. The Monuments lured them to another realm and then built a wall between that realm and ours. Every time a Monument dies, the wall weakens. Nuo is all that's keeping the realms apart and the rebel gods at bay.

This is what you do now, what *we* do now. We must protect her together.'

Sally takes a moment to process it. 'Nuo's beneath us?' she asks.

I nod. I ask her to keep her distance, and an eye out for any security guards. I kneel between the trees and sink my hands into the earth. I part the soil, sink my hands deeper and part it again.

I expose a trapdoor cut into a white marble block.

'And she's in there?'

I hesitate. 'I haven't checked.'

'You haven't checked? Finn wasn't where he was supposed to be.'

'That was because of me though.' It doesn't convince her, and now I'm starting to entertain the possibility that Nuo isn't down there. What if we guard this spot and she isn't even here? She hasn't had a Guardian in generations. 'Okay, a quick peek to confirm she's down there.'

'All right.'

I pull the trapdoor open to reveal a steep staircase carved into the marble.

'A bit dark.' I look to Sally. 'Do you mind?'

'Not at all.' She pulls a lip-balm sphere from her pocket. She squeezes it until it catches alight. The plastic exterior bubbles and discolours.

It lights our way. I begin the descent and Sally follows. The chamber below is about the size of a tennis court end-to-end, but it's split in the centre. There's a three-metre chasm – deeper than the lip-balm light reaches – that separates us and the Monument.

Nuo is mesmerising. She's made of tessellated pink and black marble pieces. The ceiling has warped above her; it droops down, as if striving to meet her raised hands.

'She's out in the open,' Sally says. She approaches the chasm and peers over. 'How does this sanctuary test worthiness if she's right there?'

I'm not brave enough to walk quite as close to the edge. 'Long jump?'

A third voice speaks. 'Well, I'm not going to tell you, that would be cheating.'

We look up. Nuo is watching from her side of the chasm, her weight on one hip.

Sally looks to me and I immediately apologise. 'Oh, we're not here for that,' I say. 'We're just making sure you're actually here, and you are.'

The Monument tilts her head. 'Is one of you my Guardian?' she asks.

'Not quite.' I don't have Darroch's sword so I can't wave it around to prove I'm his heir. I sink to one knee and tap the marble floor. It cracks.

'Darroch has an heir,' Nuo says. She blinks hard, as if finally noticing the glowing lip balm in Sally's hand. 'You are Aiden's?'

'And Finn's.'

'Three Monuments have fallen?' she asks, aghast.

'Four. You are the sole surviving Monument keeping the rebel gods at bay.'

Nuo is struck by an intense sorrow. 'They're really gone? But how? The Hounds?'

Sally stiffens. The god wants answers, and I can't give them without implicating her . . . a lot. Her search for Jivanta started all this. She endangered the Monuments and mortally wounded one herself.

I lie. I tell Nuo that the Hounds were responsible, and that we neutralised them. The Monument is quiet.

'I can't believe I am the only one left,' she says eventually. 'I need to . . . not be down here.'

'What do you mean?' I ask.

Nuo leaps over the chasm like it's no feat. She tells us she will return soon, and when I protest, she reminds me there is no danger. The Hounds have been neutralised. I mustn't seem placated, because she invites us both to come with her.

We don't have a chance to respond. The Monument clears the distance to the exit in seconds and we are dragged, as if by some invisible rope, out with her. She rushes across the grassed quadrangle and we float behind her. She springs into the air, gravity loosens its grip and we rise, rise. The wind whips at my face. We make a gentle arc and fall, fall. My feet kick at the air. The tiled roof of a three-storey building nears. Nuo lands gracefully. Sally and I, less so. I leave a dent.

'Whoa,' Sally breathes, extinguishing the lip-balm sphere and pocketing it.

I should have filled in the entrance to the sanctuary. If a security guard stumbles upon it . . .

Nuo jumps and the invisible rope pulls us once more. I slide across the tiles until I'm propelled into the night sky.

I feel like a struggling water-skier, choking on the tide, trying desperately to get the attention of the speedboat driver. And Sally's laughing. *Laughing.* I remember she told me Nuo was her favourite, now she's experiencing the Monument's power for real.

The god hops back and forth between two rooftops and then takes flight. I gasp and rocket fifty-odd metres into the air after her, over the school's imposing fence, over the road and onto the roof of a heritage building – once a bank, now a boutique hotel.

The invisible rope loosens. I can move freely again. I sink to my knees and catch my breath.

'The only family I've ever known is lost. I was underground in a marble tomb, unable to save them,' Nuo says. 'I needed to remind myself that I wasn't entirely powerless.'

'But what comes after all the jumping?' Sally asks. 'You're a god and they're still gone.'

I sense it's the beginning of a conversation I should leave them to have in private. I walk along the edge of the rooftop, searching for any sign of an external fire escape. When I accept that the only way I'm getting down is the way I got up here in the first place, I turn to see Sally and Nuo's silhouettes hugging. I give them more time. I pretend my shoes need tying. And retying.

The Monument comes to fetch me when they're done. She says she must return to her sanctuary. I'm reminded of the day I met Aiden.

'And you're okay with that?' I ask. 'Even though the Hounds don't pose a threat?'

'I am the last Monument,' Nuo says. 'The safest place for me is out of sight.'

I ask her to take it easy with the whole defying-gravity thing. She apologises for getting carried away before. I have time to brace myself before she leaps. The invisible rope yanks me and the three of us soar over the road. From above, I spot the light of the security guard's torch. He's nowhere near the sanctuary thankfully. Nuo slips into the narrow gap between two buildings. Sally and I follow. The Monument lands. We do too. Someone shrieks.

I hear the sound of brick on marble. The Monument howls. A girl is leaning against the wall, half-drenched in shadow, chest heaving.

'You threw a brick at me,' Nuo says.

The girl is flustered. A sentient marble statue is talking to her. 'I use it to prop open the gate.' She's a boarder sneaking out at night. 'I'm sorry, you appeared from nowhere and I panicked.' She squints. 'What . . . are you?'

Nuo ignores the question and inspects the damage. 'Not too bad.' She presses the point of impact and the marble cracks and crumbles. 'Okay, a little bad.'

My stomach drops. The final Monument is wounded. 'The wall between realms . . .'

Nuo looks at me. She doesn't need to say anything. She is dying. This realm's final defence will fall.

The Monument jumps without warning. Sally and I are pulled up to the roof of what appears to be the school's library. Nuo lands on her knees. She swats us away when we try to help her to her feet. She pushes herself up to standing.

'The rebel gods will return to this realm, if not immediately, then soon.' Her voice is weak. 'You must fight them, and you must win.'

'How?' I ask.

Nuo shakes her head. 'My mind is fogged,' she says. Her chest fissures and she laughs. 'The girl threw a *brick*. Cracks me up.'

The Monument looks at us, expecting us to appreciate the pun. When we don't, she shrugs like we're a tough crowd.

'The girl.' Sally's eyes widen. 'She's going to inherit your power without a choice.'

'Maybe she shouldn't throw bricks,' Nuo says. 'Actions have consequences.'

But I get what Sally's saying. The girl is going to inherit Nuo's power without a choice. Like Grace. Like me.

I speak up. 'One of us will need to become your heir.'

Nuo's left arm swings loose, barely attached. She tries to fix it in place, but it's decaying too rapidly for her to bother. She lets it fall. 'If you like.'

I can use Darroch's strength, but I'm uneasy. I don't like the idea of killing another god. Sally isn't even a little hesitant. She is determined to make sure no one will be burdened like her mother was. She steps closer and asks, 'Do you mind if I . . . ?'

'Go right ahead.'

She approaches the wounded god and lays a hand on her collapsing chest. Ice crystals spread from her palm and coat the Monument's front. They glisten in the moonlight.

'Ouch. Too cold,' Nuo says.

Sally pulls back her hand and apologises.

The god tuts. 'Kids today, you don't laugh at anything.' Frozen pieces begin to break off. 'Oh! Here we go.'

Sally retreats as Nuo's disintegration accelerates. 'Goodbye,' she says.

'You are not powerless in the face of the rebel gods,' Nuo tells us both, before turning her attention to Sally. 'You are my heir. Never forget, there is nothing holding you down. You can ...' She gasps and tries again. 'You can ... soar.' Her body fails her. She falls to her knees.

The Monument disintegrates. The air fractures above her iced remains, sliced a hundred ways by shimmering cracks that stretch for metres. Rogue fissures extend, as if they're reaching for us. Sally stumbles back, but we can't be hurt by them. At least, I don't think we can.

I stare at the spot where the web of cracks is most concentrated. And for one brief moment, in the pieces of fragmented space, I see beyond this realm. I see a pair of wide, blank, unblinking eyes.

The wall between realms is no more.

# TWENTY-SEVEN

The shimmering cracks mend, but the rebel god has left an imprint on my mind. When I close my eyes, I see her piercing gaze.

Sally is the first to speak. 'Why didn't she come through? She was standing right there.'

I have no idea. 'Maybe she doesn't know she can return to this realm.'

'Do you believe that?'

I wince. 'Not really.'

'Then she's biding her time, which is ... terrifying,' Sally says.

'Should we go after her?'

'How?'

Again, I have no idea. It's not as if the Monuments prepared a pamphlet on crossing between realms. Say they did, complete with diagrams and step-by-step instructions, and we found ourselves in the other realm, facing a rebel god – what then? We must fight the rebel gods and we must win. That's what

Nuo said. We can't contain them like the Monuments did, we're not powerful enough to do that, so we have to do what our predecessors couldn't. We must fight.

Somehow.

I word-vomit my pessimism until Sally hushes me. I wonder why, and then I hear the voices. We near the edge of the rooftop. In the gap between buildings, the girl who threw the brick is re-enacting her encounter with Nuo for the security guard.

'We should go,' I whisper.

The girl reaches the part of her re-enactment that involves trespassers flying away and the guard aims his torch where she's pointing – up at us. The beam is so bright, I'm certain there's some corner of the internet devoted to it starting campfires. We recoil.

'Oi!' the guard calls.

We need to flee, but Sally's reluctant. She's looking at Nuo's remains. 'We can't just leave her,' she says.

I never thought to move or bury the other Monuments after they crumbled. I'm guilty. But also panicked. A door slams shut below us. The guard is coming.

Sally apologises to Nuo and seizes my forearm. We run to the other side of the building and stop just shy of falling off. The ground is a long way down. I worry Sally doesn't have enough of a handle on Nuo's power. She jumps anyway. There's no arc. We simply drop. I wish the ground was a longer way down. I brace for an impact that doesn't come. The pull of gravity weakens and we float.

A burst of nervous laughter escapes my lips. Sally's too. She's surprised it worked.

Gravity rediscovers its strength. We drop the remaining metre. I bend my knees. The cement path cracks beneath my feet. The guard shouts at us from above. We sprint until we can barely hear him, past the gate that I ripped off its hinges. When we arrive at her van, Sally asks where we're headed. We can't go to her house, it's probably been cordoned off, and we can't go to mine, another me is there with Locky.

'My dad's place?' I ask.

Her eyes widen. 'Yes! Follow me.'

I'm about to remind her that she doesn't know where my dad lives, but I realise my suggestion has inspired an alternative. She pockets her keys and leads me across the road. We take a narrow laneway whose walls are colourful mosaics of stubborn poster remnants. The next block is lined with office towers, sparingly lit. We wander towards the harbour. This street's usually swarming with people during the day. At night, not so much.

'Where exactly are you taking me?' I ask Sally.

'You'll see.'

We end up in a boardroom on the sixty-fourth floor of a skyscraper, her dad's old work. They never deactivated his key card.

'I come up every so often,' Sally says, sitting on the table. 'The cleaners don't do the rounds till seven.'

The wall is all window. Sydney stretches out for miles, an incomplete connect-the-dots of roads and blinking lights. I try to find Charlton Grammar and a memory elbows its way to the front of my mind – me, six years ago, staring out at the city from the top of Founders Block.

'We're stuffed, aren't we?' Sally asks.

'I'm pretty certain we are,' I say, joining her on the table. 'But I think that bodes well for us.'

She frowns. 'I don't follow.'

'The day we met, I couldn't see a life for myself past Olly's rejection.'

'Oh, I know. It was yesterday,' she says, lips curling into a smile. I look daggers at her and she mouths a quick apology, still smiling.

'Consider what's happened since. The shape of my life has completely changed. I haven't just overcome the friend divorce, I'm a *god*. And if that's possible, then who's to say in a few years we won't be looking back at this exact moment having overcome the rebel gods? This has been such an unpredictable experience that maybe the only thing about it that we can predict is that it will continue to be unpredictable.'

'And if we're certain the rebel gods will return, kill us easily and plunge the world into an eternal war, then it's unlikely?'

'That's the hope.'

'I like that,' Sally says. She takes a long breath. 'On the hotel roof, Nuo and I spoke about moving on. She told me to mark a point in the future and walk towards it, then another point and walk towards that. It's difficult to comprehend living an eternity without seeing someone you love again, but apparently, it's manageable in pieces.' She swallows hard. 'I've decided that's the first point I'm marking, us having overcome the rebel gods and looking back.'

'But you're not certain.'

'I'd never say I was. I wouldn't want to ruin our chances.'

When we're quiet, I can't help but think about Nuo's advice. I wrestle with myself over the appropriateness of asking a follow-up question. My curiosity wins out. 'Did Nuo say how long you have to do that? Marking points and walking towards them, I mean.'

'Before the rebel gods . . . rebelled, Nuo fell in love with a human. They had an intense bond, but they never acted on their feelings. The human lived a long life, and when he died, Nuo marked a point in the future, and another, and another.'

My heart sinks. 'She never stopped, did she?'

Sally shakes her head. 'No.' Her watch beeps twice, and she's thankful for the chance to change the subject. 'It's midnight.'

I exhale. It's Wednesday, 1 April 2020, the last day I've already lived. Alek, Finn and another me will step through the portal to confront Aiden, leaving Locky behind.

I'll be there to meet him.

Sally and I don't sleep. We watch Sydney come to life at dawn and sneak out when we hear cleaners vacuuming the hall. We return to the van, disappointing the parking ranger who was waiting for the clearway to come into effect so that he could book us.

We drive past 71 McKenzie Street. There's a small crowd gathered outside, but Sally isn't too keen on dealing with that mess yet. I direct her to take the next left, and when there's some distance between us and the block of units Alek hides his portal behind, I ask her to turn the van around. There are more than three points to her three-point turn, but she gets angry at me for counting. She stops the van across someone's driveway.

All that's left to do is run out the clock. Sally retrieves her mother's letters from the glove compartment. My eyes remain fixed on the block of units.

I spent hours with Locky, but I've lived with those hours for years. We made music together and that music's only gotten better with every listen. Now we get to make more.

Time crawls. Sally works her way to the final letter and then revisits the first. I straighten up whenever a car turns onto the street, then slouch back, disappointed.

I replay our greatest hits – the debutante ball, the attempt to rescue me from Jivanta, the first time we kissed.

I yelp involuntarily. Alek's car turns into the block of units' driveway.

My heart flutters.

I look to Sally. 'Go get him,' she urges.

I don't need to be told twice. I walk towards Locky, towards our future. My heartbeat is erratic. The breaths I don't need to take are shaky. I walk the length of the building and pause before turning the corner. I hear my own voice. 'We'll be back before you know it.'

I give the other Connor time to disappear from sight, and then I peek around the bend. Locky lingers by the portal. He mutters to himself, decides something, rushes towards the opening and hesitates. He's torn. He wants to chase the group that left to confront Aiden.

I step forwards. 'Hi.'

Locky turns. His mouth hangs open. 'Hi,' he manages eventually. Then he notices something. 'You're not wearing flannel. That's a new outfit. How long have you—?'

'Six years.'

It knocks the wind out of him. 'Six years?'

I try to summarise those six years as quickly as possible. Even then, it still takes a while.

'You waited six years?' Locky asks.

He's focusing on the wrong part. The rebel gods returning. That's what matters.

'I missed you a lot,' I say.

Okay, now I'm focusing on the wrong part too.

He points over his shoulder. 'You sacrificed yourself so I could . . .' His brow furrows. He glances back at the portal. 'If Alek died, why is the portal still open?'

It's obvious. 'He hasn't died on the other end yet.'

Locky shakes his head. 'That's not right. If Alek dies, all of his portals – whenever they are – close. If he died in 2014, he shouldn't have even been able to open this one in the first place.'

I'm not quite following.

'Did you see him die?' Locky asks.

I think back to the morning I met Grace. We didn't find him in the hallway. He'd climbed through the portal and closed it behind himself.

'No.'

'Then he's still alive.'

Alek is still alive. He can help us, guide us . . . At the very least, he can teach us how to reach the other realm.

Locky and I rush through the portal and into the night. We sprint down the side of the block of units, shoes slapping on the concrete. We turn onto McKenzie Street. There's a horde gathering outside Sally's place, cautiously interested. We elbow our way through.

I open the door to number 71. Alek's there, collapsed against the wall near Darroch's sword. He's wincing, but alive. He's alive. There's blood around his mouth and down the front of his shirt. The sight of him so weak twists my heart.

'Do we take a side each?' Locky asks me.

'Nope.' I reach under Alek's knees with one arm, around his shoulders with the other, and scoop him right off the floor.

'Oh, right,' Locky says. 'Forgot for a sec.'

We leave Darroch's sword behind.

I don't know how it must look – me cradling a grown man in my arms. If we didn't rush right past them, people would've probably tried taking photos. We hurry back to the portal. The whole way, all I can hear is Alek wheezing in my ear. I need him to hold on.

I carry him into the daylight. I lay him flat by the car and kneel beside him.

Every breath seems like agony. His voice is wafer-thin. 'Aiden?' he asks.

'Dead.' I'm about to reveal that all the Monuments have perished, but I stop myself. We need his guidance, but I can't let him die thinking he's failed his mother. That's cruel. 'It's all fine. Everything's fine.'

His head lops to the side. I see the faintest smile. 'The Monuments will endure.'

My eyes sting. I blink back tears. 'They will. You did it.'

Alek's body goes soft and the portal closes behind us. His body doesn't break to pieces and crumble like the others. He looks human.

'We need to bury him,' I say.

Locky squeezes my shoulder. 'Where?'

A third voice responds, 'Jivanta's sanctuary.'

Locky and I look up. Sally is standing by the building. She steps closer.

'I came back to check everything was all right,' she explains. 'Is that Alek?'

'Yeah,' Locky says.

'He would want to be buried in his mother's sanctuary.'

When I tell her that we can't march his body through the school, Sally explains that we won't have to. Darroch dug a tunnel out of the sanctuary.

'He only filled in the exit,' she adds.

That could work.

Sally offers to fetch the van, but we have a car right here. Locky pats the dead god's pockets carefully. He finds a set of keys. He drives and Sally rides shotgun. Alek lies across the back seat. With his head resting in my lap, he seems like he's sleeping. I can't look down at him too often. It upsets me.

No one speaks for the entire journey to Eden Ladies' College.

Sally instructs Locky to park beside the sign warning trespassers. She strides into the bushes and I follow, Locky by my side and the god's limp body cradled in my arms. Sally crouches to press her palm against a patch of disturbed soil.

Nothing happens at first, and then streams of earth soar into the air and swirl above us. Sally retreats. The streams intensify and the swirl broadens. When the earth stops leaking, the displaced soil looms like a storm cloud. Where there was flat ground, there is now a gentle slope down to Darroch's tunnel, still intact.

I'm in awe. So is Locky.

We follow Sally into the tunnel. It's dark and damp. There are dips and sharp turns, then I see glowing dots in the distance. We come to the chamber under the Moreton Bay fig, Jivanta's sanctuary.

I lay Alek to rest among the luminescent buds.

I look between Locky and Sally in the almost-darkness. Their faces are tinted blue and marked by sadness.

I feel like we should say something.

'We are gathered here to commemorate the life of Alektos, son of Jivanta,' I begin, and as soon as I have, I realise this is my chance to right a wrong and give the other gods a proper farewell. 'We also pay our respects to Darroch, Jivanta, Finn, Nuo, and Aiden, not so much. I don't know where gods go when they die, but I hope you're at peace.'

We stand over Alek, and it really sinks in that the Monuments have left the world to us. We are the new gods.

I feel Locky's hand grip mine. I reach out to grip Sally's.

I'm not at all certain that we can defeat the rebel gods, and I think that means we just might.

**THE ADVENTURE CONTINUES FOR CONNOR,
LOCKY AND SALLY IN**

# REBEL GODS

*coming August 2020*

# hachette
CHILDREN'S BOOKS

If you would like to find out more about
Hachette Children's Books, our authors, upcoming events
and new releases you can visit our website,
Facebook or follow us on Twitter:

hachettechildrens.com.au
twitter.com/HCBoz
facebook.com/hcboz


Teachers notes are available from the
Hachette Australia website:
www.hachette.com.au/teachers-and-librarians/